The Circle Walkers

Cody Hathaway

A NOTE FROM THE AUTHOR

When picking up this book, please keep in mind that the main character's sex is never mentioned throughout the entire story. While reading, you will be given both elements of what our society considers masculine and feminine, and it'll ultimately be up to you to decide whether the main character is male or female. Please enjoy and thank you for taking an interest in reading The Circle Walkers.

Contact the author, or submit your artwork!

http://thecirclewalkers.tumblr.com

https://www.facebook.com/pages/Cody-Hathaway/499321173534203

www.thecirclewalkers.com

SPECIAL THANKS:

Daniel Kasper (Editor)

Amanda Feldt-Smith (Editor)

Ryan Freeze (Illustrator)

George L. Lozano (Illustrator)

Thank you all for your outstanding support and help. Without you, this wouldn't have been possible.

DEDICATED TO:

Cindy Kaebisch, may your soul rest in peace. Please forgive me. I wasn't able to publish this book quickly enough for you to read. It was an honor to be your student and friend.

Lily Stasik, I cannot give you enough thanks for the outstanding encouragement that you have given me while under your guidance in creative writing. Your words have truly inspired me to become the writer that I am today. Thank you.

CHAPTER ONE

I ran with no end in mind. My bare feet slapped onto the cracked slabs of stone and the sunlight filtered throughout the treetops, glistening off of the ponds below. The farther and faster I went through the overgrown jungle, the more the stone path lead onwards. The tiny streams that crept into the crevasses and cracks of the jungle floor radiated with neon green algae as little bugs skittered across the surface. Massive tree roots leapt through the giant stone slabs and into the air – titanic in size, eventually burrowing back down into the earth and spreading throughout the ground. It was absolutely breath taking. I wasn't home but I didn't mind. It felt good to be an entire world away, in a place that I had never been a part of or witnessed before. I could run for an eternity and never have to catch my breath. The warm breeze gently whispered down my skin, halting the sweat that I was doused in from head to toe. I could never return back and I would be content as a peach.

I came to an abrupt halt when the stone path began to merge with the dirt and soon before I could take a step further, I found myself twisting and turning throughout thick brush while attempting to avoid any spider webs or thorns. Birds that had been foreign to my ears and eyes dodged the treetop branches above while some had the audacity to attempt a suicide mission by swooping down and narrowly missing my head with a successful evasion. A few feathers had brushed against my cheeks and left the wind swirling softly in my ears. I figured that I was likely near some of their nests. Anything and everything I encountered in my journey felt magnified; heightened beyond normal means.

For instance, the very colors of the jungle were amplified to such extreme vibrancy that I could practically feel the pigments of my surroundings ingrain into the pupils of my eyes. I could smell the soil that planted itself between my bare toes just as much as I could feel my eardrums react to the vibrations of sound, emitted by various critters that lurked about in this jungle. This strange world that I was unfamiliar with carried an abundance of senses, all of which I desperately held onto. The sound of drumbeats picked up in the distance and the further I went, the louder the drums echoed.

Eventually I broke free of the thick brush and tended to my body in order to make sure I wasn't covered in any ticks or bugs that I'd have a heart attack over due to how much of a hypochondriac I was. Despite being quite the courageous person, my mind often takes turns for the worst when it comes to my health. I may find a release in running and I'm well aware that I am a healthy young adult, yet it's almost as if unknown demons sink their teeth into the back of my skull, secreting their lethal poison by creating horrific thoughts that I am going to die at any given moment and in any given scenario possible. A simple heart palpitation or a slightly elevated heart rate could trigger an episode of sheer terror. It's truly a plague to have a mind that is tarnished in ways beyond a normal human's mind, but I've learned to adapt and cope with my anxieties. I haven't much to blame for why I have such needless worries in life, and no matter how much I convince myself that fear is a man-made concept of which we succumb to, my knees still buckle at the very thought of death itself, immobilizing me beyond belief. It's never a walk in the park when you're prisoner to your own mind.

A daunting shriek came beckoning out of the jungle,

2

scattering birds in all different directions from the treetops. I snapped out of my current daydream and gained quick footing towards the general area where the scream emitted from in hopes to help anyone who could possibly be in trouble, but all I could find were broken animal bones and torn bird feathers scattered throughout the vine-infested grounds. I could've sworn the scream was that of a female and couldn't have been much younger than I.

"Are you alright?!" I yelled out in hopes to gain a response. It was futile.

A small whimper escaped the mouth of something close by and I turned my head in the general direction. A young girl struggled to crawl away and duck herself off into the shadows. The drums began to intensify as fog now loomed ominously to the floor, bringing forth a refreshing chill that battled with the heat that escaped my skin.

"Excuse me, Miss, do you need help?" I asked while heading towards her. Her face was covered by ragged hair and her thin dress was torn and covered in filth. I was afraid for her just by her appearance alone. Her right leg was completely mangled in different directions while various bruises and lacerations covered her other leg and arms, trailing upwards to her neck line and down her torso. She was barefoot like me. I extended my hand without question to help the young woman, but she sat still and silent as ever.

"You need my help. Please, take my hand. We can get you out of here." I spoke to her.

The drum beats stopped. She let out a tiny giggle, but the laughter which expelled from her throat was not right, it was not human. The tone had deepened and based on the judgment of the scream I previously heard, it couldn't have been her. Her laughter grew stronger, deeper, and her teeth gleamed as she retreated back into the fog quickly despite her broken limb. I took a step back after retracting my hand at what I had witnessed. Fear began to numb the tips of my fingers with adrenaline and what came forth from the fog next was not possible. This man, creature, or whatever it may have been easily towered over myself at nearly eight-feet tall with his stature bent in a hunch, his very bones protruding from his starving body. His skin was cobalt blue in hue and his fingernails grew out to about an inch in length, jagged and painted blood red. A foul odor lingered around the giant hideous eyesight and his teeth were in the far end stage of rotting.

My mouth opened unwillingly as I attempted to tell the man to stay back, however nothing came out but a cluster of intangible words. Eventually my body gave in and I collapsed to the ground out of inexplicable horror. He sauntered towards me, cackling in an evil manner. My stomach churned as I turned my head and tightly closed my eyes. No longer did my extremities want to work as I sat there helplessly in shock overload. I could hear him click his fingernails together and inhale deeply while the bones in his ribcage cracked.

"Open your eyes, human." he commanded hoarsely, "Do as you are told and look upon my body."

My lip quivered as I popped an eye open, his face only inches from mine. The putrid scent that rolled off of his body alone turned my face pale. The hideous man licked one of his fingernails in a gross gesture as a crow landed abruptly onto his shoulder. His face was masked by an elaborately decorated animal skull that had both horns twisting outwards on each side, one of those horns being broken nearly half way down. At the base of where the horns started were tightly tied blue jewels while dark colored red, green, and earthen brown feathers dangled about midway up the horns and were fastened by what seemed to be dilapidated hemp rope. His hair was extremely unkempt and had shown a disgusting deep jade color as it draped over his chest almost flowingly.

"What is it that you want?" I attempted to speak boldly, but forcing out the words only made the inflection of my voice crack.

He traced the outline of my eye with his fingernail and giggled. "My crows grow hungry, mortal. Your beautiful blue eyes are some of the brightest I've ever seen, which means they must be *extra* juicy."

I slapped his hand away and pushed him to the ground. After gaining my footing, I darted as quickly as I could throughout the lavish jungle. The noise of animals rang in my eardrums as the caws, roars, and screeches obsoleted the thoughts in my racing mind. I was panicking and taking in way too much oxygen. When I looked back, the cobalt-skinned man stretched his body to full length while gliding his boney fingers gently across his faded maroon-red tribal tattoos that lay spewed across his shoulders and chest line. The creature hissed at me loudly and it sounded as if he were right next to me when doing so. The vines that tangled up the massive tree trunks unwound back into the earth and slithered closer into my direction. If I were to stop for a brief moment, I would have been consumed by this demented jungle that I once considered paradise. The animals outcries throughout the jungle merged into one giant loud noise that I could not shake out of my head, as it buzzed continuously in rhythm. I tripped over a giant root and tumbled down a hillside covered in thick moss and shrubbery, completely out of breath.

There he was standing before me, already by my side as if in the blink of an eye; absolutely calm and collected. There was no plausible way in my mind of how he performed such an astonishing feat. I knew it was the end and I had accepted such a thousand times over in my head in just one split second. He knelt down beside me and cradled his freezing hand under my chin. I went limp while gasping for air, my eyebrows sinking heavily as I got a good look under his strangely decorated skull helmet. Even though a shadow was casted over his face, he appeared hungry as ever when inching closer. Oddly enough the man's face was very sharp. His strong cheekbones protruded outwards, carving out hollow indents below them. You could see that his eyes were meant to be onyx in color, yet a yellow glint resided in the center of his pupils.

"Do not fear." He spoke softly while still caressing me.

"Wh– What is your name?" I asked curiously, being completely negligent of the fact that I was mortified and had no control over any part of my body.

The cobalt-skinned creature shook his head back and forth, causing the tiny animal rib bones in his gauged ears to dangle in unison. At least I assumed that they were the bones of an animal. The yellow gleam in his eyes shimmered as he wrinkled his face with a most unpleasant smile.

"I am Sagaru, man of most unholy deeds."

Before I could interrogate the man with a bombardment of unanswered questions that I felt absolutely inclined to ask, the entire world I was surrounded by fluttered into darkness and the memory of what I saw with my very own eyes flew wildly out of control, for I had been dreaming. The ongoing noise of the animals screeching carelessly still rang out into my ears, but I was a fool to believe that it was actual animals in the jungle screaming. It turns out it was just my alarm clock going off, something that I've been planning to destroy for years now.

Stretching never felt so good on a Sunday afternoon in all honesty. I wasn't ashamed to be unemployed and sleeping in on the last day of the weekend. Heck, every day was a weekend to me. It was unfortunate to have Friday, Saturday and Sunday lose their value however, but I've worked enough thirteen-hour shifts in my life to have a little leisure time off. Yes, it often would eat away at my mind and cause a mild amount of depression, but nothing that would be detrimental to me. To this day I have never been able to fully understand the society I live in. Practically everyone I've ever come to know around my age has shown signs of power housing through their professional careers.

Do we really want to live in a society where our youth is pressured to push through their lives as fast as possible in order to sustain a happy medium between finance and labor at the expense of our happiness? Granted twenty-one years old is still quite young in my opinion, I've developed close friendships and those people have already almost attained their bachelor's degree at the sacrifice of losing their mind.

Why rush things? It's absolutely pointless. Those whom claim that life is too short to wait around are those who are afraid of time itself. My father would always tell me when I was a youngster that the concept of time was created by humans in order to claim dominance over it and that age was simply the true ruler. He'd delve into drunken rants at the dinner table often, spewing a multitude of farfetched theories and I would simply listen to each one out of respect.

It was interesting in ways. Even if he had the tendencies and habits of a drunkard, he still offered very thought-provoking scenarios that could have you pondering for hours on end. One crucial tendency that my father had was that he'd never speak ill of the deceased. My old man would refrain from also using past-tense to address those that have passed. He found it to be disheartening and that it was suggestive to us humans that we were on the road to forgetting about them. I try my best to carry on that interesting quirk from him, but I find it troublesome when people mistakenly assume that those family members still live to this day.

It must have been the Irish or Italian in his blood but I never questioned him about it and quite frankly I didn't have the opportunity to. He disappeared from our lives without a shred of evidence or a warning sign, leaving my mother to dwindle into a severe depression and eventually seek counseling – which was to no avail might I add. I kept my head held high though and carried on throughout high school. I accepted the fact that I had become a 'super senior', a term likely coined by the kids at school which meant that I had to attend school more than the standard four years. I was short three damn classes, what a kick in the pants that was. Kids used to whisper around the school that my mother murdered my father but the kids had no reasons or excuses to back it up when I confronted them about their blatant lies. I remember defending her as much as I could but it made absolutely no sense to in the first place. Why defend against wrongful accusations that were just soaked in utter falsehood? I asked myself if the kids at school did it out of spite, but I honestly could not find a reason. My mother had absolutely no motive to kill him. She was completely infatuated with the guy for crying out loud.

When my father vanished, I somewhat inherited his persona. My mentality changed for the good and the bad. I became sheltered in ways, more expressive and thoughtful in others. He disappeared when I was just starting my freshmen year in high school and the local news reporters would make sure to address it annually by making a small segment on it. I resented them for it, but my mother insisted it was the right thing to do to gain attention, hoping he'd one day be found, even if he were dead. I kept my mouth shut when she'd bring it up and in my own little world I would tell myself that maybe my father didn't want to be found. It was hard enough for people to clip at our heels about my father being gone, and the pressure of people hounding us to his whereabouts was traumatic enough. His personality would always mysteriously ignite inside my own little mind at random times and I often convinced myself that my dad likely found paradise. He had to of found paradise. Why else would he leave his own wife and only child behind?

He'd always call me his 'strange little bird' even when I terrorized the entire family in my ankle biter years. I often would be assigned the role of a messenger during family get-togethers and carried on words between the family until I grew up to about the age of seven and started telling my family to deliver the news themselves. This' strange little bird' however was set on the notion that my father was perfectly healthy and alive. I couldn't explain why, but something deep inside of me just knew better than presume he had perished. Brutis flapped his cheeks loudly, snapping me out of my daydream. I cannot tell you how many times I've had to nudge that pit bull in the middle of the night in order to get him to stop snoring, and talk about a bed hog. I love Brutis and his beautifully grey-colored fur coat but sometimes he can be such a brat. Grey has always remained one of my most liked colors. I would often quarrel with my art teacher due to her scolding me that it is in fact a shade and not a color. I paid little mind since I was a ceramicist nut rather than a drawing one. A pit bull is literally like looking after your own child and no matter what anyone may say, they make for wonderful house pets as long as you give them the proper guidance when growing up.

It was really hard for me to cope with my father disappearing, so my mother and I made the executive decision together to adopt Brutis when he was a wee baby from a stranger's home. The owners seemed to be some serious druggies so we figured that by adopting Brutis, we could bring him into a better home while in turn we would have our minds occupied by the love we had to offer his cute little butt. I was really thankful to my mother for being able to add another member to the family, as I couldn't have asked for a better buddy to stick by my side, even if he mastered the art of sleeping on my queen-sized bed diagonally.

"I had such an odd dream, booger." I told Brutis. He huffed, likely thinking the thought of getting out of bed sounded agonizing. After ruffling my bedhead hair I threw on my favorite overused shirt with some sweat pants and slapped my backside to signal Brutis to get his own butt up and out of the room. On the downstairs kitchen island my mother had left a small note as usual, but I didn't even bother to read it since her handwriting went downhill this past year. If the note has money attached to it then it means she's working late and I'll end up ordering a pizza or going out with a few friends to grab something else to feast on for a change.

The house failed to give that 'homey' appeal once mother and I moved into it in order to get away from all of the naysayers and jackasses that kept on badgering her about my father. She hardly decorated the walls with her tiny trinkets and keepsakes that she collected throughout the years. Instead, the tiny stuffed bears, rooster plates, and ceramic children figurines lay hidden in a few crumbling cardboard boxes in the attic collecting dust. I asked her if she was ever going to one day rip open those said boxes and slather the entire house with them, but she ended up slapping me across the face because I called her by her first name, Carla.

Although the walls lay bare without a picture frame or even a tiny doily on any piece of furniture, it seemed to feel cleaner that way, more spacious too. I flipped on the television and tended to Brutis' dog bowl with some leftovers and just sat bug-eyed from all of the sleep I gained over the night. The dream I had bothered me. I wasn't sure what it meant and I really didn't feel like trekking all the way across the house to dig out my dream dictionary book that I received for Christmas one year as a present from one of my Aunts. The book is amazing though and I really do appreciate it. Sometimes I'd find the answer to a dream and become completely shocked at how accurate it related to my life at the time. What the hell was that disgusting creature I ran from?

Through the noise of Brutis scarfing down his food, I could hear the television start up a severe thunderstorm warning in the background while displaying the immediate cities that were expected to be hit. A bright flashing icon on the bottom right of the television screen piqued my interest, accompanied by the standard warning colors of yellow to red as a measurement of severity. All I cared for is Miami to show up on that list and I would be a happy camper. Thunderstorms were a way of coping with my life. I felt extremely drawn to the thunderous booming that shook and rattled the house at night as the lightning temporarily blinded anyone near. There was just this immense cultivation of power that came forth when a thunderstorm hit and Miami was a definite hot spot for them. The raw power alone that comes from a storm gives me such an astounding feeling. I feel as if I'm empowered at times and my entire body becomes vitalized.

Whenever a storm would roll through my old hometown when I was a kid, my grandmother and I always used to get so excited about how much we loved thunderstorms. She'd know that a storm was approaching due to the aches and pains in her bones and most of the time she was right on the marker. I had trouble understanding how my grandmother had this absolutely uncanny and fascinating ability to predict a storm was en route to only find out that it was just due to the decline of barometric pressure before a storm rolls through. I miss that pretty lady and her gorgeous white hair, I really do. I'll have to pay my respects to her soon once my life decides to straighten out. If it ever decides to, that is.

The doorbell rang and to my surprise when I opened the giant wooden door, three of my friends ushered themselves in without even asking for permission. They were all fairly new friends since the recent move, but we all grew attached to one another pretty quickly given the allotted time we've had together thus far. I have the type of friends to where they are more on the outspoken, driven and outgoing side while I see myself as more of a reserved, collected, and observant type of person. Josiah is a total Palestinian and Greek babe. If you popped open a GQ magazine, you could flip to the hottest model in the entire magazine and compare Josiah's looks to the model's own and find virtually no flaw in Josiah but rather in the model instead.

If you were to ask me he's a total package for being absolutely and irrevocably beautiful. His green eyes twinkle so brightly when he gets a caramelized tan in the summer. What really drives me insane though is his hair and physique. He is practically a mixed Greek god. His hair has just the perfect amount of a wave to it along with being quite thick and as dark as coal while his muscles etch out his silhouette to perfection, down to a scrumptious jawline that is coated by a beautiful five o'clock shadow. I may or may not crush hard on him but I make sure to maintain a good and friendly atmosphere around the guy. I met Josiah through my mother ironically. When we moved to Miami I was having quite a hard time picking up new friendships and my mother was seeing a psychologist to cope with the disappearance of my old man and the ongoing attacks from strangers.

I really was hesitant at first to go to one of her meetings since I've always chalked up psychologists to being a pseudo career. I figured that since our society had been so skewed by pressuring young adults into careers and dragging them through some of the worst hardships in life to attain success, we had compensated our sacrifices by creating psychologists to help us understand our own mentality. I recycled the thought through my head and came to the realization that it's an underpaid profession for the tedious work they must tend to. I've learned from first-hand experience that taking on another person's problems is like bearing the weight of the world on your shoulders. Imagine what it's like to do that with several, if not dozens of people at the same time.

If you haven't guessed by now, Josiah's mother is the psychologist who my mother has been seeing to help with her mental stress. I never wanted to voice my opinion to Josiah about how I thought of his mother's career as somewhat a void, but he's helped shed light on my oblivious nature towards it and even mentions how psychologists are becoming high in demand in today's world. I'd believe anything that green-eyed angel would say. The other two friends of mine are Elowyn and Alexandria. Elowyn is the type of woman who isn't afraid to speak her mind. She's very rambunctious and has the perfect features a guy should crave over. I say the word "should" because it seems our media has yet again skewed our perception on how a woman should look. Without any regrets, Elowyn is easily following in the footsteps of Marilyn Monroe when it comes to her image. Her chest seems to always push upwards and out while having absolutely gorgeous curly blonde hair. She has the perfect curvature of a woman's body and even teases men by wearing a similar white dress that Marilyn herself wore.

I always taunt Elowyn that William Travilla is going to rise from the dead one fateful night and take back his iconic 20th century cocktail dress and she always retorts with a wrinkled nose and says "Over my dead body." when in reality it'd be over his. People often hack at Elowyn for her name, but I personally find it unique myself. It's more of an elegant name and while it doesn't suit her giddy personality at best, it still fits her regardless. I'd put a ring on her finger if I could, that's how amazing she is to me. Alexandria is definitely a character herself. She's what the fashion industry has been gawking over recently; Androgyny. Her entire appearance and the way she walks bears such an androgynous appeal that she has mastered it perfectly without even having to try. Her brunette hair on given days could be spiked upwards to sport a "La Roux" look, or it occasionally waves down across her face while curling outwards at the ends like a pixie. I admire her bravery for standing out in a crowd because she always has insane taste in her clothing styles and unique choices of music.

Even when Alexandria gets a tidbit flirtatious with a man, I still question her sexuality much like my own. Her name alone is such a powerful name for a woman, she just screams lesbian but her half-adopted introverted personality says otherwise. I say half-adopted because while she may be shy and timid, she is definitely not a self-centered young woman. She's very forth giving and I assume it comes from working tirelessly at charities and support groups across the United States for LGBT-friendly companies; another reason why I suspect her sexuality to stride towards bisexual or at most fully lesbian since we've never seen her with a boy around her arms. When all four of us were drinking one night, I almost mustered up the courage to ask Alexandria about it, but I chickened out when the thought of my own sexuality being questioned by them could come into play thereafter. Women have always had more fluidity towards sexuality while men seem to differ. I accept myself as a bisexual however and I'm proud to say I have a supportive mother who accepts and understands who I am.

It's really unfortunate to have heard so many stories of people I've gotten to know across the world through online media websites that have had horrific ordeals with their families for their coming out story. I've been blessed in ways while hindered in others I suppose. Not everyone is given the leisure of acceptance when coming out, unfortunately.

"JACKIE!" Elowyn screeched while wrapping her arms tightly around my neck.

"El. You're practically suffocating me!"

"I'm sorry loves! I just missed you like a blind kid playing dodge ball!"

"Oh my god El you can't just say that." I slapped my hand to my forehead while Alexandria and Josiah started to cackle in laughter. "Well. What brings you guys here?"

"Well, A storms a brewin' and we know how much you love thunderstorms!" Alexandria pointed out, tossing her Ed Hardy flattops under the nearby coatrack.

"You got that right!" I replied and pushed my weight into the giant wooden door to close it tight. I swear this door will be the death of me. My mother insisted when we went house hunting that the front door –must– be gigantic in size and even creak when opening or closing it. I don't understand the woman, but she has an odd fascination with doors, bath tubs, and gardens.

Alexandria reached into El's purse and pulled out about half a dozen junk food items and plopped them onto the kitchen island as everyone migrated around it. I wasn't a big nut on eating healthy, but I still liked to maintain a decent diet out of respect for my own body. It was game over though when Josiah taunted me with that handsome smile, waving around a box full of nutty bars. I swear if it's one thing that I dive into when it comes to chocolate and peanut butter, it's those damn things. I will hound them down like they're going out of business. I snatched the box from Josiah while blushing with my own smile. He was well aware that I liked to train regularly and he even offered to accompany me for some of the marathons that I have been planning to run in the summertime. One of the 5k runs I've been looking forward to is The Color Run. It's pretty expensive to register and participate in but it's worth the cause. It's nearly 'half a hundo' is what Josiah would say, which translates to fifty-doll-hairs in my own dialect, or fifty-dollars in regular terms for people who aren't adjusted to how much of an oddball group we are.

"We just want to give our favorite German some company while the storm goes through!" Elowyn said and pinched her fingers at my cheeks.

"Knock it off!" I swatted away her hand, embarrassed. The news channel flashed the thunderstorm warning once more. This time Miami and all of the surrounding cities were encased in the color red. Hail was expected to form and power outages were likely.

"You're getting pretty red in the face there, Jackie-bear." Josiah pointed out while giving me a very curious look. A part of my mind registered that Josiah knew exactly what thunderstorms did to me, but I dismissed it immediately thereafter.

"It's the storm. I can feel it in me bones!" I replied in an Irish accent.

"In ye bones, eh?!" he questioned back with an Australian accent himself.

"Aye mate!"

It was tradition for our group to always switch around our accents for what we considered fun. Alexandria is absolutely incapable of producing any other accent than a bewildered elderly Asian woman. During the times we'd drink together and get absolutely slaphappy, we'd try our best to teach Alexandria new accents but they never stuck for more than a few minutes.

"OHOHOHOH!!" Alexandria shouted enthusiastically, "YOU SOO SILLEH! I RIKE IT!"

Elowyn jumped in on the conversation. "Vut are joo dewing! Joo mush speek like dees!"

Yeah. These are my friends that I surround myself with and I love them no matter what. I find them increasingly hilarious as I get to know them and I wouldn't want to surround myself with anybody else. People may think that my friends are assholes for mocking the accents of foreign countries but I find it all in good fun, as it never hurts to live a little. If we were to rudely mock someone with a foreign accent to their face, now that is a different story.

A loud crack of thunder sounded off nearby and soon thereafter the lights flickered. Alexandria clapped her hands excitedly and then reached into her giant purse to rummage around.

"OoOooOO!" Elowyn echoed while raising her eyebrows. My friends seemed especially excited for me and I had no clue as to why. Josiah cleared the kitchen island off after I had polished off the remainder of the Little Debbie Nutty Bars and reached into his pocket to pull out some candles.

"Guys, what are you doing?" I questioned, slightly perplexed at what was going on.

"Shhh, child!" Elowyn pressed her finger against my lips, speaking in a Jamaican accent. "Dis be sumtin' we been wantin' ta show ya for sum time now."

Josiah took a lighter to the candles and sporadically placed them around the kitchen while Elowyn grabbed at the television remote and then went after the kitchen lights.

"Okay you're all starting to freak me out. Knock it off."

"Just relax." Alexandria assured me and pulled out a giant

rectangular box from her white purse.

She inhaled deeply and blew away any dust that had collected on the box. After shortly examining it, she then proceeded to pry it open as best she could with her stubby fingernails. Once the sturdy box gave in, she reached into it and revealed the contents by gently placing them onto the kitchen island.

It was an Ouija board.

CHAPTER TWO

"Hell no," I said, shaking my head.

"Oh come on. You are one of the most liberating and accepting people I've had the chance to get to know. You can't just dismiss it." Alexandria mentioned.

"Yes I can and I am now. No. Nope. Nope nope nope."

"Do you actually really believe in this heebie-jeebie stuff?" Josiah asked me while cocking his head slightly in my direction. Erg. My weak spot.

"I do believe in this 'heebie-jeebie' stuff and I believe in keeping bad juju out of my life. It goes out now."

It was hard for me to be demanding to their faces. The rain started pelting away at the sun room's windows harder than before while the flashes of lightning still carried on. Elowyn stood up from her seat and quietly tip toed her way behind me to caress my back, massaging slowly. "It's okay Jackie. We're all here together, and besides it's not even real. Just play with us."

I looked Alexandria dead in the eyes. "You're a jerk. You're all jerks. If I get an anxiety attack, you're all going to be beaten about the face and body with extreme force."

Elowyn clapped her hands excitedly when prancing back to her seat at the kitchen island, unmindful to the severe threat I just made loud and clear.

"So what we do is..." Elowyn looked over at the generic cardboard Ouija board's case, "light some candles, spread them sporadically throughout the room, turn off the lights, and keep our fingers on the eye piece and concentrate on the question we decide to ask."

"Candles are in place ma'am." Josiah spoke jestingly.

"I'll navigate the eye piece!" Alexandria offered, a little too happy for her personality.

"And I'll just watch." I said.

"I don't think so!" Elowyn squawked at me.

I'll admit that I was excited. I tried my best to hide it, really. A tinge of excitement sent down my spine with the thought of contacting those who no longer are a part of this earth. I felt like such a child but I didn't care. I was all in for it, even if it were just a silly board with a plastic navigator piece. I know Josiah or Elowyn would intentionally pull the piece anyways.

"First we need to establish a connection and then put our hands on the eye piece. Once we do, we introduce ourselves and then begin to ask as many questions as we wan—"

"Spirits come to meeeee!" Elowyn interrupted Alexandria. I'll admit we all had a good laugh from that.

We placed our hands accordingly around the navigation eye piece and went counter-clockwise to introduce ourselves by saying our names. We sat there still and silent without any questions in mind. Elowyn started to giggle for no reason at all out of the blue.

"Stop that." I demanded. "Nobody has time for your creepy laugh."

I think we were having more fun being dorks than taking this Ouija board seriously. I jumped and screamed as loud as I possibly could and to my left Elowyn flew out of her own seat. Josiah, who was to my right, sat stiff as a statue while Alexandria shook her head with a smirk on her face.

"Why would you do that?!" Elowyn slapped me on the

shoulder. I laughed, raising my hands to protect myself from her attack.

"Jackie used scream against Elowyn. It's super effective." Alexandria said. Even if Alexandria has a wicked lifestyle and is always seemingly busy, she still finds the time to pull out her Gameboy Advance and throw in a Pokémon cartridge every once in a blue moon and play until the batteries go dead. I don't blame her. I sometimes use video games as an escape from life myself.

"Come on guys. Focus." Josiah peered at us individually, one by one. The candle flame flickered in his brilliant emerald eyes, melting me like the hot candlewax nearby. Everyone placed their hands back on the marker and I drew in one longing breath to concentrate again.

This time Elowyn giggled and let out a large accidental snort. "Remember that one time, Alexandria, when Josiah launched you off of the trampoline by accident and you flew into your father's shed head-first? You were knocked out for at least half an hour!" Josiah blew snot out of his nose from laughing so hard and shook his head in agreement. The three of them grew up as childhood friends. They would often get into deep conversations about their childhood and just laugh to no end while I'd sit there laughing too at all of the insane shenanigans those three underwent. Alexandria's face turned beet red as she cackled with laughter to the point where she couldn't even respond to Elowyn at first. "It wasn't nearly as bad as Jo landing on his groin when we launched him fifteen feet into the air that day. That metal bar must've hurt, huh Josiah?"

"Screw you, Alex." Josiah retorted. "It did hurt, and not only did it hurt my manhood, but also my sanity! Never again will I go near a Trampoline with you goons. Never, I say!"

The Ouija board piece started to move at rapid speed and within the matter of three seconds it had jumbled out an unknown sentence.

Everyone who had a residing hand on the eyepiece immediately withdrew their hand in the quickest motion I have ever witnessed. Elowyn stumbled out of her seat while Alexandria's eyes bulged from their sockets. I snapped my head at Josiah and screamed at him.

"Why the hell would you do that!?"

"I sw– swear, I didn't do that. That was not me." Josiah stammered.

"You're bullshitting. This game is over. We're done with this. I told you guys." I was pissed at the thought of my friends playing a prank. "Pack everything up and turn on the lights. The storm should be over soon, just like this game you played on me."

Elowyn seemed a little startled at the event but managed to reach the lights. Alexandria sat there in complete silence, her sights affixed on the board while Josiah blew out the candles. I walked into the living room to turn up the volume and keep an eye on the storm to see how long it'd take to pass before I could send everyone home.

"It seriously wasn't me." Josiah said to break the silence.

"I don't want to hear it anymore." I turned my attention towards everyone in the kitchen. "Pack it up and we'll find something else to do. It looks like this storm is just going to get worse anyways."

Brutis started to bark uncontrollably.

"Brutis, shut up!" I yelled. My nerves were already shot, I didn't need a damn dog barking in my ears all night. Josiah jumped from his seat and pointed at the Ouija board freakishly, his limbs flailing from terror. "Look! I told you damn it! It wasn't me!"

The Ouija board cursor started moving on its own.

"Get the hell away from that thing, now!" I shouted.

Elowyn leapt across the kitchen and over the couch like an Olympic gymnast while Alexandria swiped her purse from the counter and charged right into Josiah's arms. The board's cursor spun slowly in a counter-clockwise motion repeatedly. I started to rub my forehead as best I could to cope with what was happening and I could feel my lungs starting to tighten already. No. This is just some sick joke and it has to be magnetized. After some time, the cursor started to settle. Josiah and Alexandria mustered up the courage to approach the kitchen island and observe. Soon I gained a little bravery myself and went back into the kitchen, leaving Elowyn trembling near the couch.

"Hold it down," I said, "make it stop moving."

Josiah reached his hand outwards towards the board and firmly pressed into the cursor.

"Guys put it away, now! I'm freaking out!" Elowyn pleaded. "This was a bad idea and we should've never brought it with us!"

"No. Say Hello. Ask it questions, whatever 'it' may be," Alexandria said, putting emphasis on the word "it".

Josiah let go of the Ouija board piece and we watched the cursor sail towards the "Hello" text on the Ouija board slowly. My body ceased to remain still and I could feel the goose bumps rise to the surface of my skin, along with the hairs on the back of my neck stand straight up. The board itself seemed pretty ancient, despite the cardboard casing it came in. It was thicker than you'd imagine a standard board would be that you would come across at any major supermarket. It was unique in its own sense, covered with carvings and engravings etched around the alphabet that I had never seen before, something I'm sure none of us had ever seen before actually. The sides were torn from what looked to be years of use but I figured that it was purchased as such to give the board that extra level of spooky appeal. I didn't want to buy into this crap, but there is no way for an object to move in its own without explanation.

"What is your name?" I asked. The inflection in my voice did not jump to a higher octave surprisingly, given how terrified I was. I raised my hand from the cursor and low and behold it began to slowly spell out a name.

"K-A-L-A-N-I 25"

"Are you 25 years old?" I asked.

The cursor moved to the "Yes" text.

I knew that name from somewhere, but I couldn't pinpoint it. I knew for a fact that I didn't know anybody with the name, but it sounded so familiar. Elowyn started to get worse, tears brimming to her eyelids. "Guys please! I don't want to do this anymore."

A blinding flash of light filled the room, accompanied by a monstrous roar of thunder.

"El, it's okay. Just stay calm." Alexandria approached Elowyn to comfort her.

The initial time with the Ouija board grew longer than expected. Josiah and I became intrigued while Alexandria cracked away at Elowyn slowly, finally convincing her to stand by our side after some time. We asked "Kalani" a plethora of questions and everything was answered with little hesitation. I still took all of the information that was spoon fed to me with a grain of salt. How could I possibly believe anything that was said when I couldn't even see him before my very own eyes? This claimed "Kalani" fellow came from Hawaii, which clicked in my head and made perfect sense. Kalani is a name seldom given to Hawaiian children and it literally translates into *the heavens* or *the sky*. It's actually a really beautiful name.

"Alright it's time to say goodbye." Elowyn said. "I need to

get headed home and I'm sure Alexandria has work in the morning."

"Oh you wimps," Josiah chuckled, "we were just getting to know him."

"End it, now." demanded Elowyn. I raised my hand and pressed down on the cursor with some pressure and said goodbye while dragging it to the "farewell" text at the bottom of the board. The cursor remained still.

"Good! Now we can get going." Elowyn said in a most unusual perky manner. Right as Alexandria reached for the board, the cursor began to spin wildly out of control once more. Everyone took a decent stride backwards and I gasped quietly under my breath. The cursor dragged itself to the text "No" over and over and over.

"Grab that damn thing and destroy it if you have to! I don't want to be a part of this anymore!" Elowyn grew enraged, throwing her pointer finger into the board's direction.

"Wait!" Josiah swatted away Elowyn's hand. The cursor began to fly across the board, spelling out words hastily. It repeated itself as Josiah and I attempted to pay close attention. The faster and faster the cursor went, the more frightened Elowyn became. Alexandria even started to cave in. "Okay, this is enough, guys!" Alexandria yelled.

The cursor went still. Movement halted from the board entirely. I looked up at Josiah.

"Did you make out what it said?"

The light in Josiah's eyes seemed to dwindle, his skin less resonant than before. "Circle Walkers," he uttered softly.

"What?" I asked.

"I have no idea."

"We're done here." Alexandria said and started to pack up the board.

"Alex, where did you get ahold of that board from?" I asked.

She snatched the Ouija board back into her possession and firmly placed her purse strap over her shoulder tightly. After fluffing her brunette hair, she finally spoke.

"When I went to Louisiana for spring break, I found it in one of the local shops in the city, okay? I'd rather not remember right now, given what just went down."

I didn't even bother asking what city. I really didn't want to know and I really didn't have the right mindset to even think about it any further.

"Just wondering," I replied.

The storm still hadn't completely passed, but its strength had weakened considerably. I whisked everyone out of the door after we all exchanged abrupt goodbyes. I pushed the giant wooden door tightly shut and started thinking to myself. Something about Josiah was different; something in his eyes and the way he acted. He wasn't the sarcastic or inviting person that I knew once we had fiddled with the board. He was changed, more thoughtful, it seemed. I was puzzled by his sudden change, but I decided it was best to keep it under the carpet since Elowyn had her fair share of fright for the time being. I felt somewhat bad on how I pushed them to keep going. The idea of tinkering with the board was enticing, almost as if I were drawn to it by an alluring presence. Kalani didn't seem like a harmful person, but how could I think of such a thing when I was talking to them through a twisted magical object?

I shook my head foolishly. Alexandria likely pushed the cursor. She recently took a trip to Hawaii for her job to help LGBT-friendly companies boost sales in the gay community. She probably picked up the name 'Kalani' there. There was no question about it, and it explained why she remained so calm during the entire ordeal.

On the other hand, keeping a calm face was something she was good at. While she may say up and down how she loves her job since it's second nature to her, she still loathed working with people who were homophobic. There's nothing Alexandria can really do about it though. She needs the work and gets to travel across the country for free. I'm pretty jealous, but I'd probably find myself homesick often, and I couldn't bring Brutis if I did what she does.

It's been a major band wagon in the United States to jump on the LGBT train lately, and while there are hundreds if not thousands of companies out there who truly do support equality for everyone, some do it just to fit in. I don't know if I could do it. I couldn't stand there before millions of people every day and put on a face that wasn't mine just to appease everyone. Alexandria seemed to have that perfect skillset.

"Jackie!" a familiar voice shouted from half way across the house. It was about damn time that my mother got home. "Sorry I'm late honey! There was a huge fiasco at the law firm today. Some business owner got screwed out of over half a million when one of his partners decided to go rogue. It was pretty unfortunate for the owner, but the partner successfully evaded the law since they had specific rights from a co-ownership deal . . ." She went on for a few minutes and I tuned her out. I didn't understand her line of work. All I knew is that she did her job well inside of a law firm and that she was happy with it. If it made her happy, I was happy.

"Just goes to show who you can trust, ya?" I replied.

"Most soi-tin-lee!" she said in a dorky Brooklyn accent.

My mother picked up on doing the whole 'accent' appeal when talking with people she was close with – especially when I started bringing my friends around the house. It was her way of being silly, especially once eight or so glasses of wine went down her throat after a long day at work. I always admired her blonde beauty and how she'd always wear the perfect professional outfit to work. She's a woman who values her etiquette alongside her work ethic—she likes to define herself by her particular choice of a decent-sized high heel. No higher nor shorter than 2 ½ inches. Don't ask me how I know this; I've tried to suppress memories of many spontaneous shoe shopping sprees with her.

"You just missed Alex, El, and Jo," I told her. I hadn't realized how quickly the time passed when we were all fooling around with that Ouija board.

"Oooh! How is your little Josiah-bear doing?" My mom ever so nonchalantly egged on with a taunting grin.

"Mom, stop," I sighed, shaking my head in embarrassment. "He's just a friend. I'm more into Elowyn anyways." I lied horribly and I figured that it'd be written all over my face.

"Well honey. If you ask me, Alexandria is a lesbian."

"Ma, she's not a lesbian. I can't even be–"

"Well, I'm just sayin'." She interrupted me.

"Anyways, mother. I'm going to probably get some sleep early. I have some things to do in the morning."

"Okay sweetie, did you eat?" she asked, swooping the question down like a hawk onto a mouse.

"Yes mom." I pushed the twenty dollar bill that she left on the note this morning further into my pocket.

"Okay. Sleep tight!"

I made it about half-way up the wooden staircase when my mother yelled my name from the kitchen.

"Jackie!"

"Yes?" I replied.

"You left something on the floor, sweetie."

I went back down the creaky stairs and there it was, resting peacefully on the ground, the cursor piece from the Ouija board. Alexandria must have misplaced it when packing everything up into her giant purse. I rushed quickly to the cursor piece and snatched it into my possession and resumed my trek back to my room.

"What is it?" my mother asked curiously before I could escape.

"Oh, it's just a fancy magnifying glass that Alexandria found when she was in Louisiana." I held the cursor to my eye like an absolute baboon, extending it and retracting back and forth as if it were a monocle. With my other hand I gave myself a fake mustache with my pointer finger and spoke in a bad Scottish accent.

"I'll have to give thish back to Alexshandria when I shee her next. Yesh."

My mother laughed. "I'm not an idiot, Jackie. I know what it is."

I dropped the mustache and Sean Connery impersonation instantly, afraid that I was going to be reprimanded for playing with what my mother would consider the "Devil's Toys".

"Just don't bring it around the house again. Okay?"

"You got it," I responded and then scurried up the stairs. Apparently she was in a better mood than I assumed. That's another thing I admired about my mother. Even if she would have a terrible day that dredged on for hours at her workplace, she'd never bring her attitude back home.

CHAPTER THREE

I sat with my legs suspended in the air, resting against my bedroom wall. I continued to observe the Ouija board cursor piece, pondering for some time about it. What if this piece actually did have some sort of freaky demonic power that I was unaware of? The cursor piece was old and had an odd leathery scent and feel to it. I flicked the cursor with my fingers and it made a dull thud. Solid, then. I reached for the cell phone on the table to call Alexandria, tugging away at the phone charger that was plugged into it.

The phone rang and went to voicemail. I hate leaving voicemails. I always felt super anxious about them and then felt stupid for the anxiety. I pushed aside my ridiculousness and listened to Alexandria's quirky message she recorded as an invitation to have the caller leave her a message.

"Uh, hey Alex, you um left your cursor piece at my house, girl. I think you forgot it when you were packing everything up? Call me back if you want to come back and get it. I'll, uh, probably head out to your place tomorrow if the storm lets up by then."

I hung up and sighed deeply. Thank god I didn't stutter or tangle up my words too badly, I would have replayed the screwed up message I left on her phone in my head for days. As it was, the little 'uhs' and 'ums' were still probably going to bug me for a while.

I extended and pulled back the Ouija cursor from my eye a few times jokingly after I placed my phone on the nearby table. A bright flash of lightning filled my room and I dropped the cursor out of absolute horror. I quickly scrambled to my feet as my chest tightened and I strategically maneuvered throughout my room to avoid reanimating the dreadful picture in my head. It was him. I saw him. I saw Sagaru in the corner of my room.

"Mom!" I shrieked, pulling at my bedroom door.

The door itself felt much heavier than I remember it being. I broke through into the hallway and started to charge. All I could hear in my head was the sound of him hissing in my ears.

"Mom!" I screamed louder, starting to hyperventilate.

I panicked and I felt my limbs going numb again. No matter how fast I ran, the hallway seemed endless. My feet weighed fifty pounds each, and all I could do was push my legs ahead of one another in a desperate attempt to flee. A twisted giggle followed closely behind and it felt as if I were a prey to a predator. I hopped over the staircase railing like a Parkour champion, staggering slightly once my feet landed on the floor. The entire house was dark except for a dim light that loomed over the kitchen oven. I could see my mother sitting in her seat across the kitchen island, her back faced to me.

"Mom! Why won't you answer me?! There is a man in the house. Help!?!" I yelled, checking back to see if the abhorrent creature was near.

She remained still.

"Carla, damnit!" I shouted as a last attempt to gain her attention.

She snapped her body into my direction but nothing was right about the way she looked. She didn't even have a face. No eyes, no mouth, not even an eyebrow. My brain started to pulsate with mass confusion. She placed her hands on the kitchen island with extreme force and stood up while inaudible sounds seemed to emit from her non-existent mouth. Her fingers were attached together as if she was born with a serious birth defect, pinky to pinky, pointer to pointer. I was confused, mortified to say the least. She begun to twist and turn her hands ruthlessly and I could hear the bones in her fingers start to snap. I gagged and shivered at the disgusting sound.

"What the hell are you doing!? Stop!" I tried to shout. The words caught in my throat.

It was as if my words fell on deaf ears, incapable of rising to the occasion. She tilted her head towards the ceiling and her shoulder span seemed to double in width. Accompanied by a gruesome, disemboweled screech, the flesh of her fingers began to tear apart. I could see the shattered bones in her fingers as the muscle snapped backwards. She had successfully ripped her hands apart from one another. I grew dizzy and started to shake uncontrollably. She clawed at her head and neck with her broken hands, slathering her skin in blood as it gushed out.

I could still hear his menacing giggle buzz loudly in my ears.

"What do you want from me!?" I screamed.

The room began to flutter out of control, feeling like the floor had swept out from beneath my feet. I could still feel his cold presence nearby.

"A murderer's laughter is a lullaby to the insane, my deliciously blue-eyed beauty."

His words slithered into my ear like the venom of a snake, coursing its way through a bloodstream.

"I'm not a murderer!" I shot back in anger with a clenched fist.

"I never said you were, child, for you are not the one laughing."

I retaliated as best I could. "I'M NOT INSANE! I'M NOT INSANE! GO AWAY I'M NOT INSANE!"

I turned back to the figure of my mother. Her clawing had stopped, but not before leaving deep gouges in the empty pits where her mouth and eyes should have been. I felt vomit rise in my throat as I watched the figure's maw open up as if to scream.

"Jackie!" a familiar voice called out. "Wake your ass up!"

I shot out of bed, dripping in a cold sweat. I didn't realize that I had fallen asleep. My heart was under a high amount of stress and I could feel a palpitation coming along.

"What the hell is wrong with you?" Josiah asked.

"What time is it?" I replied, ignoring his question.

"It's 11:20 in the morning. Calm down, what happened?"

"I — I had a nightmare, a really bad one, again."

"Okay?"

"No, It's not okay, damn it! I keep having this nightmare about this hideous blue creature and—" I struggled to recall Sagaru's abhorrent visage. "And every time he gets closer to me, it's like he's going to devour me whole or something. I don't know!"

"Calm down. It was just a dream."

"No, it wasn't. It felt real," I looked at Josiah straight in the eyes, fear still brewing inside my chest. "Wait, why are you in my room? HOW are you in my room?" I asked, absolutely confused.

"Your mother let me in. I wanted to talk to you about something important. Are you sure that you're not going insane or anything?"

I froze for a moment. A little manic laughter curdled in my head. There goes that word again. *Insane*. As much as I wanted to run up to Josiah and grab him by the collar and strangle every ounce of life from his body for being such a rhetorical bastard, I refrained. Instead, I looked into his eyes once more and actually took his advice—I calmed down.

"I never noticed the shape of your eyelids before, Jo; they're beautiful." I spoke softly, swatting away the sweat that had collected in my eyebrows. It looked as if his eyelids held a subtle amount of eyeliner to them.

Josiah stood there completely dumbfounded, like a young kid who just won a Nobel Prize. I felt like a complete idiot and I honestly don't even know how that slipped out of my mouth. I put my hand over my eyes and crinkled my face out of embarrassment.

"God, I am such an idiot right now," I said, slapping my forehead a few times. Josiah grabbed my arms to stop me from hurting myself any further.

"Knock that off," he said innocently, almost sweet in nature. "It's okay. I kind of wish I had your eyes myself."

I took back my arms from his grasp. I was perplexed by everything that was happening. I kept racing between ideas on how to change the subject as best I could.

Maybe Sagaru was right. Maybe I was going insane.

"Wait, you never told me why you are here," I said.

"Well, remember the board spelled out 'Circle Walkers' or whatever?" Josiah asked.

"Yeah," I paused until a spark in my brain went off. "Oh yeah, I have to give Alexandria her Ouija cursor back."

Josiah slid his backpack from off of his shoulders and tossed it on the bed. "Nah, I have the board now, don't worry about it. Alexandria got your message and gave me the board before she dropped me off. She gave it up pretty easily, honestly."

"Uh yeah, I'd give up that board in a heartbeat too. If the cursor starting spinning out of control by itself, who knows what else it could do? My mother doesn't want that thing anywhere near this house again, and I agree with her."

"But just hear me out. Please?" he pleaded with me,

pulling the board from his backpack and placing it on my bed.

"Hmm. . . No. I'm sorry, but it's going to cause nothing but trouble." I shoved the board back in his hands and turned away to comb out the knots in my hair.

"Please Jackie, you don't understand. I went to the library and started to study about this 'Circle Walking' that the Kalani guy mentioned. It's real!"

"No, Josiah, it's not. It's a load of crap and I don't want to be involved anymore in any of this. If you don't stop, I'm going to have to ask you to leave."

"It is though! Look!" Josiah threw a packet of unorganized papers on my bed and started to sift through them.

I rushed to the door way and swung open the door angrily. "Leave."

Josiah refused while scattering the papers on my bed. "I know what's after you, Jackie."

"Leave, damn it." I could feel my blood pressure starting to rise; my face felt as if it were steaming.

"I know what's after you, fucking listen to me!" Josiah shouted. He pulled a paper from the scattered pile and shoved it into my face.

It was a perfect picture of Sagaru, identical to the thing I saw in my dreams.

"Ho – How do you..." I snatched the paper from his hands. "How do you know that this is what he looks like?"

Josiah remained silent with that patented stare of his, intimidating me every time.

"Tell me right now how you know!" I yelled at him.

"Because he's haunting me too," Josiah said firmly.

I blinked at him. I let go of the door handle and walked over to the bed that was littered with papers. I remained silent, slowly flipping through the mess of paper that Josiah had collected. All of these papers held dozens of photographs, articles, and newspaper clippings of unexplainable events; deaths circulating around strange phenomena that could not be explained, all revolving around a blue flesh-colored demon. There's no way that someone could have accumulated this much information in a single day at the library.

"How long?" I asked Josiah while turning my head profile-wise towards him.

"How long what?"

"How long has this thing been stalking you for?"

"About three months."

"And when did you start to do research on it?"

"About a week after I started getting the nightmares."

"And how did *you* know that I was getting nightmares?"

Josiah did not answer.

"Tell me, Josiah."

The tension in the room created a very high-strung atmosphere. As much as I wanted to spill my guts to Josiah about this abomination of a creature that has been taunting me, I just didn't feel safe enough to yet. There are just too many unanswered questions. I was terrified yet relieved in the same token to know I was not the only one going through this. I could hear somebody walking up the stairs. There was only one other person it had to be, my mother. I panicked, shoveling the papers back into a messy pile. Josiah whipped his head left to right, aware that he had to hide the Ouija board somehow. I crammed the papers back into his backpack and zipped it up tightly.

"Honey?" my mother called out when reaching the top step.

"Yes mother?" I gulped, doing panicked charades with Josiah on where to put the board.

Her heels clicked on the hallway floor; closer and closer

she came. I mimed as forcefully as I could to Josiah and pointed to the closet with extreme ferocity. He shoved the Ouija board into the closet just as the door opened.

"I heard a commotion up here. Is everything alright?" She glanced at me and then to Josiah, who was smiling cheerily despite the sweat that dripped from his forehead. I wanted to laugh, but it really wasn't appropriate just then.

"Oh yeah!" I stood up from the bed. "I was just having a bad dream and Josiah woke me up from it. Offered me to go down to the local pancake house and everything, what a gent, eh mom?"

"Aww, I was just about to cook us all up some lunch," she said, seeming a little upset, "I was looking forward to spending some time with you before I had to go to work."

My heart sank a little bit. I felt horrible. I really did miss my mother tremendously since it felt like she was an entire world away due to her working constantly, but I needed to figure out who this Sagaru creep was. Luckily, I was able to think quickly on my toes. I didn't believe in lying to people you love, but this had to be an exception. I peered over in Josiah's direction.

"That's right Mrs. Wineberg! I uh— yeah, had to wake up the sleepy head first! Your child sure does know how to sleep."

She let out a small bout of laughter and changed her glance to the ground, her smile then retreated from her face.

"It's *Miz*," I told Josiah.

He looked down as well. "My sincere apologies, Ms. Wineberg."

I never told any of my new friends about my father, and they really didn't inquire about him either. I liked it that way. It was tedious to always retell the story to everyone individually. While I didn't consider it a waste of time, I just felt like I was digging a hole that only grew deeper. A hole filled with sorrow that my father was never going to return or reappear again. I'd beat myself up over it and had many sleepless nights since high school. I wanted my mother to move on and find somebody else to make her happy, but she vowed to never do such a thing. She's a woman with high faith and although at times temptations may shake her, she still stands strong to her word. Her entire life is consumed by her work now and she never has any time for me, let alone herself.

Why do humans find it absolutely necessary to bury themselves deep into their work when they're depressed? Why is it that we engineer our minds and bodies to the brink of exhaustion to feel better about ourselves when in reality we just turn into utter shit from doing so? I don't understand why she delved so deep into her professional life. Was it to negate the distress that washed over her from her husband vanishing, or was it because of the last night they spent together? I wish parents understood that young adults and children think too, and they bear witness to the pain they suffer from. It'd make communicating so much easier.

"Oh, it's okay darling. Please, call me Carla." She smiled gracefully as if her mind was bulletproof.

Josiah nodded hastily with a smile.

"Well, I guess I'll head to work early then and let yous-twos have your fun."

I laughed. "Yous twos? Mom, you sound like grandma," I said.

"Well at least I don't have her white hair yet," she added.

"And you know that you don't have to keep working so much, Ma. You make mad cash as it is."

My words went in one ear and out the other. She already left the room and was working her way down the stairs, the sound of her heels fading the further she went. That kind of hit me hard, but I should have spoken louder to ensure she heard it.

"So, are you going to feed me or what?" I joked to Josiah, throwing his backpack to him.

"Well, I guess I have no choice," he smirked.

CHAPTER FOUR

We sat down at a local boathouse restaurant with a pretty spectacular view of the ocean front. It had to have been a quarter passed noon, but the town drunks were already downing long Islands at the bar without hesitation towards the hour of the day.

At first I didn't understand what alcoholism really was, but once my mother started to drink heavily after dad disappeared, I began to understand why people called it a disease and see things through a new perspective. She allegedly never picked up a beer until her thirties. Luckily enough, she was able to kick the habit unscathed and if she had done any damage, it'd been only to her liver. It's quite astonishing how a human being can appear to have a fully functional life within the working world and still manage to maintain a heavy drinking addiction. I'm sure my mother's past of drinking was brought up at some point in Mrs. Ghattas' office, but Josiah knew to never discuss anything of it.

"I think I'm going to go with the blueberry pancakes," Josiah said, grinning ear to ear at the waiter after closing his menu.

I wasn't aware that a boathouse actually served pancakes in the afternoon—I wasn't even hungry for pancakes; I was just thinking on my toes with a quick lie to my mother.

"I'll take the country club wrap myself," I added, picking up Josiah's menu and handing it off to the waiter.

"Alright," Josiah unzipped his backpack and tossed some papers onto the table. "There is literally tons of information I've been collecting these past few months, Jackie. You have no idea."

"Well, from the looks of it. . . We're going to be here for a while." I grabbed a handful of the papers. "First things first though, who is Sagaru?"

Josiah leaned over the table while tapping his finger onto a crumpled paper in my left hand. "You mean that hideous creature? He's a Shaman."

"Excuse me?"

"You heard me, a Shaman."

"You mean, like the spiritual healers who do rituals and all that junk?" I asked.

"Yes! They really exist, Jackie. I shit you not. He isn't your normal ailment-curing shaman though. He's twisted. It took me hours upon hours to find out who or what that hideous creature is. I had to go back years and years, through tons of lore books before I stumbled across the root of it all. Shamanism is practiced in all different places of the world. Most people know it to be a practice of spiritual healing, but not many know that some Shaman lose their way. What Shamanism we are aware of is a western stereotype and we imagine it as just some silly little 'drum banging, hootin' and hollerin', dance-around-the-fire' Shaman to bless an item or something. There's more to it than that."

"So this Sagaru guy lost his way at some point?" I asked. I was actually starting to grow intrigued.

"Yep, I was able to look into some of the lore and legends, and I came across a piece where a group of Shaman were banished from some middle-of-nowhere place half way across the world for abuse of power. The Shaman were sentenced to death, but an entire war broke out when the village revolted against their banishment. It was almost like a mini civil war! The villagers started to feud over –"

"Wait, wait, what abuse of power? Where was or is this village located? And what does this have to do with us?" I asked, spilling questions into his head.

"That's the thing. This is where it gets a little strange and I don't even fully understand it just yet, so I need you to stay with me." Josiah mentioned quickly, shoving another bunch of papers in my face.

I grabbed the badly ordered papers and pushed away his eager hand. I tried to read the cramped scratches, but Josiah had scribbled several of the words out and left his own little notes between the lines of text. It was about the Astral Plane, and that's where I started to draw the line in my mind.

"I couldn't figure the origin of where this event took place," Josiah said, "But I did find out that the village was doing extreme practices involving trance-like ascending into the Astral Planes. The Astral Plane is like . . . this strange place where spirits reside and stuff, and with enough practice, humans can enter this plane too."

You could see it in Josiah's face that he was totally into this stuff. It kind of made me feel good that we had something in common and that he wasn't afraid to embrace his spiritual side, but he was starting to lose his marbles.

"Josiah. You do realize what you are trying to say, right?" I lowered the papers back to the table, "You sound absolutely nuts."

Josiah started to rub the back of his neck out of embarrassment and looked up towards the ceiling. "I know it sounds crazy, but it makes tons of sense! Dreams are thought to be based in the Astral Plane too. You have got to believe me, Jackie."

I looked hard at Josiah for a long moment, studying his imploring green eyes. "Go on."

"There is so much spiritualism and history linked to this Astral Realm, it's mind-boggling. You can go back hundreds of years and read about how some religions or cultures stigmatized this practice or embraced it. Greeks, Hindus, even Christians were associated with this Astral Plane at some point. It was soon swept under the rug by major western religions like any other banished practice that didn't fit at the time, and occultists and other types of underground followers adopted it as their own. Shaman still to this day practice and believe in the Astral Realm. They even claim that there are spirits from hundreds, if not thousands of years ago still walking the Astral Plane, collecting power and living as immortal beings."

"How does this fit into the Ouija board we tampered with? And what about the Circle Walkers?" I asked and crossed my arms. "And you never answered my question, jerk. How the hell did you know that I was having nightmares about this Smurf named Sagaru?"

Josiah was unable to hold in his laughter at my joke but it made me happy that he knew exactly what I was talking about — Sagaru's cobalt colored skin.

"Sagaru mentioned your name in my nightmares and that he'd soon go after you. This was about the second month into my nightmares, when he was still after me. He still *is* after me and I grow terrified to sleep at night. It was my idea to have Alexandria bring over the Ouija board. I figured that if I did, I might be able to answer some questions that weren't adding up in all of my research."

"So, that's the reason why your face went white once the Circle Walkers were mentioned through the Ouija board. I swear I thought Alexandria was tugging on the cursor. What are these Circle Walkers?"

"Exactly, it all clicked in my head. If you read those papers

I worked *ever* so hard on searching for, you'll see that Circle Walking is a practice preformed to enter the Astral Plane. There are different ways to enter the Astral Plane, Circle Walking is just a popular practice you could say. It's unknown where it originated from but the term was likely coined by the Shaman themselves. There is an entire page or two in my research dedicated to Circle Walking and how to enter the realm. I assumed it may relate to the Circles of Hell on an opposite scale, but it doesn't look that way. Instead it references Circles of Creation."

"Well, it's not like we are going to do it," I pointed out.

I knew where Josiah's train of thought was heading, and I had to stop him. There was no way that I was going to let him foolishly attempt to do such a thing, and there was *definitely* no way that I was going to risk my own life either.

"What do you mean?" Josiah asked with a slight frown on his face.

"I mean what I say. We are not going to tread into some mystical realm that you stumbled upon out of dumb luck. For all we know, it doesn't exist."

"How do you explain that I know you were being terrorized by Sagaru, then?"

I was taken aback by how quickly Josiah snapped the question at me. I felt my hand turn into a fist and my chin jut out stubbornly. He got me good. I had no explanation or justification to explain how he knew that Sagaru was after me other than the fact that he was told by Sagaru himself in a nightmare.

"No. I'm the one who's asking the questions, Jo."

"Answer me," He pressured.

"Does Alexandria or Elowyn know all about this?" I asked in attempt to turn the tables on my side.

"Answer me, Jackie. I answered you. It's the least you can do. Be fair."

He knew my weaknesses, I swear. I'm too much a fair person to ignore his question. Every time I tried my best to avoid his charming looks, something else just seemed to draw me into him. This time it was his forcefulness. I never realized how dominance in somebody could drive me wildly crazy for them. I changed my focus elsewhere and fixated my eyes onto the ocean. The waves crashed up the rocky shoreline while leaving a bubbly foam outline that slowly receded back into the water below. I concentrated as best I could to answer his question properly, but nothing still came to mind. After counting about a dozen seagulls out of a crowd of hundreds, I gave up.

"I don't know, Jo. You're right. Something weird is going on, and I'm not sure what."

"Something is, and we have to get down to the bottom of it."

The waiter came after what seemed to be a half an hour and served us our food. Maybe it was the anxiousness that prolonged the hands of time, I wasn't sure. We sat in silence while gorging our faces. In the midst of eating, I still attempted to absorb all of the information that was just thrown at me.

"For the record – Elowyn knows, Alexandria doesn't," Josiah stated abruptly.

"Well it's good to know. At least we're not the only two. Is Sagaru after her too?"

"Not that I am aware of. She says she hasn't had any nightmares about him."

I devoured the first half of my country club wrap and used a napkin thereafter. "Is that why she started crying when we were using the board?"

"It's likely. She's terrified just as much as you and I. She's more interested in this stuff than you'd think, Jackie."

"I suppose. Why haven't you two told Alexandria?"

"She's always too busy with her work. She may be a reliable friend to talk to about things, but this is a pretty hefty burden to bear."

"You can say that again. So what are we going to do? It's not like Sagaru can kill us, right?"

"I'm not sure," Josiah said stuffing back a pancake, "but if you get the time to read all of the papers I've been collecting, he's not something to be taken lightly. The tribe members in Sagaru's village died mysteriously in their sleep for no reason at all. That's what led to his banishment. He was accused of abusing the Astral Realm as a way to murder people and that's when the village went to war with itself."

"You don't mind if I take a few papers to read up on later, do you?" I asked intently.

"Go ahead. I have a few copies of everything. One can never be too careful."

"I agree. But let's make one thing clear: we are not going to use that Ouija board in my house ever again."

Josiah nodded. "We can take it to my apartment, but you have to promise me that you will not tell Alexandria about anything."

I nodded back. "Mind if I ask why?"

"She doesn't need to be sucked into this mess. If she's not having nightmares about him, then she doesn't need to know."

"She's our friend though. What if she catches on?" I asked while folding a few of the crumpled research papers and slipping them nonchalantly into my inside coat pocket.

"We'll tell her if she does," Josiah responded.

On the car ride home, my mind circled a dozen times over. I knew that trouble lurked ahead, and I could feel my chest tighten as I thought of Sagaru's brooding eyes piercing right into my own. Why does this sick man get off on hurting people in their sleep? Why did the night terrors feel so real? I could spin my head around a thousand times and get absolutely nowhere. It was right of Josiah to bring this into the light, but he had a very good point in stopping this thing once and for all. I had looked over the research Josiah had collected, and I still found it very hard to absorb it all at once. I had never heard of Circle Walking or the Circles of Creation at all, let alone what exactly the Astral Realm was. What piqued my interest instead was that Elowyn was in on this whole ordeal. I don't understand how she could keep such a straight face, but then again she was practically in tears over the Ouija board incident.

Josiah picked up his phone while driving and ranted onwards to Elowyn about how I was introduced into the equation of everything now. I tried my best to deter him from using his cell phone in the midst of driving but he completely shut me out of his mind after slapping my attempted gestures to grab at his phone. When I had to read a required book in high school, the author was pretty spot-on about some concepts in the future. When the main character's wife would listen to music through "seashells", it clicked in my head that those seashells actually resemble today's well known iPod headphones that we put into our ears, and when the author mentions that people would drive down highways at practically the speed of light, he wasn't far off the marker with that as well. Oddly enough, the world we live in has developed an irrational sense of suicide from being completely negligent of safety; case in point, Josiah ranting enthusiastically on his cell phone to Elowyn about how I was now in their "group" while speeding on an interstate and weaving through cars like a maniac.

When we reached my driveway, I let out a well-needed sigh of relief.

"Tomorrow at eight p.m. we're meeting at my place," Josiah mentioned before I could close the door to his Dodge

Charger. That thing must've cost him a pretty penny, but I bet his mother's job was able to pay for it.

"Roger that," I replied.

"Don't forget the Ouija board. We'll need it."

"Trust me, you can have it back," I replied without any hesitation. "Actually, why don't you come grab it with me? Better to have it out of the house sooner than later."

Josiah nodded, "Is your mom still home though?"

"Nah," I looked over to see if her car was parked in her usual spot inside the garage. "She's gone; you'll be okay to carry it out without hiding it or stuffing it in anyone else's closet."

I moved away from the car and up to the house. "Brutis!" I shouted out.

Once I closed the giant wooden door with some force after Josiah came through, I called for Brutis again. He was such a little pig, and it was his time to eat. If he doesn't eat exactly at 3:30, and then once again at 7:30, things in the house end up missing.

"Brutis!" I yelled a third time.

He usually always comes charging through the house when I get home. I heard whimpers coming from my mother's room. Why on earth would he be in there?

"Do you need anything?" I asked Josiah, forgetting that we just ate.

"Nope, I'm stuffed."

I went into the kitchen and on the island my mother had left a note next to the vase full of lavender flowers that I snagged from out in the backyard a few days ago. I picked them especially for my mother because she'd often tell me about how my father would go out of his way and head into the country just to bring my mother to a beautiful field of lavender when she was pregnant. During her pregnancy, she developed an irrational fear of me coming out wrong, and the scent of lavender would keep her calm and collected. I remember her describing the scenery as, "a beautiful sea of silk amethyst that gently waved with the wind, while your father and I would sit atop a small hill with a giant willow tree that loomed over us."

Sometimes, I tell my mother that I still think I came out wrong, and we both get a good laugh out of it. I snatched the nearby note from the island.

"Jackie,

Brutis has been acting strange upstairs so I locked him in my room to stop his howling. Make sure you feed him when you get home.

Xoxo, Mom."

Well that answered that question. I crumpled up the note and tossed it in the garbage. No money was attached so I figured that mother wouldn't take too long at work this time. I shouted down and asked Josiah if he could let Brutis out of my mother's room while I was headed up the stairs.

Before I had even reached the top step, Brutis had already flown passed me in a hurry. I watched him barrel down to the end of the hallway where my room was. Once there, he positioned himself with his rear in the air and his tail straight upwards, barking viciously under the door into my room. I rushed over and grabbed him by the collar for acting out of line. As much as I hated to scold my baby boy, I wasn't going to have him knocking people over and barking like a lunatic. Josiah soon arrived by my side, but when I looked up at him, his eyes were stretched with fear as he stared into my room in terror.

The Ouija board was sitting in the middle of my bedroom

floor and the cursor was spinning at a rapid pace.

CHAPTER FIVE

"That's it!" I shouted, charging into my room. "Get this damn thing out of my house, I don't want to see it anymore, and I will not be a part of this sick joke any longer!" I grabbed the Ouija board and folded it together as quickly as I could. "I don't care if you have to fucking burn this thing, I don't want to see it ever again!" I threw the Ouija board at Josiah but he fumbled it.

Brutis began barking out of control and I could feel my head starting to pound. I heard a familiar hissing in the back of my mind and vertigo started to take its course as my stomach churned. Josiah scrambled to pick up the board and the cursor but he jumped backwards in fear once the board flew across the upstairs hallway. Brutis chased after it, and I leapt after his collar to prevent him from getting near the demented thing.

"Josiah! Grab the damn board and throw it out of the house, now!" I tugged at Brutis as hard as I could with his collar entangled in my hand.

A pit bull is a gentle giant in the dog world and while they may be a docile and loyal breed, sometimes if you find the right (or wrong) button to push or trigger to pull, they can snap. Josiah's body trembled as he darted after the board. He successfully picked it up and I was able to shove Brutis in my room just in time to close the door. The two of us sprinted down the stairs at a colossal speed, likely missing half the steps. I tugged at the giant wooden door with all the strength I could muster and Josiah wound up his strongest throw and propelled the board out the doorway.

The board however would not leave. Instead it stopped in mid-flight, suspended within the air, dangling inside of the doorway. There the board unraveled and the cursor snapped itself to the board, spelling out words with the printed alphabet. I grabbed my forehead in a burst of anxiety and started to sweat intensely. I thought that I could be having nightmare, but no matter how many times I shook myself, I could not force myself awake. Everything that was happening was real.

"Come walk with me," The board spelled out.

Josiah screamed at the board as it slowly drifted to the floor. "Who the hell are you?! What do you want?!"
The board replied by spelling out more words.

"Come, Circle Walkers."

The hissing along with Brutis' barking ceased immediately. Josiah ran up to the board and as soon as he got a firm hold onto it, the board ignited and disintegrated into powdery ash in a matter of seconds. I watched the remnants of the board softly drift downwards while adrenaline still raced throughout my body. I staggered to Josiah as his hands shook uncontrollably. I turned his hands over to make sure he wasn't burned. His palms were clammy from nervous sweating, but they were otherwise unmarked. He took back his hands while his jaw chattered noisily. "I'm fine, I'm fine," he said. I'm okay. I'm fine, I'm not hurt."
"You're in shock, Jo," I told him while directing him into the kitchen.
His entire body began to shiver wildly as I went to fetch a bottle of water from the fridge. I thought of holding him, but I was too afraid that he'd take it as an invasion on my part. A loud thump sounded off nearby, and by the time I turned around, Josiah was pale on the floor and shaking madly. He was having a seizure.
"Fuck!" I shouted in panic.
I reached for Josiah's pocket in haste, pulling out his cell phone and called whatever number was first on his list.
"Hello?" A familiar voice answered.

"Um, yes, Hi! My friend is having a seizure, what do I do?!"

"Jackie?!" she replied.

"Yes, what the hell do I do!? Help!?"

She started to laugh. "If you think this is a funny joke, I'm not falling for it," she sassed back at me.

"This is not a damn joke, I have a guy who is white as a ghost on my floor and he won't stop trembling!"

"I don't know, call the ambulance!" she snapped back.

I hung up the phone and tossed it out of my way in order to tend to Josiah. There was no way that I could tell the paramedics that my friend was having a seizure after witnessing a Ouija board magically spring to life and then burst into flames—it just wasn't going to fly. I cuffed my hands behind Josiah's neck and slightly elevated his airway to make sure that he'd breathe properly. A bubbling sound started to resonate in his throat, and a new burst of fear ran through my body. It was coming. I could feel my bloodstream pulsate with energy as my mind swirled. He started to vomit, and I immediately turned him on his side. Josiah choked back the vomit as his body reflex naturally swallowed.

"Hang in there, Jo," I said, "We're gonna get you through this."

The entire time that Josiah underwent his seizure, the phone was ringing constantly, call after call. Once the vomit subsided, I resumed my attention to the phone to see that it was Elowyn who called four times in a row. It must have been her who I randomly called, and I felt like a fool for letting my thoughts become clouded in the heat of the moment. As I opened Josiah's mouth to make sure he was able to breathe, I called her back.

"Hello?!" She answered within the first ring.

"El. My god. Get your ass to my house, now!"

"Who is this?"

"Jackie. Get here now, Josiah is having a seizure!"

The phone call ended, and I took it as a sign that Elowyn was already on her way. Despite how many times Josiah put my life in jeopardy with his reckless driving, I never thought that I'd be holding him in my hands as he fought for his own life. I know that I'd do this a thousand times over if I had to in order to make sure he'd be okay. Josiah's face grew purple along with his lips and his breathing soon came to a halt. Drool started to seep from his mouth and the veins in his neck started to bulge. I cradled him as best I could, telling myself that everything was going to be okay. His neck seized up in compulsion and tears filled to the brim of my eyes. I grabbed a nearby washcloth from the kitchen table and wiped away the vomit and drool from his face. He still wasn't breathing.

I patted his back firmly as I watched his eyes bobble into the back of his head. I counted the seconds to time how long it had been. I was already up to 70 seconds with him not breathing, any longer and he might not make it. I thought of giving him mouth-to-mouth, but again I saw it as an invasion. I'd feel absolutely wrong if I did such a thing with him unaware. A gust of wind blew ash from the combusted Ouija board into the kitchen and an idea sparked in my mind. The wind reminded me about the lavender fields my mother spoke of and I decided that now was a better time as any to take a shot in the dark. I grabbed the lavender from off of the kitchen island and started crushing it in my hands above Josiah's head. My hands were dampened by a purple mush but eventually Josiah came to when the scent of the flower stifled the air. I watched him suck in air through his mouth as best as he could, still choking and gagging from time to time. It was almost as if he was asthmatic and struggling to breathe, but any breath at this point was a godsend.

I couldn't help but choke on my own heavy laughter while I teetered back and forth in happiness. The pale purple in his lips and face started to retreat. I drenched Josiah's face in so much salt and pollen in those few minutes of fear, but I was not ashamed. A wash of relief came over me, and the anxiety simply subsided. It was challenging to help Josiah up as his body jolted from shock due to the episode, but eventually I was able to get him to the living room couch.

"I n—need a blanket," Josiah stuttered, his teeth chattering violently.

I wrapped the folded afghan around Josiah that my grandmother had made for my mother and wiped away the remaining crushed lavender from his sticky cheek. I don't know if it was his drool, vomit, or my own tears, but I really didn't give a damn at this point.

"Jo, do you know what just happened?" I asked while looking carefully into his eyes. His head shifted into something I charitably considered a shake.

"You had a seizure, boy-oh."

"I ne- need to c-call my mother."

"And tell her that you fell into a seizure after you saw an Ouija board spontaneously combust?"

Josiah's eyes traveled to the afghan. He was starting to recollect what had happened just moments ago. I watched him carefully to make sure that everything was all right. Before it had been covered in lavender and puke, I'd never realized how ugly that blanket actually was, but as a child I used to carry it around the house wherever I went. I honestly don't know what my grandmother was thinking when she placed watermelon red colored yarn next to avocado green.

"Do you need anything to drink?" I asked.

"Water, and sleep." He replied fuzzily.

I went to the kitchen to clean up the mess that was left behind.

I looked back at Josiah periodically to make sure that he was alright. He had already sprawled his body out on the couch and knocked out. I smiled because I'd never realized how much of an ugly sleeper he was. It was kind of cute in a way. Maybe it was the fact that he just went through hell, though. Right as I finished cleaning up the vomit and sweeping up the ash off of the floor, I heard Elowyn's heels clicking through the front doorway.

"Hello?"

"In the kitchen, El," I responded.

She rushed into the kitchen and threw her purse onto the table. "Where is he? Is he alright!?"

"Yes, he's sleeping behind you on the couch," I said while

picking up the shattered vase.

I wasn't aware that I tossed it across the room in a state of panic. It was my mother's favorite vase, and now I'd have to tell another lie to her in order to evade the truth.

"Well, what the hell happened?"

"A lot happened. Come outside with me so we can let him sleep."

We stepped outside through the sun room's door, and I dropped down into one of the patio chairs, finally able to relax. I sat there for a few brief moments while enjoying what I could of the warm breeze. Elowyn pulled up a chair nearby, and I watched her stare at my own face as I looked at the sun-kissed freckles on her cheeks.

"We were coming home from the boathouse after he threw me into this whole mess. He told me about Sagaru and he introduced me to this "Circle Walking" albeit in brief."

"So you know about the entire Astral Pla–"

I waved my hand dismissively, "Yes. I'm well aware of everything, and I'm starting to believe in it more and more after what had happened. When we went inside after we arrived at my house, Brutis was acting strange so I went to go check on him. When he darted upstairs passed me, the Ouija board that you guys ever-so-kindly brought into my home was going bat-shit crazy."

"I'm sorry," Elowyn said.

"Sorry for what, El? That you and Josiah kept this hidden from me when bringing that board into my house?"

She looked downwards once she saw the disappointment in my face. "We didn't know that it was going to do that, Jackie."

I sighed. "You're right," I said while I linked the fingers of my hands behind my head, "and you surely didn't know that it was going to fly across the floor upstairs, let alone burst into flames after conveying a message."

Elowyn looked up quickly, her eyes flashing in confusion.

"Before you ask, the board was talking about Circle Walking. El, we're going to have to find out more about it, and soon. When the board finished conveying it's message, Josiah grabbed at the board and started to go mad. That's when it burst into flames. I led Josiah into the kitchen to calm his nerves, but by the time I looked back, he was foaming at the mouth on my floor."

"How long did it last?" Elowyn asked, her concerned tone growing sharper.

"El, it was bad," I looked up to the clouds in the sky, "It was really bad. His face turned purple, and he stopped breathing after he vomited blueberry pancakes all over my floor."

"So you called me out of panic?"

"Yeah, I figured to call anyone as soon as I could and it so happened to be you, since Josiah called you last on our way back from the boathouse. It auto dialed as far as I can remember, I just mashed buttons."

"Why didn't you call an ambulance?" She asked curiously.

"I'm not going to lie to a team of medics. There was no way they'd believe what happened. Nobody would believe it—I wouldn't believe it if I didn't see it with my own eyes."

She nodded. "Understood."

"Thank god I took med term in high school, never thought I'd be resuscitating a friend anytime soon."

"They actually taught you how to revive someone in that class?" Elowyn asked.

"Yep, we were given these broken hand-me-down dolls and half the guys in the class fondled them jokingly and ended up never becoming certified. I didn't even pass certification. The questions on the test can be ridiculously confusing," I was babbling. I wondered if I was going into shock this time.

Elowyn and I sat there quietly for a while as the breeze blew her golden curls over her shoulder. I rubbed my thumb and pointer finger together to get rid of the sticky feeling on my hands that I was given from crushing up the lavender plant frantically. Rubbing my fingers together was usually a nervous tic I would also often do. I figured it was better than biting my nails or pulling out my hair like some folks do. Today was just a clusterfuck of unimaginable events that I did not ever want to repeat.

"I could really go for a drink," I mentioned out of the blue.

"Jackie, what if it was Sagaru who was on the board?" Elowyn asked.

"It couldn't have been." I replied, denying any chance of it being so. I didn't want to believe it.

"Then who?"

"I'm unsure." I said.

"Then what are we going to do now?"

"We're going to find out how to do what the board asked of us, El."

"And that is?"

"We're going to find out all about Circle Walking. We're going to practice it and pay a visit to our faithful friend, John Doe." I spoke assertively.

"Who's John Doe?" Elowyn asked dumbly.

I stared at her for a moment and then started to chuckle.

"It's a name used in place of an unknown identification, El."

"OH!! You mean like when they say 'Who's our John Doe' in those Law and Order shows, right!? Oh my god I can't believe I'm now having the epiphany about that name." She let out a dorky giggle.

"El, I think your blonde is showing. You should run inside before the Miami sun bleaches your hair any further."

Elowyn and I headed into the living room to check on Josiah. I was relieved to see that the color in his face had fully returned. Elowyn tickled her finger on his nose quietly while holding back an absurd amount of laughter so she wouldn't wake him. Occasionally Jo would swat at his nose and let out a snarled grunt while shifting his head and Elowyn would look away while clasping her mouth shut. Somehow she always knew how to make you smile even after having one of the worst days of your life.

I wiped the ash off of Josiah's phone and started making

calls around Miami for any places that'd have a better understanding of what Circle Walking might be. I stumbled upon psychic hotlines and even ended up speaking with a woman on an native reservation who spoke with a thick accent. Nothing concrete seemed to be forthcoming as of yet, and I was growing tired of the "special deals" that I was being offered that were likely a scam. I looked back at Elowyn to see that her terrorization attempts on Josiah had faltered, and she was soon caught in a snare by Josiah's arm.

"Jackie, help!!" Elowyn screeched, her mouth half smothered by Josiah's hand at the time.

Josiah had her in a not-so-serious headlock while he rubbed his knuckles onto the top of her head. They can be very cute together as friends, and I'm pretty sure they're kindred to one another at times. It must be a real treat to find your kindred spirit early in life. I really wanted to jump in so bad between the two and wrestle with them, but I already knew that I'd play favorites. The phone call that I had dialed picked up, and I ended up having to leave Elowyn's desperate plea in the wind.

"Yes, hi, I'm looking for anyone who'd know something about Circle Walking?" I asked, completely unrestrained.

The phone hung up.

"Or not, jerk," I said to the dead phone.

I still became distraught at the thought of what unfolded earlier. It still comforted me to know that Elowyn was raising Josiah's spirit however. I could hear them thudding and thumping around in the living room.

"Hello? I'm looking for anyone who knows about Circle Walking perhaps?" I asked into the phone on another call.

"Hello?" I asked again. The line went dead. I called several different places after that with still no luck at all.

"Oh my god," I walked into the living room and slammed Josiah's cell phone on the table. "I can't believe it. That's like the third or fourth person to hang up on me. What gives?"

Elowyn and Josiah made truce with their wrestling, given the fact that their faces were beet red from probably choke-holding one another.

"She can put up a pretty good fight," I said to Josiah.

"No kidding!" he replied with his eyes still locked on Elowyn.

"Don't even get me started!" Elowyn put up her arms and crossed them tightly together.

"Calm down, sailor," I said to her. "We've got other issues on the horizon to tackle." I then turned my attention to Josiah. "It's good to see that you've made a full recovery though."

Josiah rubbed his stomach. "Yeah, no kidding about that either. I've never had a seizure episode before. It sure does make you tired and hungry thereafter. How bad was it?"

"Do you really want to know?" I asked in the hopes that he'd dismiss it.

"Yeah."

Elowyn leaned in. "It was pretty bad. You're going to have to see a doctor about it. I knew a girl from school who would have them in class sometimes and from what Jackie described to me, your first seizure was pretty severe."

"Wait, you weren't here for it?" Josiah asked her.

"Nope, I came when Jackie was cleaning up your vomit and everything else."

"Oh man, I puked?"

"Oh you sure did," I said, "it was like a possessed person chugged a bottle of Ipecac after going to the bar and downing four pitchers of beer."

We all started to laugh.

"But it still is a very serious matter, Jo," I said. "I don't want to see you go through that again. You stopped breathing too, and I was literally at wits' end on what to do. When you do have the time, go to the doctor. Who knows, maybe your mother can help you out."

"Fat chance," Josiah said.

"Why say that?" Elowyn frowned.

"Well, there's no history of seizures in my family that I know of, but then again nobody in my family had a wooden board explode in their hands either."

"It could have just been caused by sensory overload. So much has happened in such little time," I pointed out.

"True," Josiah said and headed straight into the kitchen to raid the refrigerator.

"I've called practically every place in our local range with no luck, guys." I tossed Josiah's phone back at him after sweeping it off the table.

"Yeah, and it was with my phone too."

"Haha, sorry about that, if you get any calls from any psychics about super-hot fortune telling deals, just tell them you've got bigger fish to fry."

"Hey, I know someone who might be able to help!" Elowyn clapped her hands excitedly.

"Oh?"

"Yeah, my mother used to go to this psychic woman who'd do readings for her in Key West. I bet she'd know!"

"First off El, that's way out there. Secondly, how do you know always know somebody that relates to our lives at any given point? It's very creepy."

"What can I says?" Elowyn flipped her hair self-righteously with a giant smirk. "I'm just a social butterfly."

If her eyes rolled any further with her exaggerated hair flip, I was afraid that she might become permanently blind.

"We don't even need to go see that psychic," Josiah added, heading back into the living room with a plate full of home-made pasta salad that I made the other day. "It's simple. No need to pay a psychic, no need to waste gas. We can get onto the Astral Plane with a good amount of practice. Ever heard of Astral Projection?"

Josiah made a good point. Circle Walking seemed to sound familiar in comparison to Astral Projection. Astral Projection itself is claimed as an out-of-body experience where the soul leaves the body temporarily and enters the Astral Plane. I've attempted it before with no luck and figured that it was just a myth.

"I've done it before," Elowyn said.

"You've literally Astral Projected before?" I questioned her, my eyes squinting in denial.

"Yes. I swear on everything, it's very much doable."

"You do know that it's considered a form of witchcraft, right?" I peered at her.

"What're you gonna do, burn me at the stake?" Elowyn whipped back.

"Enough, guys," Josiah butted between us. "this may be our only chance to actually enter the plane."

"I agree. It's a shot worth taking."

"What's a shot worth taking?" a familiar voice asked from the kitchen.

I turned my head around to only feel my adrenaline pump quickly inside of my stomach. Elowyn stood up quickly and started to speak before I could even conjure an idea.

"We're going to Astr–"

I quickly looked to my side and shoved Josiah into Elowyn with all of my strength, knocking her to the ground while Josiah intentionally saved the pasta salad. It was the only thing I could think of to do in time to get Elowyn to stay quiet. My mother didn't even agree about having an Ouija board in the house, what would make her think that her own child performing Astral Projection would make things any better?

"We're going to ASK Alexandria if she's able to pitch in," I jumped in quickly, still eyeballing Elowyn like a bulls-eye target.

"Pitch in for what, sweetie?"

These little lies were starting to build in number and quite frankly they started to grow disheartening.

"As you can see, Mom, Elowyn has been a little clumsy today. We were all rough-housing in the living room when it led into the kitchen and..."

"And..?" My mother asked while dropping her keys into her purse.

"And we broke your vase." Josiah finished my sentence.

Elowyn stood back up and straightened out her jeans while huffing. "We're really sorry Ms. Wineberg. We know how much it meant to you."

My mother looked over into the trash bin for a brief moment. I could see it in her eyes and it wrenched at my heart. The vase was extremely important to her because she had made it with dad. When I was about 7 or 8 years old, he bought her an intricate ceramic starter kit and even built her a wheel to spin pottery on. My mother would spend hours in the basement spinning out pots, plates, and even giant bowls that she'd place around the house as decoration. She was pretty artsy with her crafts and if she found a very sturdy string, she could suspend entire gardens in bowls she made herself, hanging them in the windows of our house. Her artistic side ceased completely once father disappeared. I admit that I've thrown a few action figures or bath tub toys at the hanging bowls and may or may not have broken one or six of them, but I was just a kid. This time however there was no excuse.

I took a few steps forward and outreached my hand to her. She looked back at me and dug her hand into her purse quickly without saying anything.

"Ma, I'm really sorry."

"It's okay honey!" She pulled out a bottle of superglue, "I raised you and still to this day I've learned to keep super glue with me wherever I go. Same goes for Neosporin, Band-Aids, tissue, and whatever else life throws at you!"

"You know that super glue isn't going to work on ceramic, ma," I said softly, feeling the familiar guilt that I remembered years ago.

She sighed. "You're right. I'll just head to the store and find something that will, then."

"You're home pretty early too, what's up with that?" I asked

"Yeah, I should probably share the news now," she said while looking up to the ceiling.

I could see her fighting back the urge to cry. She dug her fist even deeper into her purse for no evident reason before finally giving in.

"I've been laid off," she uttered.

Elowyn scurried to my mother's side and gave her a big squeeze of a hug. I shifted my feet uncomfortably while Josiah continued to stuff his face with pasta salad. Apparently I was wrong, today was just the day when the news could get worse. The last time my mother was laid off, she fell into a serious depression. We would get under one another's skin easily, and her temper was worn pretty thin. I saw how hard it was on her. To be a single parent who was now unemployed, having to deal with people scrutinizing her for allegedly murdering her husband, and on top of that she was battling a near drinking addiction. If it's one person who deserved props though, it was her, for keeping her backbone strong through thick and thin.

She reached into her purse and pulled out her keys and cell phone. She tapped one of the keys on the kitchen counter in contemplation before ultimately tossing the cell phone into my possession.

"Where are you going, and why are you giving me the cell phone?" I asked.

We used the cell phone together as a family phone. Relying on landline phones seemed to be outdated and we didn't know if we were going to be staying in Miami once we moved here.

"I'm going to grab some glue that'll bind the vase together for good. I may have lost my job, but I'm not going to lose something I hold dear to me."

"And the phone?" I asked again.

"Some guy named Kalonkie called asking for you. He said that it was urgent."

"Who the hell is Kalonk—"

Then it clicked inside of my head. She meant Kalani.

CHAPTER SIX

I twiddled with the cell phone on the table absentmindedly. I was confused and scared. How did a complete stranger that I've never even spoken to know how to get ahold of me? Despite the fear that came with the message that my mother had given me, I was considering what was going to unfold before me in the following days. I could walk away and hope the nightmares of Sagaru would cease, or I could make this one phone call and likely get some of my questions answered. The fact that Kalani found me in only hours through the Ouija board certainly indicated to me that he is not to be the type of person you underestimate.

"Should I call him back?" I asked Elowyn and Josiah with a sliver of uncertainty.

"If you don't, I will," Josiah promised. "He knows things that we don't, and he's the one who we spoke to with the Ouija board. It had to have been him who told us to join him earlier."

I dialed the number. Josiah always knows how to make for a very valid point. My stomach churned with nervousness as the phone rang. Right when I was about to end the call, he picked up.

"Aloha, Jackie!" The voice spoke enthusiastically. You could hear the wind in the background causing interference with the call.

"Uh, hi, can I help you?" I looked at my friends and shrugged while glancing back and forth.

"Help me? Well, it's nice to hear your voice for a change!"

I eased up about twenty minutes into the call. Kalani didn't seem too bad of a guy to be honest and he had an interesting accent. His voice was very proud and inviting. He sounded much like what I pictured a big brother would sound like. I had my doubts as any stranger would (and should), but it seemed that Kalani was a natural born Circle Walker. I asked him dozens of questions on that phone call, like how long he had been Circle Walking for, how it's done, what it is, what the Circles of Creation are, and even why he has gone to the lengths of attempting to contact us to do Circle Walking as well. Turns out Kalani has been keeping track of Sagaru for a few years now and is very aware of his motives.

"He's a very bad man, Jackie," Kalani said, "I've been reaching out to those who have been haunted by Sagaru. We need to stop this man."

"How? How do you know who Sagaru has been tormenting?"

"In the Astral Plane, Little Bird, anything is possible."

My heart froze. It has been nearly 10 years since I've been called Little Bird and there was only one person in the entire world who would call me that. The hand that held up the cell phone to my ear started to shake.

"How do you know my nickname? Answer me right now."

"Well, a little bird told me, of course."

"Don't play mind games with me."

"Come to the plane and visit us. We've been waiting for a long time."

The phone went dead. I balled up my fist and forced myself to keep from chucking the phone across the room. Hot anger started building within my chest. The longer that I sat there, the more red I could feel my face grow. Blood pounded in my ears, and I could see Elowyn and Josiah watching me. I didn't understand why I was so infuriated.

"Calm down. I can practically see the steam pouring from your ears," Josiah said, firmly gripping one of my shoulders. "What did he say?"

"He said something that only my father would know to say. There's more to this than we thought. Tonight we're going to attempt at the Astral Plane, and I know exactly how we're going to do it."

I sat there and explained to them about Kalani's instructions. Running through the whole thing helped me collect my thoughts, even if Elowyn was flipping her hair since she already had done it before.

"We're going to Astral Project, much like how Josiah said. Simply picture yourself rising out of your body when you go to sleep tonight. Make sure that you picture any objects in the room you are sleeping in as grey, imagine all the edges are softened, and make sure that you remove any dangerous objects. Do not think of anything negative or evil when picturing yourself rising out of your body."

"Thanks," Elowyn said while throwing her hands into the air, "Now I'm going to think of evil things, and I've done this before!"

I shook my head. "You cannot. As you picture yourself rising out of your body, imagine yourself floating up to the ceiling so you have an entire birds-eye view of your room. It's a slow process. Repeat it over and over if you have to. You must concentrate. Do not become distracted, and it's best that there isn't any noise nearby either."

Josiah nodded carefully as he listened to the instructions that I relayed to him.

"Don't tell anybody what we are doing, unless you want to look like a fool."

"Not even Alexandria?" Elowyn asked with a tiny frown.

"Not even her," Josiah answered for me. "Keep her out of this."

Elowyn nodded. "But what if one of us doesn't make it? And what did he tell you about the Circles of Creation?"

"Just focus on getting into the plane for now. He was pretty vague about the Circles but we don't have much to go on as is. I wish I could brief you more about it, but now you know just as much as I do. Something tells me that we're in for a treat if we do cross over," I said.

"Cross over?" Josiah gulped.

"Yeah, basically, who knows what's to happen after that. If we don't all make it, we'll have to deal with what we are given. Please do not call one another either, just resume your day like the normal human beings that we are. We could still be in the plane."

"We're all really not that normal, ya know," Josiah added to the conversation.

"I know, I befriended a buncha weirdos."

We sat in silence for what seemed a good chunk of time, just pondering everything and anything. There were so many things I still did not understand, but deep inside of my mind I knew that I was on to something. Something amazing waited for me on the horizon and I grew more and more eager to discover it. It felt as if the world was finally ready to unravel at my fingertips, and I was ready to seize the moment.

"Why don't we go out to eat and enjoy a night out on the town?" I suggested to them, breaking the long silence.

"Yes! Please!" Elowyn exclaimed with happiness.

"No drinking though."

"I agree," Josiah said. "I'm sure we don't want to be drunk as a skunk when we go to the Astral Plane."

Lo and behold Josiah drove—as always. We were just another car among hundreds, if not thousands, buzzing through the bustling city at an increasingly alarming speed. Twilight had reached where the earth met the sky, and I quietly hummed in the passenger seat, muffled by Josiah's loud music. My chest vibrated as the speakers pounded through his car, yet somehow my mind raised above the loud music. I questioned my sanity in that car ride for a good half an hour. There was no way that I could have gone twenty one years of my life without knowing that I was slightly mental, and there surely wasn't any mental illnesses running through my family history. Maybe I was just over-analyzing things like I often do.

We headed to one of Elowyn's favorite restaurants, Hosteria Romana, located right on Española Way. Miami Beach had slowly grown on me after we moved here, but I was secretly certain that it was the amazing Italian food that won me over. It's some of the best that I've ever had, and the restaurant is always crowded with a great atmosphere. I knew Elowyn was part Italian so I found myself asking her about half a dozen menu items that I wasn't familiar with. Between the outdoor seating, the exchange of Italian accents, the music, food, and good company, I felt at home in ways I couldn't explain, like an honorary member of the family.

We finished up eating and decided to hand in the towel early. Josiah seemed eager to return home. We all really didn't talk much on the car ride back. It was almost as if our night was hindered. Hindered by the lingering thought of what we were going to do when we went to sleep. Not one of us could focus, no matter how hard we tried to have a good time—it just wasn't working. I gazed out of the car window with a deep feeling of uncertainty, my eyes spellbound at the city lights that lit up the night sky. I could feel the melancholy in flying through the interstate with a giant city just at your side, and the feeling of being alone rang out deep inside of me. If you've ever had the chance to head out into the city at night with friends, make sure you don't wear your heart on your sleeve. The feeling of being alone seems to magnify when you leave without someone wrapped up in your arms.

You know, it is a fact that when you enter the big city as a young adult, you want to have the time of your life and chances are most likely that you will. You will dance with attractive strangers that you haven't even met for an hour of your life because you just downed four long islands at the bar and you will play charades with those attractive strangers because the music is so loud that you cannot hear each other. You will press your body up against theirs in hopes that they may be able to hear your voice due to it being deafened amongst the crowd, but in turn you are able to smell their favorite cologne or perfume they put on prior to going out. You will fall in love with a complete stranger, much like how you can in a dream with someone you have never met before.

You will become irreversibly entangled in love with someone and your hearts will intertwine in the matter of minutes. An infestation of emotion will kindle deep inside of your thoughts and you will relish in the electrifying feeling that the potential for love actually exists. You can remember feeling their breath trickle down your neck while their hands barely grazed the surface of your skin as you danced with them. A friend will then pull you from the crowd by whimsical chance, be it to leave or a sudden bizarre event, and you will never see that person again. You may remember their face for the following days, weeks, and maybe even months after, but you will never come into contact them again.

That is the feeling of what it is like to leave the city as you watch the giant skyscrapers overhead. You crunch your thumb and pointer finger with your eyes as if the buildings are only inches tall from your current distance on the highway, when in reality they are hundreds of feet in height close up. You count the lights that fill the tiny squared windows on each floor of the sky scrapers and wonder if just one of those people living in those cramped apartments happened to be in love or happened to find their lover much like how you did by mere random chance tonight while you were dancing. Sometimes meeting someone for the first time can often be the last.

It's best to look at it like this: regardless of never being able to see that person again, they will forever remain immortalized in your life as one of the most amazing people you have had the chance to get to know. You will never learn about their flaws nor will you ever learn about their insecurities. All that you two shared were a few hours of happiness and smiles together with some infatuation on the side, perhaps a kiss or a hug, and that alone you should be thankful for.

I said my goodbyes and gave out my hugs to both Josiah and Elowyn. Rain started to pelt down to the ground by the time I was in the doorway. Brutis greeted me as usual, and I was sure that he was ready to get a good night's sleep. Mother was knocked out on the couch with a bottle of Arbor Mist wine that was half depleted on the table. I figured she deserved it after what happened today. I reclined back in my bed after kicking off my broken-down and faded combat boots, and I nuzzled my baby close. Brutis wasn't much of a cuddle buddy, but I took what I could get since I was sure I'd wake up with his paw in my face sooner or later.

After about half an hour of remaining completely still, I grew tired of picturing myself floating out of my body over and over, always having to reset the thought because my conscious mind would interfere with the process or Brutis would startle me with a snore. I groaned, slapping my hands to my face. Maybe I should have had a few drinks when I was out to help me relax. There was nothing better to do than to watch the hands of the clock on my wall slowly spin around, ticking away. Every second stretched into minutes, every minute became hours. A strange silence befell me soon enough, a kind of silence that was accompanied by an odd ringing in my ears. Perhaps it wasn't silence then, because I could also feel a sensation of lightness come over me soon after, as if I had begun as a brick but had become a feather.

"Well it's about time!" a voice called out from the corner of my room.

I shot straight out of bed in terror.

"Who are you and what are you doing in my room?! Get out!" I screamed at the top of my lungs.

"Calm down!" The large man gestured his hands in a downwards motion as he approached me.

"Don't come any closer. Get out!"

"Ya don't have ta be so rude, mon." Another voice emerged from the unknown, feminine in nature and off in the direction of my room's dresser.

I quickly shook my head from left to right while holding my hands to my temples, absolutely confused. The large man who had to of been in his mid-twenties or early thirties still gestured for me to return to a calmer state – something which was not going to happen while there were two strangers in my room.

"Answer me! Who the hell are you guys and what do you want?!"

"We want'cha to settle down, ya." The woman spoke, her Jamaican accent curling off of her tongue. She was sitting askew on my dresser while tapping her long fingernails together. "Don'cha know who dis be?" she motioned her head towards the robust man.

"It's me, Kalani." He insisted.

I lowered my hands from my head.

"I. . . No. There's no way that. . . No, I can't be dreaming already."

"You're not dreaming, little bird. You're walking on the plane."

"Don't call me little bird!" I shoved my finger at him, "You're not my father!"

"I swear Kala, why do we get all da crazy ones?" the Jamaican woman asked.

With fear enveloping me at that given moment in time, I studied the woman's face and body carefully. Her eyes were not of this world, one was a deep crystal blue while the other was a vibrant emerald green. Freckles lightly traced around her cheeks and nose while her light, earthen skin appeared soft as freshly spun silk. Her hair was tied back in a style I have never seen before. The dark onyx strands were twisted and folded in giant rows after being woven together on both sides of her head and pushed back to only be suspended by a giant femur bone that resembled a war-hawk type of hairstyle. It was essentially a Mohawk but improvised with thick, knotted hair. This strange woman who sat atop my dresser was absolutely stunning in appearance. I took a step closer in her direction with my mouth suspended slightly open as her piercing eyes howled into my own. I felt heightened to look at her, as if I were a wolf gazing at the moon. The closer I approached, the stronger the inclination grew to become acquainted with her.

I traced my eyes down her breast line. Her chest was

pushed upwards from a tightly strung fur corset that ended with a thick veil of war-torn rags covering the upper part of her hips and thighs. Her skin was uncovered all the way up past her knees and upper legs, bearing perfection that seemingly went on for miles. She swung her delicately crossed legs over my dresser while placing her hands subtly behind herself, maintaining a most sexual poise as if she were a pin-up chick who was sun bathing at the beach. I couldn't help it one bit, I was enticed by her absolute beauty and there was not a chance in the high heavens that I was able to hide it.

"Do dey always do dis?" She asked, cocking her head sideways.

"No. . . Not rea—"

"What is your name?" I interrupted Kalani.

A rose-red blush started to surface underneath her freckled face, "Shajara." She extended her hand, "But you may call me Sha if you so desiah, sweetness."

I snapped my head backwards in fear that Brutis was to soon lunge at one of them but where I presumed he was sleeping, he was not.

"Where's my dog?" I asked while looking under the bed and all over the room.

"He hasn't crossed over."

"But I was sleeping right next to him, I swear it."

"Maybe it seemed that way, or we can animate him to appear, but that takes much work." Kalani folded his arms.

"Animate?" I was baffled.

Shajara let out a high-pitched giggle which resembled that of a witch. "You have much ta learn, child. We ganna show ya da ropes soon, den we'll bring ya to Astraga once ya ready."

"Astraga?"

The rate of comprehension and that of explanation did not equal out. I struggled with bewilderment at first, but as the two covered the essentials over and over, I started to get a firm hold onto the new world that I was in. Kalani and Shajara seemed to have a bountiful amount of insight about the Astral Plane, and all I could do was sit back and absorb everything that was thrown at me like a sponge.

"In da Astral Plane," Shajara twisted her hand with extended fingers to convincingly invoke suspense, "objects change shape, colors can become strongah. Ya senses be honed."

"The Astral Plane does not abide by natural law like the real world, Jackie," Kalani added. "You will see things, people, even creatures of both beauty and horror that tread this realm. The Astral Plane is where people retreat to in order to grow stronger, physically or mentally – be it for malevolency or for greater deeds."

"Some remain here, child, because dey are stuck here, unaware of where ta goh. Much like how you were."

"Wait, what? I was here?"

"Yes, my dear." She accentuated the the 's' with a slither. "I could smell ya soul da minute you walked into da Astral Plane for da first time. You was lucky!" Shajara's gorgeous eyes widened. "Lucky dat Sagaru didn't feast on ya soul."

Shajara was talking about the first time I had encountered Sagaru, with the dream I had in the lush jungle where I was running. It had to have been, there's no other account that I can remember of, especially when a dream like that was so vivid. I turned my gaze away from Shajara and onto Kalani who nodded his head. His hair was shaved on both sides of his head much like Shajara's, but the top part of his oily brown hair was long and tied back by a red rubber band that matched his dirty red muscle shirt. Kalani had a very muscular build, massive shoulders along with giant arms that were laced with the perfect lining of fat that covered his entire body. I could see that if somebody happened to piss him off, he'd be able to truck right through a wall of pure steel to get to them. Even though Kalani's appearance was intimidating, his voice was still brotherly, loving, and caring like a gentle giant.

"It must mean he has a strong Silver Thread, Shajara," Kalani said. He folded his arms with a burly smile.

His smile was so big that his cheeks pushed up into his

eyes while his arms bulged like massive cannons.

"What is that?" I asked, confused.

Shajara picked up my hand while looking at it, "Wave ya hand a little bit ta find out, ya?"

I swayed my hand back and forth a few times until an almost translucent thread appeared near the tip of my middle finger, tied about half a knuckle's length down. I raised my hand upwards above my head and dangled the thread—only inches in length—awed by its twinkling shimmer. It was fascinating to watch, looking as if it had been spun by a spider during a heavy downpour. As I tugged on the thread with my other hand, the string grew. The more and more I tugged on the Silver Thread, the further I followed it until I reached the end of the string. There my body lay in my bed, soundless and motionless. My eyes were closed and I looked peaceful. Brutis was still nuzzled in my arms, safe and sound.

"Ya see, Jackie," Shajara said, placing her hands onto my shoulders while leaning toward me. She spoke softly into my ear, "Ya Silver Thread keeps ya soul connected to ya body when ya visit da Astral Plane. It is ya guidance home for when ya wake – da bindin' dat keeps ya alive even while ya soul is elsewhere. " Shajara twisted my body by the shoulders to face her own. Her face became stern in a flash." You must neva break ya Silver Thread, Jackie! Do ya understand me?!"

I nodded as quickly as I could. "I understand."

"If ya do, you won't be able ta return to ya body."

"So... I die?" I asked with a lump in my throat.

"You could say that," Kalani answered. "It's more like being comatose. You won't be able to properly wake up, and then Sagaru would likely have his way with you. We cannot allow such a thing to happen."

A loud whisper soon infiltrated into my ears. I clasped onto my head as the pounding continued but all I could hear was my name being repeated several times. "Jackie, Jackie. Are you there?" I heard over and over. The magnitude of sound that shook my ear drums was nearly unbearable and I collapsed to the ground screaming.

"What is going on?" I shouted. "Who is saying my name?!"

Kalani knelt down beside me and patted my back firmly with his thick, callused hands. "It's okay, Jackie. Stay focused. Someone is trying to contact you. Answer them back."

"What?! I can't hear a thing you're saying! The voice is too strong!"

"Jackie, it's me Elowyn. Are you there?"

"Speak duh name of who is tryin' to call to ya, child. Remain calm!" Shajara whispered at me.

I panicked when I closed my eyes, thinking of the first thing that brought peace to me. When I opened my eyes back up, sunlight started to filter through a giant willow tree's branches. I could feel the soft wind graze my skin and if I listened closely, I could hear the flowers brush up against one another. I somehow ended up in the lavender field that my mother spoke of and I had no clue as to how. I felt so serene standing in the thick tangle of flowers. The potent scent of lavender traveled far and strong. Tranquility itself came with my surroundings, beckoning to me like Narcissus to his own reflection. I felt weightless, as if my body was suspended on pure thought. I was without consequence. I could trip or fall down the hill I stood upon and I'd never bruise and I knew this in my bones. I could feel that pain did not exist in this place—the pain of living, of time, had fled, as if this was a place outside of both. Soon the intense ringing ceased and I opened my mouth. A whisper escaped my lips.

"Elowyn? Is that you?" I asked as I felt my breath exhale into the field.

"Yes!" her familiar voice answered back. "I'm glad you made it to the plane, Jackie."

A familiar silhouette appeared off in the distance of the lavender fields.

"How can I hear you from so far away?" I whispered while waving my hands in the air.

"It's the Astral Plane, silly. Anything is possible. Sound in the plane is free to do as it pleases. We could hear each other's voice from half a world apart as long as we whisper each other's names first. You can get ahold of anybody on the plane."

"This is so. . . WICKED!" I shouted.

"Ouch, Jackie! Not too loud, geez."

"Oh. Sorry El. Heh."

"I see dat'chu found out how ta whispah and move yaself aroun'." Shajara said.

I peered off into the direction of her voice. There, Shajara sat perched on the willow tree with her natural elegance as a few of the nearby willow tree branches twined down her arm. Kalani was not far away, his back resting against the trunk of the willow tree. When I looked back to see if Elowyn had made it any closer, she was already standing beside me. I jumped a few feet into the air; she giggled.

"Where's Josiah?" I asked to Elowyn. She shook her head.

"I don't think he was able to make it, but congrats on making it yourself! First time, wow!"

I stuck my nose up into the beautiful summer sky, pompously in jest. "Well, I am a natural after all."

Elowyn gave me a good shove and eyeroll, and then she pointed at Shajara and Kalani. "Who're those two?"

Shajara tugged on the willow branches that tangled around her arm and gracefully swung to the ground before us, landing softly on her bare feet.

"Shajara," she mentioned in half bow, "Priestess of Astraga. The pleasha," she paused dramatically, "Is all mine." She finished with a wink.

Kalani dissolved into a giant cloud of smoke near the willow tree and then reappeared to my side. I flinched out of excitement of what just happened but attempted to keep my cool about it. Elowyn wasn't kidding when she claimed that anything was possible in the Astral Plane.

"El, this is Kalani, you remember talking to him, right?"

Elowyn looked sternly at Kalani in disapproval.

"You mean the one who burst the Ouija board into flames and gave Josiah a seizure?"

I looked at Kalani and waited for him to answer the question. I was curious if it were true. I had completely forgotten the turmoil that I had endured due to that particular trick, and I could feel a slight amount of agitation flicker in my eyebrow. Kalani shook his head. "Not me."

"My apologies, sweetness," Shajara giggled. "Dat was my biddin'. Kalani was bein' too soft on ya."

Elowyn scowled. I saw the uncertainty in her eyes when she glanced heavily at Shajara, but Elowyn was not the one who had to deal with a close friend shaking uncontrollably on the floor while they foamed at the mouth. I peered downwards to suppress the replay of memories when Josiah struggled to breathe and noticed that everyone was barefoot. It was an ongoing theme that seemed to appear and I couldn't fathom why.

"Why is everyone barefoot?" I inquired.

"Well, you don't necessarily go to bed with your shoes on, now do ya?" Kalani asked.

"Good point," I said. "What is Astraga?"

The sparkle in Shajara's eyes flickered brightly as a grin painted quickly on her face, bearing nearly perfect teeth. I felt a warm gust encircle the four of us, round and round as the gentle wind toyed with everyone's hair. Elowyn's curls bounced elegantly to the front of her shoulders as she looked at me, just as puzzled.

"Astraga, my child, is da city of where all da Circle Walkers gatha. It is da mecca of cities, much like a capital to a state. Circle Walkers from all over da world go to Astraga to congregate."

"You will meet people from all walks of life there," Kalani said mysteriously. "You will be welcomed by people who have lived only for a few years in the waking world, but have lived hundreds of years within the plane. It may even be on the contrary as well. I hope you can keep an open mind, kiddo. While you may come across astounding beings, you will also find that the Astral Plane houses those of which are corrupt and foul. We refer to those people as the Umbrage Walkers."

"Da Umbrage Walkahs," Shajara said while shifting her eyes left to right. "Evil bein's who have wavered off from what it means to be a Circle Walkah. You may tink dat you are safe from dem and dat'chu would never veer off course, but da power dat is promised to ya is enticin', Jackie! Dey are foul men and women who use sly tactics and trickery."

"Sagaru must be an Umbrage Walker then," Elowyn pointed out.

"Yes, he is, along with the Necromancer and many other vile people," Kalani said while shaking his head in disdain.

I staggered back and forth for a moment from a surge of light-headedness. The scent of lavender that infused the air dissipated and the flowers themselves begun to retreat and disappear into the earth. The massive willow tree on the hill withered before my very own eyes, and my eyebrows sank as my mind muddled at what was happening.

"What is going on?" I asked quickly, extending my hands to keep my balance. My head was swirling.

"You're leaving us for now, Jackie. Elowyn will soon too."

"What?" I asked.

I couldn't muster the strength to properly stand anymore, and I ended up collapsing onto the cold ground. At first the tall blades of grass softly bent downwards to catch my fall, but soon after, they wilted as the entire field was stripped of all greenery and left with only dirt in return. I felt the Silver Thread on my knuckle tighten as the bark of the willow tree crumbled into nothingness. I lifted my arm with all of the might I could gather and watched the Silver Thread bear its glittering prominence as it grew in length. My soul was tossed from the fields as if traveling at a thousand miles in the blink of an eye. By the time I was able to take a deep breath from the onset of shock, I was already awake in my bed with Brutis snoring savagely in my ear.

CHAPTER SEVEN

It worked. It literally worked! But how?! All I could remember was resting my head and watching the time on the clock tick away. I actually visited the Astral Plane, holy crap! I stood from my bed in triumph to only see that it was already nine o'clock in the morning. It felt like I was only asleep for ten minutes at most. When I stretched, I felt completely revitalized. I could feel the raw energy resonate throughout my body. I poked myself several times just to make sure that I was actually awake and not still in a state of slumber. I walked into the kitchen where I found my mother cooking over the stove top.

"I'm making your favorite," she said.

There was nothing that I craved more in the world towards breakfast food than a well catered to grilled cheese sandwich. My mother wore the same clothes she did every day that she had to go to work in; dark nylons with any type of given high heels, various jewelry pieces, a white button up covered by a grey top suit, and knee-length skirt, yada-yada-yada.

"What's the occasion, mom?" I asked while rubbing the tiredness out of my eyes.

"Just felt like cooking today, sweetie. I never have time for it anymore." She passed the orange juice and an empty cup to me.

"No, I mean, what are you dressed up for? I thought you were laid off."

"I am, but you should know me by now darling," she smiled knowingly. "I have an interview in forty five."

Here we go again. Whatever front my mother builds up as a loving mother, it always ends up being just a façade. Her career comes first and has for the last five years of our lives. Are humans not afraid that one day they will wake up and yesterday was twenty years ago?

She's still young. I give her props, and I appreciate her making me breakfast, but I know she has enough savings to live comfortably for at least three months before she starts carrying the world on her back again. Sometimes I figure her work is a security blanket. If only my dad would appear out of the blue, things would be different. She'd kick off her heels in a heartbeat and sacrifice her own career to be the stitching that held the family together. I admire a working woman, but it hurts to watch the one you love drown themselves carelessly in their profession out of pain or denial.

I tinkered around with a tiny little porcelain teddy bear that my mother seemed to have placed on the kitchen island this morning. I started to examine the room further to notice that trinkets and homemade knickknacks were spread sporadically throughout the house. I couldn't help but feel the ends of my lips start to curve. It was bittersweet in a way to see that my mother started to decorate overnight. One evening my mother and I drank so much that we rearranged the entire house together after eating half of the food in the kitchen in our previous home. This is when we were dirt poor and had nothing to lose. She was a free spirit then, even if finances ate away at her mind constantly.

"Don't go breaking that too," she said sternly with intimidating eyes.

"Yeah yeah, whatever, it was an accident. Where did you put the vase by the way? I noticed you started decorating."

"The vase is safe and sound in my room, and I must say that I did quite a spiffy job fixin' it up." She shook her purse happily to signify that she bought proper glue for the job.

"That's good." I smiled after she handed me the grilled cheese. "Remember that one time we got so plastered that we decided to rearrange th—"

It didn't matter. By the time I had spoken half of the sentence (after taking a huge bite of the grilled cheese) she was already struggling to open the giant wooden door to leave. I was teeming with emotions, anger presiding over most of them.

Regardless of how upset I was on how my mother and I played a game of tag to attempt to stay close with one another, I skittered to the giant door to help her open it.

"You know, you could have chosen a different house, mom. For one, this door is insanely heavy, and for two, this house is way too big for just two people."

"I know honey, I just loved this giant oak door. It's just complements the house so nicely!"

"And mom, you know it is alright okay to take off for a while. You're always working yourself to the bone. Relax some. Before you know it, you'll have a head full of grey hair."

"Not if I can help it, sweetie," She flipped her hair jokingly. "Hair dye works wonders!"

"Remember how we used to dye our hair together late at night?" I asked, attempting to convey a yearning feeling to stew within her.

"That was so long ago, darling. I don't have time for that anymore."

"You never have time anymore."

"I'm sorry, dear! It's nice to reminisce and all, but life must go on!"

"Except yours hasn't!" I burst out in rage. "Ever since father disappeared, all you do is work tirelessly until your develop bags under your eyes. You come home absolutely drained – sometimes half passed two o'clock in the morning – you never find the chance to enjoy time with your own child, you're always ranting on about work, and you just now found the time to actually decorate the house after we've been living here for half a year. You're becoming a spineless zombie who digests extreme amounts of labor to satisfy your constant need to silence the ongoing thought that you will never find love again, that it's your fault that dad is missing, and that if you're not working, you're not happy. It's not true!"

I spilled. I could no longer contain it for another second. I grew infuriated and I could feel the sweat starting to boil out of my pores. I took a step back from the door as my mother sat in silence, staring at me like a deer in the headlights.

"I'm sorry, mom," I said in a hushed tone.

Elowyn slipped through the doorway seemingly out of nowhere with a smile on her face. She was wearing giant aviator sunglasses and a massive brimmed sun hat.

"Good morning!" Elowyn shouted perkily.

My mom didn't say a word. She trailed her eyes off into the invading sunlight that crept through the doorway and gave me a silent nod. It felt so justifying to actually discharge all of my anger and hatred onto my mother. All of the feelings and resentment towards her that I suppressed for years flowed out of me like a river dam breaking apart all at once during an earthquake. I could have gone on for half an hour solid. After my mother nodded, she took her leave in stony silence. I cringed as the onset of remorse took over. Every step she took, her heels clicked further and further away from me down the brick sidewalk. I wanted to grab her and just give her a giant hug and tell my mother that everything was going to be okay, but I knew it wouldn't solve anything.

"What is wrong with her?" Elowyn asked while helping me shut the door.

"Nothing, just stress."

We took the conversation into the sun room. I flipped on the television in the adjacent room to create background noise in hopes of expelling the mild frustration in my head. I should have been happy that my mother already scored an interview, but something just wasn't clicking. Instead I thought of the Astral Plane how it was an entire world away from home. I wanted to retreat back to Kalani and Shajara already to see if they were still walking the plane.

"Well...!" Elowyn spoke when sitting stoutly on the pearl-white sofa across from me. "Was that fun or what?!"

I smiled tightly, "Yeah, It was pretty amazing. I can't lie. It's really fun to visit there. Who knew it actually existed."

"I know, right?!" Elowyn said in an extremely flamboyant manner.

"El, your attitude is at a ten, but I'm gonna need ya to bring it down to a five or six please," I jested to hint at her over-excited feelings.

"Oh shut up." She fluttered her eyelashes while tossing a pillow at me. "It's sucky that Josiah wasn't able to make it with us for the first time, though."

"I agree! He would have had such a blast with us. I'm sure we would have traveled all over the Astral Plane if he was by our side."

Elowyn continued to speak while my mind drifted off. Josiah. I almost forgot he existed this morning. I was still thinking of the alluring gaze in Shajara's eyes when she looked into my own, and how the icy blue battled with the lush forest green in vibrantly colored warfare. I thought about how her body curved just to the right angle in every place as she kicked her crossed legs to and fro, and how her plump lips would smile and cause her beautiful light freckles to collide on her silken skin. Shajara was something different all right. You could bet your boots that I'd be more content with counting the freckles on her face than counting the stars in the heavens.

"Jackie?" Elowyn snapped her fingers at me. "Hello? Earth to Jackie?"

"Huh, what?"

"Your phone, it's ringing. Answer it."

"Oh, right."

I patted down my pockets and pulled the phone from my right pocket along with some lint that was jammed deep down. "Speak of the devil," I said, pressing the speaker button. "Morning Jo, you're on speaker phone. El is here too." I placed the phone onto the coffee table that sat between the two of us.

"Oh my god you guys!" Josiah shouted. "That was amazing!"

I crunched my eyebrows together, confused. "Uh, what was amazing?"

"The Astral Plane!"

"Wait, you actually made it onto the plane?" Elowyn asked

into the phone as she removed her aviators and sun hat, listening attentively.

"Uh yeah, where were you guys?!"

"We were there, too! Why didn't we meet up?"

"I have no clue! I was in some place called Astraga, it was amazing! Holy crap! There were so many people there from all over the world!"

"What?!" Elowyn shouted jealously. "How did you get to Astraga so quickly?!"

"I was with a guy named Dante. Some war veteran from a long time ago. He helped me find it!"

My mind roared into a state of excitement at what Josiah had said and I picked up the phone as quickly as I could, turning it off of speaker. "What did you say? Who were you with?"

"Dante, a war veteran."

"You're sure of this?"

"Yes, I am sure of this, Jackie. What's going on?"

"Was he wearing shoes?"

"What is going on, Jackie?" Elowyn asked, concerned.

"Yes, he was wearing shoes, torn combat boots actually, entire camouflage getup and everything. Now that you mention it, I was actually barefoot myself. Huh, weird."

"Did you get a good look at his medals or pinstripes?"

"Jackie, what the hell is going on?"

My father served in the Military as a Marine back in his youth. As a combat field medic, he served for roughly six years before he met the end of his militant career reluctantly after he was nearly killed by an anthrax bomb. He was on duty when the bomb set off just a few feet to where he was standing, completely blowing up his friend Dante to pieces before his eyes. My dad ended up having to scrape Dante's mangled body parts off of the ground while still bleeding from a dozen or so wounds that were brought on by the bomb and nearby debris. He then sat in decontamination for weeks from the anthrax until he was assessed by the Medical Evaluation Board to see if he was still fit to serve. Ultimately my old man decided to hang up his dog tags even when they cleared him.

This all had happened a many years ago. As a firm reminder of his service, dad was given a permanent limp along with severe PTSD that lasted for a nearly a decade thereafter. We had to buy specific types of soap, hair care, and hygiene products for him. The anthrax had completely destroyed his ability to handle practically any type of chemical that could be found in everyday items. Chlorine from pools would turn him red as a cherry and I remember throwing a fit when I was a young kid about how I always wanted him to swim in the pool with me. As a memento for his deeds, he took Dante's combat boots since Dante's dog tags were unable to be found in the disaster. The boots however didn't fit my father. His feet were too big so he opted for me to have them when I came of age. Ever since then I've worn them like they were going out of style. The shoes were tattered out to all hell, but I felt that it was what made them unique. My mother still holds onto dad's dog tags somewhere in the countless bins and cardboard boxes we have yet to scour through.

"Nothing," I said. "I was just wondering if he served our country, that's all."

The conversation ended about Dante and nothing was further asked as to why I was so curious about that fellow man. I figured if I wanted to know if it was the Dante that my father knew, I'd be able to find out firsthand myself. The three of us continued to converse together about how fascinating our trip was in the Astral Plane and how eager we all were to return – this time together as a trio. We all agreed that we'd meet in a place that we were all well aware of this time, a local park not too far from my home that Josiah and Elowyn played at growing up.

Josiah mentioned a critical point that the Astral Plane is uncannily parallel to the actual world we live in. Mirror like, even. When we asked how he knew of this, he had told us that he had the privilege to roam around several places of the world with this Dante fellow before making the final stop to Astaga, the Circle Walking capital. He went on to tell us about how rooms, cities, landscapes, public places and the like all over the world look exactly alike in the Astral Plane as they do in the waking world. Josiah was right. After all we were technically out of our own bodies when treading the plane.

"Dante said with enough practice, you can phase out from the Astral Plane and into the waking world while still being out of body!" Josiah exclaimed.

"No way!" Elowyn gasped.

"Yes way!" he replied. "I can't wait to go back!"

The best way to describe the feeling of being out of your body is that you feel ultimately free. You feel free of the physical weight your body naturally brings down upon you, allowing the ability to release your true potential from your consciousness that was once impeded. You are not bound by gravity when you are Astral Projecting; instead, you float weightlessly through the atmosphere, undisturbed and unencumbered by the waking world. We still weren't totally certain how we could interact in the waking world by trying hard enough, The three of us assumed that it worked on a similar scale to how spirits attempt to convey messages to those who are still alive, sucking the energy from the room in hopes to conjure a speckle of an event that could be noticed by the living.

A week's time had passed as the three of us continued to attempt the Astral Plane. Elowyn and Josiah were fortunate enough to consecutively reach the plane day after day. On the other hand for myself, I was not lucky enough to make it that far. I was too disoriented, bent out of shape from unleashing upon my mother so angrily. I made amends with her by going out back and plucking fresh lavender and lilies of the valley, but they remained on the kitchen island to only wilt where I had left them. In the week that I was unable to reach the plane, Sagaru had visited me twice. Technically from Sagaru visiting me, I had reached the plane but on a level to where I could not control my actions adequately as I wanted to like how Circle Walkers could. There was an apparent difference between what it meant to be in the Astral Plane as someone who was asleep compared to someone who was able to Astral Project efficiently and effectively. I was feeble, susceptible to whatever Sagaru had in store for me. I'd try my best to flee from his ghastly terror but I just couldn't.

The minute that Sagaru would attempt to reign over my body and devour me whole, one of my comrades would come to my aid in my stupor. Be it Kalani, Shajara, Elowyn, or Josiah, no matter who would valiantly appear at the given time, I'd be rightfully saved. The audacity that Sagaru portrayed was frightening and quite frankly every time that he was forced to retreat, you could sense that he was growing stronger. Kalani and Shajara had walked the plane plenty of times to know the basics of how to put up a good defense against Sagaru while Josiah and Elowyn would taunt him successfully in order to trail his attention off of me since they were just as weak as myself. Sagaru was a coward and preyed viciously onto poor souls who could not lift a finger to protect themselves when sleeping.

"I can smell the weakness in your muscles as you sleep, little one." He cackled maniacally. "I can taste the salt in your sweat that pours from your very body here in the plane. You're helpless without your friends." He dragged his decrepit, ice cold finger down my cheek. "I will soon have the chance to devour you whole, Jackie."

"Go to hell, Sagaru." I clenched my fist, frozen in terror.

"I've been there before, bahaha," I watched his onyx eyes gleam brightly as he burrowed his head on my shoulder. "I prefer fresh, vibrant souls such as your own. You need to have an acquired taste for the burnt souls that are tortured in the infernos of hell."

In an explosion of smoke, Kalani and Shajara came forth in triumph, ambushing Sagaru with a bombardment of attacks that I had figured would have never been possible from the likes of them. Sagaru was taken aback quickly and his very image distorted, eventually disappearing into the darkness from which he came. Shajara sat beside my frail body, nodding her head softly that everything was going to be okay. I grew sulky, angered that I was helpless to defend myself until I was able to Astral Project once more. I woke in a cold sweat after my dream had fluttered out. It was strange being able to see my friends in the Astral Plane via dreaming, almost as if I were talking to someone directly through a television screen while they acknowledged my existence.

I could faintly hear rain hitting the roof of the house as I vigorously scratched Brutis to wake him up. He puffed out a generous amount of air that flapped his cheeks, indicating to me that he'd rather remain sleeping than get up. My sullen feeling deepened as I tried to find the answer of why I couldn't reach the Astral Plane correctly, until I was able to come up with an idea. I went into the upstairs hallway and popped open the cubbyhole that loomed right above my doorway, leading right into the attic. I scavenged throughout the various giant cardboard boxes until I had finally come across my mother's sewing kit that was lodged in a deteriorating box. The box harbored a decent amount of mold that must have started to fester once everything was moved into the attic. The sound of the rain hitting the roof had increased. I coughed at the copious amounts of dust clouds that smothered the already-stagnant air when I picked up the kit and headed out of the cubbyhole with it wrapped tightly in my arms.

I placed the sewing kit onto the dining room table and twisted the knob that popped it open. I poked my finger around curiously until I had found what I was looking for: a spool of Silver Thread. With the thread in hand, I unraveled it just enough and cut off the thread with a tiny scissors that was provided to me from the kit. The scissors were honestly meant for someone with extremely small fingers, as I had troubles removing them thereafter for a good half a minute. I stuffed the thread firmly into my pocket. The doorbell rang as I tossed the scissors back into the kit.

I quietly peeked through the window blinds near the giant wooden door to see an older woman standing there. She fastened her bonnet tightly and swatted away the remaining rain that glided off of her leather gloves from the gutter. She placed a piece of folded paper between the door handle after she pressed the doorbell once more. I looked her up and down with extreme prejudice and couldn't help but snicker. Maybe it was my own oblivious nature to be a punk about it, but just the way she dressed bothered me.

Her maroon fleece long jacket affixed giant buttons about the size of moderate kiwi's, but were olive in color with checkerboard 1970s red pin striped pants that cut off at the ankle. Her pants were ironed so perfectly that I cringed at the thought of one of her grandchildren running up with sticky fingers and ruining her entire day's worth of work on maintaining a beautiful image. She looked to be the type of woman who'd break your heart without knowing because she'd be dining alone, inside of a bustling restaurant all by herself. You'd just know she lived a wonderful life. She most likely lived her prime during the World War II era and she became an unwilling widow to a man who served the country.

You could watch her for the entire stay at the restaurant and yet a tear would never escape your eyes despite how much you yearned to know her story. I still watched the older woman walk down the crumbling street with flyers in her hands, and I started to resent myself for thinking like an ignorant fool. I was too quick to judge on the fact that her apparel and sense of fashion had permanently stuck in the 1970s, and that she was simply going door to door in hopes to speak to people about the praise of the big man upstairs. I felt wrong. She, who had to of been in her late 70s by now, still found the time of day to pin her hair back into beautiful giant white curls and tie it down with a colored bonnet that matched her given mood or the current season, and would iron her clothes every morning while slathering on her favorite powder, lipstick, and most likely her ancient perfume just to feel sheltered and preserved, while I, a young judgmental kid who wore a stained sweater and sported disastrous bedhead hair, laughed at her.

I laughed for all of the wrong reasons and a piece of me on the inside really grew dark that day against my will, as dark as the mundane clouds that loomed over the city that night. I closed the blinds to the window and refused to judge her anymore, but instead I thought of what life was like for her back in the day. Back when women were on the rise in the industrial age, how fashion began to take electric spinoffs, leaps and bounds. I pictured her again in that restaurant, but this time she was not old and not eating alone. Instead she was a young and energetic person such as me. She had danced the entire night to an old jazz mash up with her wedded love, and had the grandest time of her life. In circles she spun in and out of the crowd while holding his hand, and just for that mere second I realized that I gave life to what I once mocked in my mind. I felt better about myself. When I looked back out of the window to make sure she had made it safely down the street, I saw her accompanied by another elderly woman. My heart dropped a little as the other elderly woman fluffed away at her gaudy black fur hat with a matching black purse on her elbow.

I wondered if she could have a similar story such as her friend, being a widow and all, waking up every Sunday morning and dolling up her appearance just to go to church alone. I pondered on it harder than I should have, but after a brief moment of indescribable uncertainty towards why I was flustering my mind over two old goons, I soon immortalized her alongside her friend as a youthful woman herself, dancing by her side in that parlor restaurant. I really do miss my grandmother, and it's moments like these that I wish I was home where I first grew up, in the suburbs of Illinois.

There was a good reason as to why I felt like I always left my heart in the city whenever I would go out with Josiah and Elowyn before this entire Astral Plane adventure started. Initially before I arrived in Miami, I actually did leave my heart behind, right smack dab in Chicago. I met a wonderful man during a Blackhawks' game that I was attending with a couple of my high school buddies. We kept eyeballing each other throughout the entire game. I mustered the bravery to approach him after the game and it was the most well invested 20 seconds of insane courage I have ever undergone. He was the punk rock type of guy who spiked his jet black hair and wore faded black jeans that were cutoff at the knees. His converse shoes were so torn apart that you could see his white socks poke out at the tips of his toes when he walked. I remember when we used to spend time together for hours on end after school. I would twine my finger through the loose linen strands of his jeans and pull them off. Whenever he'd light up a cigarette, I'd take his lighter from him and burn the ruffled linen strands to the brim of his newly formed shorts. I wasn't too fond of smoking, but it was something that I generally blocked from my mind when he did light up.

His name was Cid and he possibly had the most muscular jaw that I had ever seen on a man in my entire life. His chin was squared off and in the center you could see it fold inwards to a perfect degree while being subtly traced by facial hair. Cid was decently sized in his bone structure, making his body weight average around 160 to 170 while he stood at a good 5'11" in height. I envied him for that but I promised myself that I would never show it. I didn't want to jeopardize him ever looking at me as if I were insecure. Cid was, and still is as far as I know, bisexual, just like myself. We were two peas in a pod and eventually after dating for a year solid, we rightfully brought our true feelings into full fruition and consummated under a half moon, taking one another's innocence. I will never forget the fella. He was one of the only people in my entire life that actually treated me right and respected me for who I was at the time.

He was there for me when the going got tough. When my mother was having mental breakdowns due to my father disappearing, he took the burden onto his own shoulders and took care of me. I admired his stalwartness and I always promised that I would be just like him, especially since he could maintain such a loyal persona while still pulling off that bad boy appeal from his looks and attitude. Unfortunately we didn't make it through. We had a fall out when I was forced to move but I made a vow that one day I would see him again, even if we went separate ways. I still expect to fulfill that vow.

I shook my head to dispel the trip down memory lane that the elderly woman provided for me. I opened the giant door to retrieve the folded paper that she had stuffed in the handle. I figured it was going to be a brochure on religion but to my surprise it was not, instead it was addressed my mother, Carla Wineberg, to attend the biweekly bingo tournaments that were held down by Miami beach where all of the old fogies flocked to in the morning. It was sweet of the elderly woman but I think my mother still had quite a few years to go before she'd be seen as a rowdy old blue haired woman screaming "D3, Bingo!" after landing a successful bingo line. I almost ripped up the paper but instead I folded it back together and stuffed it into my back pocket.

The day dwindled on slowly, rainy and damp as ever. Mother arrived home after shopping for food at the local grocer and stuffed the entire kitchen with plenty of food that I actually fancied for a change. I helped her unload the groceries after I tossed the wilted flowers on the table into the garbage. The entire week I had wished a thousand times over for the hostility between us to vacate our lives, and it turned out that my wish was granted. She brushed away the rain that beaded onto the last plastic grocery bag and unraveled its contents with a grin full of intent on her face. There she took out two bottles of hair dye, one being a walnut brown, the other being a bleach blond, and then continued to pull out two giant bottles of Arbor Mist wine. I tried to resist as best I could from smiling, but it was impossible. She won me over.

"Mom," I said when she wrapped her arms around me. "You didn't have to."

"No, you're right. I've been caught up in my professional life and for that I am sorry. It's time that we have some quality family time. What better than to spend time together and get drunk while coloring our hair, right?"

I laughed with pinpricks of happy tears in my eyes. I firmly hugged her back and pulled a bottle of wine toward me. "Aye aye, captain, you don't have to tell me twice!"

"But I will tell you to take off those damn boots in the house." She scolded.

She really wasn't really fond of the combat boots and never has been for that matter.

My mother is a natural blonde so I went after the bleach blonde hair dye since it'd be useless to her. We gloved up for the coloring process, taking generous swigs of our wine bottles and let the session commence. Arbor Mist wine is extremely sweet and a guaranteed hangover if you get annihilated on it. I was more of a hard liquor fan, but when you live with my mother, there wasn't a chance in hell that you'd find a bottle of the hard stuff lying around.

"Do you remember when father always used to carry a bottle of scotch in his study room, mom?" I shook the bottle of dye chemicals together vigorously.

"I do. Every Friday night he'd spin off the top and pour a little bit into a glass full of crushed ice. He was a hard-working man and deserved every drop of it, but it didn't do too well with his skin."

"Aye, that he was, and you're right." The inner pirate can come out in me when I drink at times. I squirted a heavy amount of dye into my hands and started to douse the tips of my hair. I decided that I wasn't going to go completely blonde this time but instead just dye the tips of my hair. My mother squirted the entire bottle of brown into her hair carelessly and massaged it in. Now that's the woman that I know, I wish she'd still made bold choices all the time.

"He sure loved his job. There is no denial in that." Mother added.

"Agreed. Speaking of love, my heart has been all over the place myself."

"Oh yeah?" she came over to me and spiked my hair upwards into a giant mohawk. "Spill."

"Well, between still thinking about Cid, I still question Josiah and who he is. I dunno ma, many things just really attract me to him, but I don't want to risk ever losing him as a friend, ya know? And then there is Shajara too, who I—"

"Shajara?" she interrupted me while tilting her head.

Great, I get all liquored up off of half a bottle of wine and almost spill the beans. I darted my eyes around the kitchen while thinking of yet another fib to tell her. It was the second (third? fifth?) time lying to my mother and it had to continue. I just wanted to come clean over every single detail about what was going on in my life, but I knew she'd become absolutely dumbfounded. I gave her an intense stare and for a given second I almost did.

"It's an online screen name she goes by. I met her on some social media website, nothing special."

"Ah. That name sounds kinda funky." She snorted and then took a drink from her bottle.

By the time we rinsed out our hair, the clock was already reading 9:45. It didn't bother me that neither one of us prepped up something to eat in the meantime; we often would eat solo since we lived separate schedules. I screwed my nearly empty bottle closed and stuffed it deep in the refrigerator. My mother flipped her towel-dried hair over her shoulder and gave me a concerning look.

"You're not leaving me just yet, are you?"

"Uh it's nearly bedtime for me." I pointed the clock.

"I don't care," she let out a huge hiccup. "We still have to decorate."

I couldn't help by grin. "You really want to decorate the house finally after living here for so long?"

"Hell yeah," She rose her bottle into the air. "Besides, you've already been rummaging through the boxes upstairs."

"How do you know that?"

She pointed the narrow neck of her bottle towards the dining table which had the sewing kit still resting on it. I completely forgot and I almost reached into my pocket to make sure the Silver Thread was still there out of remembrance.

"Oh yeah, " I tugged at the collar of my neck, "I had a rip in my shirt, had to fix it up."

"Since when do you know how to sew?"

"I did it manually. Brutis popped a little seam when we were wresting," I said nervously. "Are we gonna decorate or what?"

"Meh, I think we can another day."

Phew, successful evasion by the skin of my teeth. I watched my mother slap off her stained gloves and toss them into the garbage.

"I'll be off to bed now, then. I love you," I said while scurrying upstairs.

"I love you too, darling."

Brutis clipped at my heels when I headed up the stairs. I tripped halfway up and blamed it on the wine. After I entered my room, I instantly retrieved the Silver Thread and tied it carefully around the knuckle of my pointer finger, determined as ever. I nudged Brutis onto his side of the bed and burrowed myself deep under the covers. I sat there, picturing myself rising out of my body continuously. The more I pictured myself floating upwards, the less the world spun around from the alcohol. I tossed and turned a couple of times until I found the perfect position, and before I knew it, I was greeted by Kalani himself.

CHAPTER EIGHT

"Good to see you again," Kalani said, extending his hand. I pinched his cheek instead. "I missed you too, honey," I replied. He laughed as he knocked my hand away. "Do you know if Josiah and Elowyn have made it through?" I asked.

"You don't have to ask me. Why don't you whisper their name and find out first hand? Or first ear rather?"

"Right," I replied.

I still wasn't used to all of this bizarreness. There is an abundance of information to ingest after you're introduced to a world that you thought didn't exist. I felt sort of childish while Kalani waited for me to attempt a whisper. Kalani encouraged me to begin by waving his hand in circles.

I closed my eyes tightly and concentrated. "Josiah?" I whispered.

Nothing. I whispered louder, "Josiah?"

"Jackie?" I heard a faint whisper in my ears.

"It worked!" I shouted to Kalani. Kalani put his pointer finger to his mouth quickly. "Shh! Not so loud! You're going to blow his eardrums out."

"Oh, right. Sorry."

I turned away from Kalani and whispered again. "Yeah, it's me, Jo. Where are you? Is Elowyn with you?" I asked in a hushed voice.

"She is! Come to us! We're at the Wainwright Park."

I concentrated as strongly as I could to picture the park. Josiah and Elowyn always spoke of how beautiful the view of the bay was and how they spent many days there with their family. I envied them for it.

When I was younger, I would always tread down by Lake Michigan. I basically visited the lake every day for three years solid when I was having troubles in my life. There's just a sense of peace that a large body of water provides. One summer night, Cid and I walked down the local pier and sat beside a massive red lighthouse; we watched a thunderstorm pummel the waters overhead. Eventually, after the storm dissipated, a chilly cold front came through with a dense fog that rushed right off of the lake and enveloped us. It was an easy twenty degree drop in temperature, and I remember huddling next to him to keep warm. I used to pick away at the broken cuticle skin around his fingernails when he'd wrap his large arms over my shoulders. I thought about the water and the cold, and I felt myself start to move.

I could hear the waters of the bay rush up against the rocks and echo throughout the ground. Soon I could hear the tiny pieces of sand and pebbles rub against one another as the water escaped from around them. I concentrated harder to picture the Wainwright Park with everything I could. My skin shivered as goose bumps rose, and the heavy scent of seaweed lingered in the air. Before I opened my eyes, I whispered Elowyn and Josiah's name quietly with a smile, feeling that I had reached my destination.

"Elowyn? Josiah? I think I'm there." I waited quietly.
The sound of the waves grew stronger and I could also hear the branches of the trees knock together from the wind.
"No, silly, it's me. Who are those people?" A voice replied with an adorable laughter that followed.

My heart sank and I instantly opened my eyes in shock. I shot my eyesight around in utter confusion, searching for their face. I was not in Wainwright Park. Instead I found myself standing under the giant red lighthouse. Apparently I hadn't concentrated hard enough to my specific destination and crossed my thoughts together. I swear the voice I heard was Cid's, it had to of been his voice but when I looked around, nobody was to be found. I called out Elowyn and Josiah's name by whisper and waited a brief moment. There was no response.

"Great, now I'm screwed." I attempted to whisper their name again along with Kalani and Shajara but still wound up with nothing.

I was alone, or I thought I was. I walked quietly, my bare feet gliding across the cold stone pier pavement. I took in what I could remember of the place. A sense of nostalgia overcame me as the waves crashed violently against the beach. I was actually somewhat close to my first home again, and it really tugged hard at my heart. I was back where I shared my first kiss, where I confessed my first love. I sat down and kicked my legs over the side of the pier, dangling them loosely while looking up at the night sky. The thick clouds were dense and almost veiled the entire moon. I howled loudly like a feral wolf, like the way that Cid used to when a full moon hung in the night sky.

In my head I pictured his twinkling earthen brown eyes that would become crunched when he'd purposely smile big. I remembered that I used to trace his jawline and chin with my finger while asking him nonsensical questions about the future. He used to snap his teeth at my finger out of nowhere with a growl and startle me. I'd punch his chest as he cackled at seeing me surprised. Somehow he always knew the perfect moment to startle me, no matter how much I prepared for it. Just to be in his sturdy arms again was a dream. I laughed and shook my head in dismissal of such thoughts. No matter how much I thought about the past, it really didn't matter; it just would never be the same. A smile would still stretch across my face when I thought of him. I looked down at my finger nail cuticles and thought of picking the broken skin.

"That's a pretty impressive howl, I must say," A strange voice said from behind me.

I fell off the edge of the pier and into the water out of fright. I quickly swam back to the surface, choking on water. I hastily climbed back up the ladder due to an absurd fear that a giant fish was going to devour me whole. By the time I reached the ground level of the pier with my eye level barely above the pavement, I saw a pair of eerily identical combat boots approach the ladder. A rough hand extended out to me as I looked up.

"You okay there, sailor?" he asked with a grin on his face.
"No thanks to you," I responded sarcastically, declining his help.

I wrung out my shirt and roughed my hair up a bit to get rid of much water as I could. While looking at the strange man, I was instantly able to surmise his identity by the attire that he wore. He was dressed in full Battle Dress Uniform and his posture was as straight as an arrow, perfect and stalwart, much like how my father would stand. The BDU was accompanied by the combat boots my father had given to me that I still wore to this day; they were a perfect match to my own, bearing the exact same tar marks and holes. It took a few moments to collect my thoughts on how to approach the situation. I inhaled a deep breath and looked into his bold eyes.
"I take it you knew my father," I said.
"You look just like him, kiddo."
"So it's true after all. You are who I think you are. Dante, right?"
"That I am, little bird."
My stomach pumped a small amount of adrenaline from hearing my childhood nickname. I felt indifferent that strangers such as Dante and Kalani knew and used that nickname without even thinking twice. I grew upset that my father would share such personal information and still at times it didn't add up when I thought about it.
"The name's Jackie, not little bird."
"Roger."

"How do you know that nickname? Did my dad tell you?" I asked.

"He's been around the plane a few times." Dante trailed his vision elsewhere. He folded his arms behind his back promptly, pumping out his robust chest. He looked pretty strong physically, although he didn't have much height on him. His skin was a darker hue, as if he had sat out in the sun for a good month or two solid and earned a heavy bronze tan. I turned my attention off into the distant waters. I watched as the crashing waves barreled over each other forcefully.

"And Kalani?" I asked without hesitation.

"He's my son."

I didn't want to inquire any further but I just couldn't resist. Despite the yearning feeling of wanting to know of my father's whereabouts, I knew that I'd have to step over a fine line to get to them.

"Nice combat boots," I said abruptly.

"Thanks. It makes me happy to know they're in good hands now."

I looked down to the pavement as I wiggled my toes. The way that Dante and I conducted the conversation was as if it were an inside-only understanding. I knew that Dante was dead, and I knew that, despite seeing the combat boots on his actual feet, I was the sole owner of them now in the waking world. It's uncommon for people who are alive to wear shoes to bed when attempting to Astral Project if you truly think about it.

"I take it my father talked about me quite a bit."

"Leo always did when he found me here on the plane, and always did when we were on the field together, too."

"If you don't mind me asking, what exactly happened?"

Dante hesitated. He shifted his hands nervously behind his back and gave his head a small shake to rid himself of the recollection. It felt wrong to ask so soon. I figured from his initial reaction, Dante still suffered from the memory of the accident.

"It's alright. You don't have to explain. I'm sorry for asking." I said.

Dante ignored my apology and continued onwards.

"That night I was assigned to stand watch with your father. We were making a round when out of nowhere I heard a loud scream and before I could act, all I remember was everything going white. I don't remember seeing the explosion. The last thing I actually saw was your father's face. It was burned into the back of my mind for quite some time afterward."

His hands twitched slightly behind his back.

"All sound became obsolete and eventually all colors disappeared into darkness. I was lucky. I didn't feel a thing. I remember floating above the place of impact for hours, perplexed about what had happened. I didn't understand, and a part of me still doesn't fully comprehend. Time itself didn't match up to what I remembered. Time was slower, much slower."

"Then I felt an overbearing freedom, as if all the weight in the world had vanished. Physical pain was that of the past, but my memories were still very strong. I could feel my psyche ache in agony. Even though I lost the ability to feel physical pain, the emotional pain was very traumatic and still very real. After all of these years there is still no way to fully describe or articulate the misery that I endured. The anguish that feasted on my soul nearly swallowed me whole. I trembled at what was to come."

I watched him carefully. He turned towards me and took a step closer. It was as if the flesh on his body started to carve out the wounds from the bomb that had killed him. His jaw unhinged while the skin of his eyelids disintegrated. I watched as one of his eyes became crushed by his socket, violently buckling inwards. The smell of burning flesh invaded my nostrils and his face deformed into unrecognizable, hideous scars and lesions. I turned away as quickly as I could out of sheer horror. The stench that rolled off his body made me gag, and I covered my mouth as I stepped away. He laughed maniacally while I squinted at the sight.

"Enough!" I shouted. Dante took a step back and the moonlight glistened over his necrotic flesh, soon returning it to a soft, plump and natural state like before.

"Sorry. I always like to freak out the newcomers. " He laughed loudly.

"Job well done," I affirmed.

"After the explosion, I somehow stumbled upon this place. I remember drifting in between worlds for a time. I was lost and confused with nobody to give me any guidance. The plane is not much of a home, but it's the closest thing that I have. You'd think that I had seen enough crazy shit in the military and that I'd be used to what I see here on the plane, but not a day goes by to where I'm not astounded – not that day and night actually exist here on the plane." Dante mentioned.

"I still have so many questions for you."

"What, you're not going to thank me for my service?" He asked.

My father always used to detest when people would shower him constantly in thanks as a veteran. While he was thankful for the recognition, he considered his duty a second nature when he was in the military and that there was no need for such common courtesy or generosity all the time. I apologized to Dante and gave him my thanks for his services but he didn't reply right away and seemed to have his mind set on other things.

"You know, Leo is a humble man and always has been. He was one of the most kindhearted men I knew. He always kept an open heart and open mind." Dante said proudly.

"You talk about him as if he's still alive," I added quickly.

I hadn't realized how my thought process immediately jumps to the conclusion now that my father is dead. Perhaps I had lost my hope. I quickly grew ashamed and sunk my head downwards. I was just so used to always thinking the worst when it came to him and it was much easier to accept that he died years ago than to hold onto the thought that he was still alive and kicking.

"I can't give you a concrete answer if his heart is still beating, kiddo, but I can tell you that he's visited the plane a few times these past years. He's older now than I remember him being."

"If he's so great, then why did he disappear from my family and leave me behind?"

"That I can't say." He reached out and put his hand on my shoulder. "It's not that I don't want to, but because I don't know the answer. I'm sure he has a good reason."

I jerked my shoulder away from Dante's grip. He was a young man when he died, I'd say at best he looked like he was barely twenty five. For how much time that has passed since his death, you'd think that he'd be hitting half a century in the looks department. I suppose it's true that age is a mortal curse. Those that are dead are lucky enough to be lifted of such a curse. The more I spoke with Dante, the more I paid attention to his looks. To be quite frank, Dante and Kalani didn't look much alike. Maybe it was the tiny scars that were spread across Dante's face, or the fact that Kalani was much taller and broader.

I could feel my heart flutter a little as my palms sweated. Actually getting some news that my father could possibly be alive after nearly a decade since his disappearance ignited something inside me. I had remained optimistic and hopeful throughout my entire teenage life, but a smoldering feeling of resentment brewed deep within me now. Resentment from him leaving my mother behind and causing a traumatic chain of events for her, resentment for leaving his own child to fend at a young age. How could he do something like that? *If I ever get the chance to see him again, I'm going to ring his neck and relish watching every second that I squeeze the breath from his lungs,* I thought.

My mind turned endlessly, spun by the idea that I could once again have a fully-functional family in my life. I felt my lip quiver and I was unsure if it were out of happiness or rage. Dante took a step forward and offered his hand out to me with a gleaming smile, nodding his head slightly. I didn't fully comprehend the gesture, but my initial reaction was to reach outwards and accept his invitation.

"You don't have to hurt anymore, Jackie," Dante spoke softly. "I can show you a better world — a new place where your emotions won't consume your very mind."
With a deep breath, I wiped the sweat from my hands and shook them free of any trembling. "You can take me to Astraga, right? You helped Josiah get there."
Dante nodded, but I didn't feel very assured by it. "Yes, but I can give you much more. Take my hand. I promise."

Before I could accept his handshake, I was tossed to the ground by an explosion of smoke and dust that filled the air between Dante and me. I coughed and swatted my hand from side to side and squinted to see what had happened.

"Run, Jackie!" A voice called out from the dense cloud. It was Shajara.
"Shajara? What the hell are you doing? I know this man!"
"You do not! Flee now!"

I stumbled backwards, trying to get my feet underneath me while an unimaginable amount of fire filled the nearby atmosphere. Shajara's hands crackled like a raging inferno as giant waves of fire discharged from her fingertips towards Dante. The fire reflected wildly off of her beautiful eyes as her eyebrows narrowed in disbelief and hatred.

"What the hell are you doing!?" I shouted in complete shock.

I watched the flames roar around the two. I had never before seen such a performance here in the plane. What trembling I was able to rid myself of undoubtedly returned when I stumbled around the giant red lighthouse. My eyes bulged from their sockets and I couldn't properly get air into my lungs. A threatening laughter echoed throughout the immediate area as more people appeared from thin air. Sagaru along with two others I had never seen before emerged from the darkness. Before I could raise my hands in defense, my body was torn from my stance as yet another cloud surrounded my body. I felt a rough tug on my left arm and I was whisked away, off of the pier and into the midnight sky by a well-known force.

Kalani nodded bravely towards me when we met eyes. We soared high above the ground at incredible speed. I looked back in terror as I watched the pier explode into an inferno of fire as Shajara defended herself. I fought to break free of Kalani's grasp and he shook his head at me in disapproval.

"What the hell are you doing?! She's outnumbered!" I screamed at Kalani as I shoved my free hand into his face.

"She'll be fine, Jackie!" He fought back.
"Why are you attacking my friend!?"
"He is an Umbrage Walker. He is not your friend!"

The world I was in went silent as I watched the onslaught below me unfold. The further and further Kalani carried me away from the encounter and into the sky, the more angered I grew. I could still see Shajara fend off the Umbrage Walkers and it shattered my heart that I wasn't able to help her. With one final attempt to break free of his grasp, I pushed with all of my might away from Kalani and dove downwards like a vulture, hungry for flesh and blood. The clouds in the heavens let out roaring bouts of thunder as lightning streaked across the royal blue sky. I whispered to Shajara quietly.

"I'm coming. Don't worry."

My own muscles flowed with raw strength, as if powered by pure electricity. With my fist clenched shut, I made immediate contact with the pavement, sending a tremendous amount of energy through the ground. The pier shattered into a hail of splinters and spread outwards from impact. I could feel the lighthouse shake violently nearby. Shajara jumped as high as she could to avoid the debris while I watched Sagaru and his two henchmen become shredded by the ongoing fragments of stone. His pale blue skin leaked blood from his wounds but his teeth still shined brightly in the distance, smiling like the wicked scoundrel that he is. Dante flanked Shajara's heroic jump, cultivating an immense amount of energy at her side which sent her plummeting through the air and eventually splashing into the water. I picked up my broken hand and reached out towards her but she had to of been a hundred yards away by the time I was able to witness it.

Kalani soon came into the fight and grabbed Sagaru from his back, winding him around in circles until he gained enough momentum and let go. I watched as Sagaru streamed through the air helplessly. Time itself had slowed down and soon I could feel my breath become shallow. I heard Sagaru's body whistle passed me as the feathers from his skull headdress ruffled. Our eyes met in that fraction of a second, deadlocking with one another. The same yellow shine in his onyx eyes that I remembered from the first moment I met Sagaru flickered brightly. I turned my head and raised my hands to protect myself as his bone-etched body met with the rusty iron lighthouse, going completely through both sides and leaving behind a trail of dark smoke behind like a comet soaring through space.

Shajara broke free from the waters below and accompanied Kalani and I by our side. She shook her head violently to rid the water from her warhawk hair.

"Are you alright?!" I asked, frightened, still trembling with the raw energy that thrummed down my limbs.

"Neva bettah!" She shouted, curling a ball of fire in her hands.

"No!" Kalani grabbed Shajara's hand, "It's over, for now we retreat."

"Retreat?! Ovah my dead body!" Shajara exclaimed.

When Shajara was pissed, you could tell. Her accent would magnify to the point where you could barely comprehend what she was speaking. Her eyes would furiously glow with the thirst for revenge, accompanied by sunken eyebrows that would cast impending doom on any unfortunate soul that happened to obstruct her path. I could feel the fury teeming off of Shajara's body as if the anger were that of my own. She eventually came to and extinguished the sphere of fire by clamping her hands shut and gave her braided war-hawk hair one last shake, making it well known that she was the victor of today's battle. Sagaru and Dante, along with the other two unfamiliar Umbrage Walkers were nowhere to be found.

I lightly traversed my bare feet throughout the pavement rubble and took a good look at the massive hole that Sagaru's body had made through the lighthouse. Without any doubt, Kalani had to have thrown Sagaru through at least three to six feet of iron without even thinking twice. It was completely astonishing how power in the Astral Plane was practically limitless, how people could not perish from such titanic attacks brought onto them. I wasn't even aware that I was capable of such brute force.

As someone who still lives in the waking world, it's downright unbelievable. I waved my broken hand softly in the air to assure myself that I wasn't dead. My hand didn't hurt much given that I likely pulverized every finger and bone in it. The glistening Silver Thread that was tied to my knuckle soon appeared and I held it up to the moonlight with a smile on my face.

"You must be careful, Jackie," Kalani said, stepping closer to me. "You may feel invincible in the Astral Realm, but I'm afraid to inform you that you're *not*. Wounds and pain can still transfer over into the waking world if you're careless."

"You mean. . . I'm going to have a broken hand when I wake up!?" I started to panic, thinking of excuses to tell my mother.

Kalani let out a hearty laugh. "No, but you may have a bruise or two on that hand now. Not all of the damage you obtain here is transferred over, just a minimal amount. The Silver Thread that binds your soul to your body cannot fully protect you. The thread itself not only act as a gateway to visiting the plane while out of body, but is also the link to your senses. This includes the ability to register pain from wounds."

I nodded my head in understanding. "Next time I'll be more careful, I promise. I didn't know I could do that."

"We didn't know eitha," Shajara said with a proud grin curling on her face. "Dats very impressive, I must say. Usually it be takin' weeks, if not months, for a Circle Walkah to accomplish da powah you displayed before us."

I raised my head gallantly to the sky while planting my hands to my sides, elbows bent outwards. The heroic posture that I performed caused both of them to snicker.

"You know," I said after a moment. "You guys still haven't told me about those Circles of Creation I've been asking about. Remember?"

Kalani wrapped his giant arm around my neck and burrowed his knuckles roughly into my head to give me an undeserved noogie. "Well, kiddo, we can talk about all that jazz and fill you in on everything once we get you to Astraga."

I gave Kalani a strong jab to his side with my elbow and pushed him away. "Stop calling me kiddo. You know you get that from your father, right? And what gives? Why is your father, who used to be good friends with my father, an Umbrage Walker, huh?"

He slightly frowned while looking back at the giant hole in the lighthouse. "I'll cover that too once we arrive to Astraga, I suppose."

I looked around and noted that even the destruction that had happened here tonight at the pier wouldn't show up in the waking world. There wasn't going to be a massive hole in the lighthouse that Kalani had profoundly made with Sagaru's body, and there wasn't going to be shattered pavement scattered throughout the pier. If anything, it was just something that I merely witnessed from my wild imagination, something fictionalized that would never make sense to anybody in the real world. I was suddenly bothered that I couldn't share this story with people, but I knew that I still had Elowyn and Josiah to talk to.

Shajara caressed my broken hand and started to rub my palm in a gentle rhythm. With a little bit of force and several cracks later from added pressure, my hand seemed completely up to par as if I never even touched the pavement. I felt the soothing warmth of blood circulate my hand properly once more. I waved it gently and nodded in approval of Shajara's healing magic.

"Good as new, yah?" She smiled, collecting the freckles together on her beautiful face. "Dank you for comin' to save me back dere. I didn't expect dat many to show."

"Sure thing, pretty lady," I said with a cheesy smile, my

eyes glued to hers in awe.

"Now let us get ya to Astraga, ya?"

"Yes, please! But how?" I asked.

Kalani answered. "We have to take you there by flight. Since you've never seen the place before, you cannot possibly picture it in your mind. It's much too hard to explain in detail from how beautiful Astraga really is, Jackie."

"By flight?" I said, confused.

"Yep! Just follow what we do. Kick your legs from the ground with all of your strength like you're Peter Pan."

"Seriously, Kalani?" I slapped my forehead in laughter at how silly he sounded.

Kalani walked right up to me and flicked his fingers on my nose. "This is no joke. After what we just went through, you should have some respect that Shajara and I don't banish you from the Astral Plane. That was a ballsy risk you took back there."

"You guys can actually banish people from here?"

Shajara looked at Kalani warningly. "Well. . . Not really. Perhaps da Necromanca or Heilige, but we can't."

"Wait, who is this Necroma—"

Kalani interrupted, "Yeah, once were in Astraga we'll explain, sheesh."

Shajara squatted to the ground and then kicked off with all of her strength, sending her body rocketing into the air at an astonishing speed. Before three seconds had passed, she was already a spec among a thousand stars in the night sky. I wanted to gasp in amazement but held it in as I shook my head. I had a slight fear of heights and kept it well hidden. I withdrew in a few deep breaths and shook my hands to rid myself of the jitters.

"You'd better hurry," Kalani said. "Before you know it, she'll be long gone."

I pictured myself running in the lush jungle, much like the one I was a part of right before I met Sagaru. I remembered the sweat that poured down my skin and the sunlight that sifted throughout the treetops. I started to run, hitting my cold feet onto the broken pier pavement. I pictured the green algae infiltrating the broken rubble much like in my dream and by the time I reached the end of the pier I had kicked off the ground with all of the strength that I could muster. I soared high into the heavens without thinking of ever looking back. The wind blew harshly in my face and my eyes watered no matter how much I squinted to protect them. I turned to see Kalani flying to my side with nodding approval and then took the lead. The further and further we went up into the beautiful night sky, the lesser my fear of heights became.

I stretched out my arms in one of the most freeing moments of my life, twirling and spinning round as we broke through the giant clouds. There, the glistening moon rested peacefully on the fluffy white expanse, humungous in appearance. It was similar to how the sun would radiate off of the horizon during a morning sunrise, but instead it was a giant white sphere full of craters and mystery, silently staring back at you. I locked the beautiful sight deep inside my memory to never forget. If I were to never return to the Astral Plane, I knew that at least I'd be able to cherish this moment until the day I died.

I continued to speed through the air like a bullet cutting through the atmosphere, following Shajara's trail with my arms tucked closely together. The wind lashed at my skin, but I had not a care in the world, for I was free. After several dips in and out of the clouds, she paused in midflight and stuck out her arm, causing me to come to a screeching halt. With her jagged fingernails, she flicked her fingers carefully ahead of her while leaning in to listen. You could feel the sound waves ripple through the atmosphere as a low hum chimed in all directions. She had exposed a massive translucent blue shield that had to have been a hundred football fields across, if not larger.

The circumference of this spherical shield that was revealed was monstrous in size, much bigger than anything I had ever seen before. Inside of this giant shield lay a floating city, resting calmly in the epicenter, suspended by absolutely nothing. My eyes dazzled at the spectacular sight and I had wondered how something so magical could possibly exist. It was as if a titan had dug their claws into the earth, ripped the very foundation of the city from the ground and launched it far off into the sky. Massive temples lay scattered about the city, both in congested areas and on the outskirts, while village homes and smaller establishments huddled nearby. Some places were left completely intact while others lay in ruin, teaming with lush overgrowth.

"Dis be Astraga, child," Shajara said enchantingly while our bodies slipped through the translucent shield. "Da City of da Circle Walkahs. Welcome."

CHAPTER NINE

We landed on the very edge of a city street with our bare feet in a fog. The street was made of brick, but abruptly ended as if an earthquake had torn it apart from something it was previously attached to. I turned to look off the edge. I kicked some rubble and watched the bits of earth helplessly fall from beneath this marvelous place. The fragments of earth stayed suspended inside the massive shield, looming carelessly, unaffected by gravity. I peered over the edge even more, watching white wisps of the fog curl down among the floating dirt while I fought with my sense of vertigo. I took in a deep breath and realized that what I was standing on was real, or as real as things ever were in the Astral Plane.

Kalani motioned his hand for me to follow him and Shajara. The three of us made our way down the ruined brick street and I could hear the buzzing of the strange floating lights, as if they were ordinary streetlamps. The fog made avoiding the missing and cracked bricks difficult, and my feet began to ache. I tripped over several tiny growths of moss and vegetation that were spread liberally among the cracks. It seemed obvious that this city had been abandoned for decades.

Once we emerged from the thicket, I could see the giant tower-like buildings placed sporadically throughout the city streets, in and among the glowing greenish lights that hung over darkened alleyways. One of those giant towers seemed to be a bell tower, connected by a massive cathedral made out of a dark, muddy stone.

The further we ventured into the city, the more I was

taken aback by the Astraga's beauty. The architecture was astounding, full of gothic flourishes and windows cheek by jowl with weather-worn gargoyles, choked for water. Influences of Greek structures accompanied this, having massive stone pillars surround nearby temples with a Parthenon not too far in the distance. Sooty brick pavement paved the city streets, and a giant marble sculpture of a naked man and woman spewed pristine water in a nearby fountain. Shajara rested herself against the fountain and glided her fingers gently across the surface of the water. I watched the water ripple softly, the reflection of her eyes pulling at my mind. The water moved much slower than what it would have in the waking world.

"Isn't she beautiful?" Shajara asked, peering at the sculpture of the two naked lovers, etched and entangled close together by marbled cloth. I looked more carefully at the statue, and I could see that the marble actually shimmered as if it had veins of twinkling stars running through the stone. The lovers held each other closely, lips close to touching as if they breathed one another's air. It took me a moment to realize that Shajara was referring to Astraga.

"Yeah..." I said, twisting my head around and trying to absorb everything.

Astraga looked exactly as I imagined Europe some time ago, a clash of many different images and cultures, accompanied by an overarching sense of nature with a dark and gothic vibe. It was a disparate city, a place that could never have existed on Earth together at the same time.

"She sure is beautiful."

"Thank you!" Kalani said, scraping his thumb off of his scruffy chin.

"For what?"

"For the compliment. I helped build this place you know. We wanted to give it a Renaissance feel with other European influences throughout time."

"Dun be fooled, Jackie. I helped too, ya. Everyone does at some point," Shajara added.

I didn't quite understand what they were referring to, my eyes still transfixed on the city. Delicate glass windows of nearby buildings glowed amber in tint from the lights on the inside. At first when we had arrived in Astraga, it had been empty, with only the three of us wandering the streets, but when I finally stopped to listen, the sound of shoes started to click against the pavement. Men and women danced and cheered heartily while clanking their brews together inside a local pub. Intoxicating perfumes and scents suddenly filled the air, and I could hear the laughter of the old and young as people conversed in a strange, musical language. Confused, I arched my eyebrows at the abrupt appearance of so many people. Before I could look out of the disarray to ask why such strange things were happening, dozens, if not hundreds, of people surrounded me in a bustling city at night, smack dab in the middle of the crowd.

Astraga came to life before my own eyes. A confusing blend of men and women of all ages scurried across the pavement gracefully. Some of these people bartered with one another while others casually walked in groups and bantered. I staggered backwards as more and more people flooded the city street, bumping into me as if everyone had a destination in mind, and I was standing in exactly the wrong place. There were as many kinds of clothes as there were individuals in the crowd. Some wore fully modern clothes like sweaters, jeans, and sneakers, but many more people wore clothing decades out of date, and there were quite a few wearing some strange mix of the two. I saw one woman wearing a bright royal blue and white laced polonaise, accompanied by a man with a monocle and top hat, his weight supported by an elaborately designed cane. He looked rakish in a flat-ironed suit. A little girl wearing something like burlap, eight at the oldest, accidentally bumped into me, carelessly dropping some burnt baked goods onto the damp ground. I looked at her frozen-red cheeks and nose, knelt down aside her and helped her pick up the bread as quickly as I could.

"Are you lost?" I asked while placing a baguette into her dirty woven basket.

She shook her head and I watched the shadows on her face dance under her hollow cheekbones. Her eyes were bark brown with darkened circles under them.

"No? What's your name?"

She, at first hesitant, pulled the basket closer to her stained dress and lowered her head.

"It's okay." I said after a few moments of staring at her.

She raised her beady eyes to mine and muttered softly.

"Ariella."

"And where are you from, Ariella?"

She tucked the basket under her right arm and fled. The moment I heard her tiny shoes hit the brick road, my heart dropped into my stomach. I looked at Shajara and Kalani confused, wondering if I had done something to upset the little girl. I know I'm not the best person when it comes to children but I don't think that I'm terrifying or anything. Shajara shrugged her arms and Kalani slapped his giant hand onto my back.

"Sometimes it's best not to question things in the plane." Kalani spoke.

I nodded my head.

"She's dead, right?" I asked.

"It's likely if she's wearing shoes. Poor girl, did you see her arm?"

"No, I didn't. Was she hurt?"

"She had a tattoo."

I looked back in the direction that Ariella had run, though the mass of people meant she had long disappeared. Before I could think of my next question, my body was squeezed tightly from behind by two ivory arms.

"Jackie!" she shouted.

I spun around, reciprocating the hug. "Elowyn! Hey! It's nice to see you!"

"It is nice to see you too!"

Elowyn broke from my hug and took a gracious bow, picking up her beautiful dress with her thin bone-white gloves.

"What on earth are you wearing, girl?" I chuckled.

"You don't like it?" She frowned and twirled, letting the fabric of the dress flair up for me to see.

I watched her curly golden hair bounce around as she spun. When she stopped spinning, her hair delicately draped over her shoulder and met with her breast line – a breast line that was being generously pushed up by an extremely tight emerald green corset. Her silhouette looked magnificent. She wore a laced dress over the unusual corset, which showed flashes of the corset through the fabric as she moved. From the hips down, her dress ruffled in a thousand shades of forest, cascading outwards towards the ground. She was stunning from the top of her head to the bottom of her bare feet.

I clapped my hands together and shouted. "Bravo, a true beauty!" and blew her a kiss. She caught the kiss and smiled graciously.

"It's for the upcoming event. I thought you of all people would like the dress," Elowyn said.

"I do! It's beautiful. Now if only we could get this fella to dress up." I pointed behind her.

Josiah stepped forward from the crowd, stopping not too far from Elowyn's back. He was still dressed in ordinary clothes with that same beautiful face and eyes even deeper green than Elowyn's dress. It was a relief to know that my clothes weren't going to make me the odd one out.

"We thought we lost you back there," Josiah said, a concerned little smile unraveled on his face.

I had almost forgotten that I had missed my target destination when traveling throughout the Astral Plane.

"Sorry about that. I tried picturing the park, but I ended up somewhere else."

I briefed them about Sagaru's ambush and why it had taken me so long to arrive. We carried the conversation to the local pub which was filled with an array of "interesting" characters to say the least. Men with massive burly beards of every shade surrounded the bartender's main table while plenty of others filled the air with loud chatter. For every table, a dozen to two dozen steins surrounded a dim lit oil-bleeding lantern, some lanterns even laid suspended above the tables, buzzing harmoniously. Every man with a beer-drenched beard was accompanied by a woman with a rather revealing dress, some showing skin more leisurely than others. The diversity the pub brought together was amazing in feeling, like we were all one big family.

"There is a Masquerade coming up!" Elowyn said cheerily as we walked through the pub, once again flaunting her Emerald gown. "And you're invited!" she added and pointed to me.

"Is that so?" I jazzed back. "What is the special occasion?"

"Astraga holds annual events during autumn to welcome those who find the plane and also to honor those who still walk it." Kalani mentioned. "It's a time to pay our respects, but also a time to celebrate in festivities. This year we've chosen a Masquerade to spice things up."

"Your attendance is mandatory." Shajara gleamed when

she looked back at me.

"Consider me there." I replied.

Josiah and Elowyn continued to chatter amongst themselves while Shajara instructed Kalani on some subject I was unaware of. I kept to myself, continuing to observe and analyze the crowd around us. It was a nasty habit, but you can never been too comfortable in unfamiliar waters. In such a mysterious place, one minute you could be in the presence of a man from any given war that dated back hundreds of years ago, and the next you could be standing alongside a village woman who lived for nearly an entire century in a rural city, deeply hidden half way across the world. The possibilities of whomever you happened to encounter here were endless. This was something that I was absolutely fascinated by. I wove in and out of the crowd with Elowyn and Josiah. Shajara and Kalani walked not too far ahead until we were able to find a decent table that'd seat all of us.

I wiped a blob of brew suds from my sleeve, gotten from a local pub patron who ever-so-kindly splashed onto me when he clanked steins with a fellow mate. I sat at the table and turned the woven wick higher into the lantern to increase the flame's size. A wooden bowl of dried fruit and stale bread chunks lay next to the lantern. The sight of the food made me pause, wondering how people on the Astral Plane could eat, or, for that matter, drink beer. I looked carefully around the room; based on the red faces and poor balance of the people around me, it was clear that alcohol had a similar effect here as it did in the waking world. I kept the thought to myself, remembering that Kalani had warned me against bringing attention to myself like that. I decided to go with the flow.

Kalani nudged me by the shoulder. "You see that table over there?" I looked in the direction that he was indicating.

The table that Kalani was referring to sat tucked way back into the pub's corner, abandoned with cobwebs spread across it with broken barstools nearby. Moderately sized char marks smeared some of the table and chairs as if they were lit ablaze at one point in time. Everybody at the pub kept their distance from the table as it lay isolated, deserted in the shadows. I watched how carefully the other bar patrons moved around the area, keeping their distance as if they walked along an invisible wall around it.

"What happened to it? Did Shajara blow somebody up?"

I heard Shajara let out a loud giggle as she popped a few pieces of dried fruit into her mouth.

"Not quite. Are you ready to have some of those questions answered?"

"Lay it on me." I said eagerly, mimicking Shajara by grabbing a few pieces of dried fruit to eat. I tried my best to choke them down, but the acrid taste got the best of me and I ended up spitting them out. Shajara winked her blue eye at me mockingly.

"Years ago, there used to be a coven of witches who would congregate frequently. The founder went by the name of Elizabeth. They sought a means to empower themselves and soon started to dabble in foreign practices of which they had never endeavored before. Eventually one of the coven members stumbled upon the Astral Plane and presented it to Elizabeth in high hopes. Elizabeth took the member's claim seriously and eventually she wound up in the plane after much practice. The five witches spent days, weeks, and even months perfecting themselves on how to enter the plane. By the end of three months, they had made astounding progress and soon they could visit the Plane in mere minutes. The witches deemed this practice as what we call it now, 'Circle Walking'."

"Circle Walking entails Five Circles of Creation and Five

Circles of Destruction in total, ok?" Kalani sternly beamed his eyes at me.

"Okay. What are these circles and why are there two different types?" I asked.

"Boy!" Shjajara swatted at me, "He will get to dat. Listen!"

"Anyone who walks the Circles of Creation are simply known as "Circle Walkers" – such as yourselves." Kalani pointed to the three of us. "Those who walk the Destruction Circles are known as Umbrage Walkers, like Sagaru. Both the Circles of Creation and Destruction follow the same tree, but start to diverge by the Third Circle and I'll explain why."

Kalani cleared his throat and took a deep breath. "The First Circle we walk is Astral Projection, which often does take time to grasp ahold of with much practice. Humans can walk this circle by accident and not even realize it, but mostly it takes weeks, if not months, to fully understand the concept. The Second Circle is when you begin to test your abilities by counting on Aether. Aether is a substance that allows us to retain magic in the plane. Using too much Aether by exerting an excessive amount of power can and will weaken you. The magic that you've seen Shajara cast? It's from a cultivation of Aether. As a Circle Walker, you depend on Aether greatly in combat. It's basically an invisible energy that we cannot see, but the atmosphere can often tilt into a dangerous direction if too much is absorbed, a sort of ebb and flow if you will. You will notice that if a fight between two people is ongoing, the weather may change dramatically. Rain, thunderstorms, even quakes have been witnessed. The plane does not heed well to the Aether being drawn from the atmosphere for your own power. There is a balance to everything after all, right?"

Kalani continued to speak on the matter, his words filling

my head like a barrage of infinite insight.

"Do not abuse the Second Circle at all. It is a privilege and the Heilige will see fit to banish you if you do choose to abuse it. There's a reason why Umbrage Walkers are expelled from Astraga."

Shajara nodded strictly, eyeballing the three of us. "And don't'cha dare become an Umbrage Walkah! I won't hesitate to send ya off!"

"Wait, wait. Who is the Heilige?" Josiah asked.

A flare in Shajara's eyebrows sparked. She didn't even need to speak a single word for Josiah to already know to keep quiet.

"I'm sorry. I retract my question. Go on please hehe!" Josiah prompted, scooting a few inches closer to Elowyn.

"Anyways, "said Kalani. "Now this is where the two types of walkers start to differ. In order to enter the Third Circle of Creation or Destruction you must mend or destroy a Silver Thread. Destroying a thread can yield you to walk the path of an Umbrage Walker whereas healing a thread will remain you on the regular path of Circle Walking. As you know, threads become damaged over time, even broken. Repairing these threads are what only Priests and Priestesses are allowed to do, and you as new Circle Walkers are forbidden to enter this Circle. You mustn't go beyond the Second Circle unless you follow under the Heilige's tutelage. This is where many people often succumb to Umbrage Walking, wishing to enhance their powers in the plane. Do you see now why temptation tends to eat away at people?"

"But can't people just become Priests then if they want to enter the Third Circle?" asked Elowyn.

"No, not necessarily. There are a set of rules here in the plane, instructed by the Heilige. Only Twelve Priests and

Priestesses may act on his council at any given time, no more or less. Six men and Six women. Shajara is one of them." Kalani looked over at Shajara.

Shajara nodded once again. "Da otha Priests and Priestesses are spread through Astraga and the plane, helpin' young Circle Walkahs like yaselves. We're given da duty ta protect'cha from falling off the path of Creation. So don't'cha dare!" she ordered.

Kalani went on with the story of the witches.

"Once every coven member was able to walk the Astral Plane in ease, the Witches started to cultivate an immense amount of power by practicing the Second, using up all of the Aether they could. They had a staggering strength that had never been seen before, unrivaled by others to the point that they could move entire mountains at a mere thought, shifting both the Astral and the earthly versions." If you ask me, human beings shouldn't have access to power like that."

"Elizabeth kept a close eye on her coven and watched them carefully. Any attempt to prevent corruption within her small gathering proved futile, for problems started to arise, and fast at that. A few of the members started to toy with fate and push the boundaries of what was possible or wise, switching their Silver Threads with one another when out of body, which in turn caused their souls to switch bodies when they'd wake. Elizabeth banned this practice after it became widely known by the entire coven, but by then it was too late.

"Soon, her followers invented other, darker kinds of power in the Astral Plane, and their minds grew twisted by the surplus of magical power that they developed. These witches started to terrorize the Astral Plane, carving up the world with massive glaciers of ice and comets of fire along the way. If two witches worked together, they could conjure thunderstorms that could rip cities and people apart before wiping them out entirely, especially with the help of abusing the Aether in the air."

"What?" Josiah asked quickly, "How is that possible? You lie. Do the cities still look like that now? All wiped out and stuff?"

"Hold on, let me finish!" Kalani said. "It truly did happen, but here in the plane some things are easily repaired. Cities can be restored in a matter of minutes if we get a team of Circle Walkers to help, but it's still a costly and dangerous undertaking. And even as we restored one city, another would fall. After the Circle Walkers brought it to the attention of the Heilige, he summoned the witches in order to straighten things out. Elizabeth accepted the punishment of the two witches and demanded that she would suffer the consequences, however even if that were the case, the two witches who were at fault ended up retaliating against the Heilige of Astraga. The Heilige, or also known as the High Priest, banished Elizabeth and her coven from ever stepping bare foot back into the Astral Realm."

"Elizabeth accepted this fate reluctantly, disbanding the coven and all further practices of Circle Walking. All five coven members were to immediately wake thereafter, else their Silver Thread would be forfeit to the Heilige and Astraga as a whole, meaning certain death. Everything seemed to go according to plan, but the Heilige was not strong enough to keep the two young witches away for long, and that is when the Umbrage Walkers were coined soon after. In a concerning gesture, the Heilige and the Circle Walkers of Astraga constructed a massive shield to protect the city, but the attempts to keep the conniving witches away were in vain at the time. The young coven witches started to abuse alcohol and drugs to enter an even deeper slumber, staying clear of Astraga while still cultivating as much power as possible. For years they worked together, and even Elizabeth herself could not keep away."

"The witches learned to hide their visage well under certain witchcrafts, altering their looks, giving them the chance to enter Astraga once more and interact with the common folk. It wasn't much longer until Heilige could feel an ominous power starting to brew in Astraga. With a little searching, he cornered the witches here, in this pub, and that is when a war ensued."

A barmaid approached the table with five giant steins filled to the brim with bubbling brew. "Ya shoolda seen it! Tha entiah roof went KABOOM!" she exclaimed in a heavy Scottish accent. I watched the bar maid slam the steins on the table in a burly gesture, whipping her frizzy knotted orange hair to the side.

"Yes, yes. Thank you for that lovely addition to my story, Crissy." Kalani intercepted.

"ANYTIME SWEET CHEEKS!" Crissy shouted while pounding her giant legs off to tend to the other drunkards.

"Anyways, yes, the entire roof went 'KABOOM!' as Crissy had previously mentioned. In fact, the entire city of Astraga shook that night by the abuse of Aetheric power. It was described to me as chaos, while Circle Walkers watched helplessly as the Heilige and the five witches battled furiously against one another. Thunder and lightning bombarded the city streets of Astraga while ice began to encase everything it came into contact with. A cluster of elements really took over and even the city folk were scalded in flames. The Heilige was able to successfully kill one of the witches, however, he was struck down in battle soon after. This is when the Circle Walkers took action to protect the High Priest, some putting their own Silver Thread on the line.

"It was soon revealed to everyone on that eventful night that in the Astral Plane, power surpassed our standard human capacity of what we knew from the waking world. We all didn't know the potential we had as far as power went in the Astral Plane, so in a way we were lucky for the witches to have shown us this. Many people lost their lives and were bound to Astraga for eternity by having their Silver Thread severed and ultimately shattered. Upon what is suspected to be one of the first Silver Threads shattering ever in the history of the Astral Plane, one of the coven witches grew immeasurably dark that day. Shadows engulfed the witch, and soon after a second followed with another Silver Thread shattering, thus the Umbrage Walkers were born."

"Elizabeth witnessed this and grew envious of her coven members. The very eyes of the witches turned dark as graphite and their veins coursed with the blackest of blood. Elizabeth descended into the crowd of Circle Walkers for a very Silver Thread of her own to break, but was overpowered and betrayed. One of the coven members took her hand, slicing it clean off and tearing off her Silver Thread. You would think that maybe she would have remained in the Plane from that moment on, but she did not. Instead she simply dissipated into thin air, never to be found or seen again. The Circle Walkers still fought valiantly. They were able to take down one of the witches that hadn't succumbed to Umbrage Walking just yet, but more Circle Walkers died.

"In one last courageous attempt, the Heilige cast down a massive pillar of light onto the Umbrage Walkers, causing them to flee from Astraga. Their wounds were grave, but nothing that would have ended their lives. Now before I forget to mention, the Fourth Circle is only obtainable by the means of having your own Silver Thread severed. Once your thread is plucked away from your body, you are extremely vulnerable. Many turn twisted and evil from doing this, buckling at the power that is offered to them. Understand that all of the circles are circumstantial in their own way. Some people immediately enter the Fourth Circle without even knowing. For instance, my father, Dante, entered the Fourth Circle against his will when he was killed by an anthrax bomb. He went straight from the waking world, right into the Fourth Circle within the blink of an eye, and never had he experienced the other circles prior. Also take note that not everyone who loses their mortality by passing away is expected to enter the Astral Plane. As much as we are tutors to you, the Astral Plane is as much a mystery to you as it is to us. It's silly to think that souls only end up in this place and this place only."

Shajara raised her hand to intercept, giving Kalani a chance to catch his breath for a moment.

"Ya do not need ta follow tha circles in a specific, exact orda ta obtain da next. Remember dat! Dis is why humans are often bewildered or incredibly confused once dey pass away. To be launched dat quickly into something people know so little about is a shock to da system, for lack of a better term. Ya could literally assume dat tha Fourth Circle translates to death itself, but it has much more meanin' den just dat. You are strictly forbidden from entering tha Fourth Circle, just as much as you are forbidden from surpassing tha Second in order to go into tha Third! Suicide is not condoned to obtain a higher circle and you will be punished even in tinkin' of doin' such a thing. Do I make myself clear?" Shajara spoke sternly.

The three of us nodded in unison.

"Good. Da Fourth Circle is nutin' speshal anyways," Shajara said. "In fact, da powa of ya senses weakens for da time bein'. Ya vision becomes less, much like ya sense of smell n' touch. Ya feel isolated because ya loose ya mortal connection wit da eart'. It be nutin' ya want to discova until ya time is at an end, as tha Fourth Circle should be entered naturally, ya."

Kalani took hold of the conversation again. "The Fifth Circle, however," Kalani spoke, "not many know what lies within. Only few have returned. Some suspect that Elizabeth and the two coven witch apprentices are trapped inside of the Fifth Circle, others claim that paradise awaits, possibly even limbo. It's apparent though that you lose your sanity upon returning back from that said circle, case in point: Sagaru and the Necromancer."

"Sagaru and the Necromancer attained the Fifth Circle? What!?" Elowyn gasped after guzzling down her stein.

"Yes, they have, and they're both bona fide Umbrage Walkers. In time, the Heilige will bring them to their demise, but for now he's safe within the Cathedral with his council. Also, everyone is expecting you to attend the masquerade ball so that you can see him." Kalani tipped off his non-existent hat to Elowyn in a charming manner. She reciprocated with a nod and a cheeky smile.

"So, that doesn't explain the burnt table still." Josiah pointed out.

"You're right, child," Shajara answered. "No matta how much da Circle Walkahs tried to repair da entire city of Astraga, the table would not be fixed. It is permanently scorched from da inferno of the fight that went down when da Heilige confronted da coven. To sit at da table is to wish a bad omen upon yaself, so don'cha dare sit there, boy."

"The locals are always coaxing each other to sit in the burnt chairs, teasing and taunting their friends, saying that it will make them men." Kalani said, finishing off his stein of beer. He wiped the suds from his mouth and belched loudly. "People can only stand the horrid stench of burnt flesh and wood for thirty seconds at best. Anything thereafter, people claim you hallucinate. Remember though, these are drunks we're talking about."

"I'm gonna do it." Josiah braved, taking a stand and heading to the table.

Before Josiah could even attempt three steps towards the

cobwebbed and scorched table, Shajara was already standing before him, pressing her curled fingernail deep against his throat and sending him back to his seat with force.

"You will do no such ting on my watch, foolish child."
"Yes ma'am." Josiah peeped with bulging eyes, planting his feet onto the floor.
Elowyn and I chuckled quite a bit, but the look in Kalani's eyes was still very earnest. He continued onwards in his story.

"Now about the Necromancer. . . If you ever happen to stumble across the Necromancer, you might wish that you hadn't. Your mind will enter vertigo if you linger around her presence too long. Her odor has been known to intoxicate all who stride too close, rendering them ill beyond belief. After she had attained the Fifth Circle, Sagaru attempted to form an alliance with her but she rejected his offer. The Necromancer continued to manipulate the lost souls that'd enter the Plane while Sagaru continued to feast on them in his own ways. The Necromancer isn't known to take sides and Sagaru saw this as a threat, marking her for death. It was foolish, being that she is –the– Necromancer and is already dead, so to speak. They both devour souls relentlessly to satiate their appetite."

"How come we've never met the Necromancer before?" I asked.
"You have, kind of. The Necromancer is my father, or will be soon at least."
"I don't understand, you said the Necromancer is a she?"
"Exactly, this is where it gets confusing."
Kalani paused before speaking further and looked around him. The entire pub went silent. It never dawned on me that Kalani's father, Dante, could have ties to the Necromancer somehow. I felt pity towards Kalani, watching his own father surrender to the evils of the Astral Plane.

I outreached to Kalani to give him my hand as a gesture of kindness, but he raised his stein instead and blocked it, cheering to the barmaid for another brew. The tavern resumed its loud chatter amongst the people after a hearty "AYE!" bellowed from the swashing bellies of the drunken, followed by a strong clashing of brews. I wanted to ask Kalani so much more about Dante since Dante used to be a part of my father's crew before he died, but I figured Kalani spent many days with him after his unexpected death. Maybe it was one reason why Kalani frequented the Astral Plane, to pay his respects to his own kin.

I glared at Elowyn's glazed eyes as she let out a few hiccups. Oh dear.

"Is everything alright, El?"

Elowyn stood up and took a few sauntered steps towards the bartenders table, shouting profanities that she be served more alcohol at once. Her posture was even more outgoing than before. Despite the strong aroma of beer rolling off of her breath, she held her poise as best she could. The rugged bartender laughed, squeaking a stein clean of its contents while the burly men alongside the table looked her up and down like a piece of meat. Josiah approached Elowyn's side once he witnessed this, wrapping his arm around her waist side to give the men the impression that she was taken. It's moments like those that make me proud to be Josiah's friend —a true friend who has your six no matter what is going on. He has done the same for me when in public, and it just makes you appreciate a guy that much more when they're paying close attention.

Elowyn stumbled to the floor and her very body shattered into a thousand tiny flickering lights, as if a bustling cloud of whizzing fireflies had taken flight harmoniously. The tiny lights soon dimmed and Elowyn was nowhere to be found, her Silver Thread making a prominent sparkle before fading away. I stood up in shock and rushed over to Josiah's side. He soon also repeated the exact same scenario. Right as I caught Josiah in my arms as he fell down, tiny little balls of light emitted from his body and nuzzled my skin with warmth. The tingle to my skin felt as if I were being kissed by the sun on a hot midsummer day in the middle of July.

"Josiah! Elowyn!? Whats going on?!" I looked up at Shajara and Kalani for immediate answers, panicking frantically.

The entire pub began to cackle in laughter, pointing at me. Some men had crammed stale bread into their mouths as if it were popcorn and continued to laugh hysterically until their faces turned purple. I could feel my own face grow red in embarrassment.

"Look at tha scared lil' Threadie!" Crissy belched out, holding her rather large gut.

Threadie? What?

"Dun' worry, child." Shajara came to me and placed her arm around the span of my shoulders, lifting me to stand. "Dey simply woke up is all, you do it too when ya leave da Plane. All people who are still alive do it. It's nuh-ting ta worry ya pretty little head about."

"Why don't we go watch the sunrise before you wake, Jackie?" Kalani suggested. "You've all had quite a bit of absorb tonight."

I peered at both of them still with a sliver of muddle in my head. I nodded and we left the pub, paying no mind to the onlookers that teased and berated me about my amateur ways. In the corner of my eye I could see Shajara snap her fingers near the face of one of the prude men who had laughed at me, sending a bolt of electricity towards his beard which then ignited it into flames. The husky bearded man became startled and patted away at the small fire anxiously. Crissy grabbed a nearby stein and had poured all of its contents over the balding man's head, and another round of mocking laughter echoed through the building.

We sifted through the crowded city streets of Astraga and had made our way back to the edge where we first landed. I watched Shajara take a running leap into the sky and swoop down like a hawk through the translucent shield. I looked back at Kalani for approval, and he nodded to suggest that I should do the same.

"You want me to. . . jump?" I gulped.
"Yes. Nothing to it."
"But..."

When I took a quick glace over the edge of the cliff, my posture faltered as dizziness erupted in my head. I heard Kalani laugh and, before I knew it, he nudged me off of the cliff and into the sky. I tried to scream but the wind had muffled my voice and restricted my airways, and the view—the view left me breathless anyway. I embraced the fall, clamping my hands to my sides and straightening my body like an arrow, whistling through the star-lit expanse ever faster than before. I looked back at Kalani with excitement and then watched Astraga shrink into the brightening sky until I couldn't even see it against the day.

Astraga: The otherworldly City of Circle Walkers. I will never forget this place.

We nearly made it half way through the atmosphere when I witnessed Shajara burst into a thousand small spheres of light, shooting dramatically across the dawn. As I swooped passed the firefly of lights that remained from her body, they tickled my skin soothingly with warmth. I bid Shajara good morning in a small whisper and I felt the waking world calling to me, blurring my vision as my body began to wake. I tried my best to stay asleep for Kalani's sake, but when I looked back once more at his location, he too had already exploded into thousands of bits of light.

CHAPTER TEN

I woke to Brutis' paw jammed deep in my ribcage. His cheeks flapped continuously as he snored like a slumbering giant. I didn't move. Instead I combed my fingers through Brutis' grey fur coat while watching the sun break over the horizon. It was the sunrise that I was supposed to share with Kalani and Shajara. I noticed that my hand was bruised a shade of yellow-green from when I had made impact with the pavement at the Pier. I ignored the slight pain; it was nothing compared to my experiences in the night. For the first time, I was finally able to visit Astraga—the sounds and strange scents, the constant smiles and foreign laughter that filled the air under the shield-distorted galaxy. I let the memories wash over me, trying to make sense of the wonders I had seen. Waking up in the ordinary world was such a let-down, everything seemed so faded and ephemeral, compared to the bright reality of Astraga.

There are hundreds of people across the World that visit Astraga every night when they sleep. Just imagine the infinite possibilities. Imagine if you found your soul mate, destined star-crossed lovers across the Plane. Imagine if you found a lifelong friend you hadn't seen in years. Imagine finding a beloved family member that had passed away years ago, striding in the Plane, waiting for you with open arms and a warm heart. I felt my eyes sting at the thought of my father and what Dante had said. Is my old man still around? Is he still the same man as I remember him?

After a half hour lying in bed with my thoughts, I pulled myself from the bed. Out of habit, I reached for my combat boots, thought about it, and then I shoved them aside for my jogging shoes. Brutis popped one eye open and quickly closed it thereafter, moving his lazy butt onto the warm spot I'd just left. I ruffled the top of his head and gave him a kiss on the nose. I don't know what I'd do without my baby boy.

I left the house, pulling through the giant wooden door and started my slow paced jog, picking up distance as time went on. From being in the Astral Plane, my body was teeming with energy, as if I were a young kid again at the school playground. Not an ache or pain would dare seep into my bones or joints.

As I ran, I could see the sunlight stretch across the canvas of the hills, strewing the dawn shades of red, yellow, and orange over the world. For some reason I used to adore this sight. It was something that I would look forward to seeing in the morning since I'd often sleep through the day. I passed a few joggers with a friendly wave, but nobody waved back. People in the South were different than what I was used to in the Midwest. Southern hospitality overloaded some parts of Florida, while in other places, not so much. I shrugged and continued on my run, breathing in and out.

The waking world wasn't as lively. I couldn't help but notice the little flaws in the faces of the morning people. Last night's lipstick smeared the face of one woman, and her hair was tangled in brown knots; another man reeked of coffee, and his beer belly hung heavily over the belt that struggled to keep his pants on. The birds that chirped when hopping through the morning dew grass did not seem happy either, gawking madly at one another. The noise of cars driving down the street annoyed me in an unfamiliar way. I paused my running on the Miami Beach bay front and looked around at the mundane life that surrounded me. I wanted to cringe. A knot tightened in my stomach, and I tried to suppress my unhappy thoughts. There was no way that I could live in this world if I weren't happy.

Running was a way to alleviate my stress, not bring it on.

Everything felt ass-backwards. My head clogged itself for minutes on this train of thought, toying with the idea of what death exactly meant. I realized that people who described their near death experiences were uncannily accurate to how it felt to be in the Astral Plane. Pain became obsolete, the strength of colors enhanced, hell — all of my senses were enhanced in the plane. I quivered in unease as I thought about how it was possible that every night I entered the plane, I could be severing my soul from my body. In all honestly, the feeling was addicting.

I became easily distracted in perplexities but my daydreaming was struck down soon by an old voice.

"Bingo!" An elderly man shouted, waving his hand rapidly in cheer while sitting on the beach front.

He wore a plastic green visor, the trim around it being white cloth. His shirt was striped with bright pastel colors to reflect the sun's scorching heat. Even though he was wearing the proper attire to prevent the sun from harming his skin, it really didn't say much since his face and hands were covered in sun spots. I assumed the old fella was native to Florida because of his leathery skin, that or he was used to always being out in the sun his entire life. He grinned from ear to ear, showing everybody his scraggly teeth.

"Baby needs a pair of shoes, yee-haw!" he said with a quirky laugh.

I shook my head and was about to resume jogging when I remembered the flyer in my back pocket. I wasn't wearing the jeans I had been in yesterday, but I decided to join in anyway. Why the hell not?

I scoped the crowd for a good seat. There couldn't have been more than a dozen people, all of them well into their blue-hair age. I took an empty seat at one of the back tables while the announcer congratulated the old man, giving him a firm pat on the back.

"Oh, what a beautiful child," she said, her voice quavering in her old age.

It was the same woman who had placed the flyer in my

door, still dressed in her luxurious style. She winked as I pulled up my chair. I couldn't help but blush.

"Do you mind?" I asked, taking a bingo sheet and motioning towards a few bingo chips.

She reached out her frail hand and dropped a few chips into my hands. I thanked her and she gave me a gracious nod.

"What's your name?" I asked her, smiling courteously.

"Deborah, sweetie, and yours?"

"Jackie. Nice to meet you, Deborah," I extended my hand.

She shook my hand with a most pleasant smile on her face. Her arms were weak and trembled as she struggled to keep them up. It boggled my mind why she was wearing a white fleece sweater in the dead heat of Miami, under the scorching sun, but I really just wanted to pinch her cheeks for how cute she looked.

"Likewise," She replied, scooting a few bingo chips onto her sheet.

The announcer went onwards calling a few more numbers, E7, A3, and when he had reached D1, Deborah's eyes popped open quickly as she waved her hands into the air jerkily.

"Bingo!" she hollered.

It was as if she had just won the lottery, and I couldn't have been happier for her. I applauded in glee at Deborah's bingo victory until I saw the sleeve of her white fleece sweater fall down, bearing a tattoo with digits on her forearm. I didn't know what to say as my hands froze in place, eyes affixed to the engraving. She caught my stare and quickly covered her arm back up, walking to the podium to claim her small prize. The announcer put on a plastic smile for Deborah, wiping the pouring sweat from his forehead. When she returned, she refused to make eye contact with me.

"I saw it," I said, unrestrained.

Was it wrong of me to bring it up? I felt horrible that I practically blurted it out. Deborah nodded at me, but she said nothing, still looking down at her bingo card.

I apologized. "I shouldn't have said anything." I stood up to leave as another game began, tucking in my chair and letting out a deep sigh.

"Wait." she said, extending her shaking hand for me to resume my seat. "Come talk with me."

I nodded and sat back down.

"What would you like to know?" she asked, her beady brown eyes darting back and forth into my own.

"Everything," I replied.

I was never in my entire life such a solemn person but this particular conversation had definitely warranted such. Deborah pulled back her white hair and tied it into a knot. She then pulled up both of her sleeves and laid her arm on the bingo table, revealing the faded tattoo with the numbers "18542".

"I was placed in Auschwitz. I was lucky in ways, I suppose." She looked over the oceanfront. "Lucky that I wasn't separated from my family,"

"You don't have an accent though." I pointed out.

I didn't realize at the time how immature and undereducated I sounded. I tried my best to dance around the subject lightly. I could see the pain welt in her eyes.

"You're right. I don't. I was young. Seven or Eight possibly, I can't entirely remember that much anymore." Her voice swelled in her throat.

"I lost my accent when I had made it to America after some time, but when I was in Auschwitz, I went through most terrible things. My family practically starved to death in the concentration camp. Whatever morsels of food my parents were able to collect or steal, they'd hand it off to me or my sister. It wasn't very long before my father was caught doing this. He was tied to a wooden pillar and whipped to near death while having to watch my mother become sodomized by the end of a soldier's rifle. Ultimately, the soldier pulled the trigger after she begged for him to stop several times. After the soldier pulled the rifle out of my mother, he aimed it at my father and shot him in the temple."

Deborah cleared her throat and closed her eyes tightly,

strengthening her posture and ignoring her shaking hands.

"I screamed as loud as I could while I cradled my twin sister in my arms. I still remember to this day the look of that soldier's wicked smile as he wiped the blood from his weapon and approached us. The soldier snatched my sister from my hold and dragged her by the hair across the camp and threw her in the mud."

Deborah choked up for a brief moment, withholding her words. A long pause filled the conversation until she swallowed hard and continued to speak.

"After he aimed the rifle to the back of her head, he pulled the trigger once more. It was the last time he'd ever fire a gun, as the camp went into chaos and the people revolted. My screams were soon muffled. It did not matter how hard they tried to hush my voice, I was too outraged to be silenced."

I witnessed the look in her eyes grow somber as if fueled by rage when she reopened them.

"In the midst of the fight between the soldiers and camp goers, I was able to find that man's rifle in the crowd and shoot him with his own gun. The sound echoed in my ears like a firecracker, I say. I could hear the people's bones crack and shatter while the soldiers bludgeoned the starving. I ran with blood spatter all over my dirty dress. There was a hole that I was able to slip passed in the fencing while the guards were distracted. I don't remember how many days I had traveled, but eventually I came to a small farm that was being tended to by a darker-skinned couple. I was on the brink of collapsing from exhaustion when they spotted me. They harbored me into their home and took care of me. To this day I still owe them all of my gratitude."

I watched Deborah's hands shift together several times

and break apart. Nervousness still bombarded her when she recollected the memories. I honestly did not expect her to be so open right off the bat. Perhaps she was a lonely woman who was in dire need of company.

"Eventually they sent me off to America with all of the money they had. I was just a teenager at the time. They came along with me on the boat ride as well, but they both fell gravely ill and didn't make it. Maybe it was better to happen that way. Back then in America, people didn't see too kindly to anything other than white. I wouldn't ever want them to go through what I had to. It's a horrible thing to say, but nevertheless it is true."

Deborah carried on in conversation. At times she'd be timid to answer my questions, while at other moments she'd be open as a book. I admired her immense bravery for being willing to speak on such a touchy subject. Even if her voice would at times shake, her memory was still solid as steel despite what she claimed.

She paused, letting out a heavy sigh. "Anything else you'd like to know?"
I looked over Deborah's face, which beheld a sorrowful expression.
"What were your family's names? And who took care of you after?" I asked in a softened tone, feeling a wrench in my heart.
"I don't remember the names of the dark-skinned people, but my father's name was Mitch, my mother's name was Anne, and my twin sister's name was Ariella."
A spark went off in my head.
"Ariella," I repeated to her.
"Yes. A beautiful name, isn't it?"
I crossed my arms after a moment of silence.
"Yes, it is a beautiful name." I replied.
My head spun around in circles. Could it possibly be?

Deborah smiled at me politely and excused herself when her friend approached us—the same friend that I saw handing out flyers with her on that rainy evening.

"Oh, and don't worry, dear. Many people ask when they see this tattoo." Deborah spoke, finally walking off.

"Wait." I said.

"Yes, dear?" she asked, turning her attention to me one last time.

"Why are you sharing such a private event of your life with me? I'm a complete stranger to you."

"Are you a complete stranger?" she replied back in question, winking her eye.

I didn't understand what I was feeling. I rose from my seat and looked back at Deborah, who was a decent distance away by now. She had taken off her white fleece sweater and draped it over her right arm, feeling safe in the company of her close friend. Something gave me the feeling that Deborah didn't trust many people in her life after what she had gone through.

I shook my head. It didn't matter. I didn't want the question answered. I felt privileged enough to know that she trusted me. That alone put my mind at ease and filled me with a glimmer of joy. After I wiped a few tears from my cheeks, I let out a small bout of laughter.

CHAPTER ELEVEN

The weeks had flown by and now summer started to quickly transition into autumn. Watching the plum colored maple trees shift into a palette of golden-red, amber-orange and lemony-yellow was really one of my favorite things when September hit. Here in Florida? Not a chance in hell of such a thing happening. Even the branches of the willow trees refused to change for the season. I missed what it was like back home, especially since my birthday was approaching.

I used to curl up into a fetal ball on the porch with a flannel blanket and slowly sip on a hot cup of cherry cider with Cid's arm tucked around my shoulders. We'd watch the wind whip throughout the trees, sending down a colorful rain of leaves to the damp ground below. I'd pick at his punk-rock torn jean shorts with my hands as he'd whisper sweet nothings into my ear. My mother didn't mind me having him around the house all the time. It surprised me that she didn't mind his bad-boy persona. I yearned for the taste of his lips, and how we'd both kiss each other's collar bone, but those days were long gone.

Still, I found myself more and more reminded of Cid as I grew closer to Shajara. They had so much in common — defiant, outgoing, and never afraid to instigate when needed. They both enjoyed getting into trouble and knew that they'd come out unscathed, an adorable "I didn't do it" kind of grin on their face.

I visited the plane through the beginning of autumn. Shajara became my teacher as I learned to tap into the Second Circle by using Aether, while Kalani reigned over Elowyn and

Josiah to do the same. Still though, after all of this time, I didn't really know much about Shajara. Despite how much she reminded me of Cid, she remained closed off from me. She and I sat in the field of lavender, practicing away at magic.

"Where are you from, Shajara?" I asked
"Jamaica." she said, straightening out my arms.
"Ya hold ya arm out like dis and snap ya fingahs. Make sure ya picture a flame comin' from ya hands when doin' so. Feel da Aetha around your body—imagine absorbing it into ya skin."
I nodded. Shajara seemed to have been a priestess for decades. She studied under the Heilige of Astraga, who I was eager to meet once the Masquerade happened tomorrow night. She gently walked her fingers down my straightened arm and nodded. I snapped my fingers while in concentration and a small spark had emitted from the tips.
"Good. But'chu gonna need to do betta. Sagaru is much strongah den dat."
"Can we even kill Sagaru? I mean...hasn't he been dead for hundreds of years?"

Shajara didn't answer at first, still making tiny hand gestures for me to adjust my position and try again. A tiny flame kindled in my hands for a brief second and soon disappeared into a puff of smoke. I tried harder, but I couldn't feel the raw power the way I felt at the lighthouse. She shook her head.

"To be honest, I dun know if we can get rid of him," she said. "But it is best dat we be prepared and dat you be ready to defend yaself. We don't want'cha Silver Thread hangin' on da water fountain in Astraga, ya?"

I thought of the marbled sculpture that lay in the middle of Astraga's square — the two lovers who were closely held together by marbled cloth. It was tradition for the people of Astraga to take the broken Silver Threads of those who had fallen by the hands of the Umbrage Walkers and string it onto the sculpture as a means of respect and honor. The Astragian Priests and Priestesses would conduct an annual ceremony that'd be held on the coming of the New Year, honoring the newly dead that had lost their lives when visiting the Astral Plane. On rare chance would the Heilige offer to mend a Silver Thread off of the statue with the help of his council if he deemed it appropriate. The giant statue is said to illuminate with the brightest of neon blue lights from the thousands of threads that are attached to the limbs of the sculpture, much like how some beaches shimmer from the thousands of bioluminescent algae that lay scattered across the shorelines, glowing like a constellation of blue stars in the dark night sky.

I pushed the thought away and refocused on the lesson. I outstretched my arm and snapped my fingers once more, yet only a fizzle came forth.

"Not good enough!" Shajara shouted. "Tink of sometin' dat enrages yoo. Somtin' dat will cause ire to stir within ya."

I tried my hardest to picture Sagaru's face on the nearby tree. I jolted my arm outwards to only conjure a mere cloud of smoke. Shajara sauntered to my side, whispering quietly into my ear.

"Ya fatha hates yoo, Jackie," she said.

I snapped around and stared Shajara down. Her two-colored eyes sparked with deceit.

"Excuse me?" I asked in shock, "What did you say to me?"

"You heard me. Ya fatha hates ya guts." She scowled.

"You don't know who he is and have no right to say such a thing."

"Leo told me himself." she shoved me backwards, "He even spat at da ground when sayin' so."

"That's not true. Stop it." I deflected her hand from shoving me again.

"Sure it is, Jackie. Have a look for yaself."

"Get away from me!"

I attempted to maneuver around Shajara's grasp but she

had firmly planted her hands onto the temples of my skull while cackling at me in a mocking fashion. In a burst of energy, I could feel the muscles in my head pulsate. I tried my best to focus and push Shajara away, but her eyes grew hungered as the grin on her face darkened. In a flash of light, my vision was clouded and before me I could see my old man speaking with Dante.

"You know she misses you, right?" I heard Dante mutter.

"Yeah, yeah," His raspy voice replied. A voice I hadn't heard in years.

"And so does your kid. You should go back to them."

"Fat chance, my little bird will do just fine without me."

"Are you sure? You know, I'd kill a thousand men to be alive again with my family, Leo."

I watched my father spit to the ground. "I'm not going back. It's too late now."

"It's never too late, man. The only time it's too late is when you're dead."

"I said I'm not going back! Damn it, Dante! They'll fend for themselves!"

The flash of residual light brightened once more, returning my vision back to normal. Shajara giggled at me while removing her hands from my head, tip-toeing away.

"I tol'ja. . . He dun care for yoo or ya motha. Ya nothin' to him. Just garbage."

"You're lying! That wasn't real! You made that up!"

"Ya saw it for yaself, Jackie. Daddy's not comin' back." She laughed menacingly.

I caved in. My hands shook violently as I aimed at Shajara with intent to harm. She withdrew her footing, still scoffing at me with faces and cruel laughter. With a deep breath in my lungs, I closed my eyes and pictured myself beating my father to a bloody pulp. Every blow that I successfully landed onto his face caused the blood in my veins to explode with rage. I could feel vigor seethe out from my pores. In a swift motion I opened my eyes and screamed at the top of my lungs. A cluster of ice emitted from my hands into the shape of a jagged spear. I exhaled my remaining breath and the spear of ice shot forwards at magnificent speed, piercing the willow tree through its thick bark exterior, nearly missing Shajara by inches.

Shajara flinched at the sight of ice that had whizzed furiously past her face, a strand of her hair taking to the wind. Slowly the strand floated upwards and then softly drifted back down to meet again at her face. I darted towards Shajara and started to apologize as quickly as I could.

"I'm sorry, I wasn't thinking! You got me all riled up!" I stammered.

"It's okay, dun worry. Ya did good!" She curiously walked around the tree to examine the other side. "Ya made it through de entiah tree!" she yelled back.

"I did?"

"Ya did!" She came back around the tree, nodding with approval.

I choked back on my laughter, happy that Shajara was okay. I entangled my arms around her and hugged tightly. "I'm so sorry!"

"It's fine." She muttered while gasping for air. She pushed me backwards from my grasp and tapped onto my nose. "Now dat we know how ta channel ya powah, we can be prepared for anyting."

"I wouldn't be so sure about that." An ominous sounding voice growled in the distance.

Instinctively Shajara had put her arm out in front of my body and knelt low beneath the willow tree, waiting for the blackened cloud of smoke to reveal the person within. She gripped at my shirt and pulled me down to ground level with her.

"Whisper for ya friends quietly, Jackie. . . We're

outnumbah'd."

The cloud lingered about a good 20 yards from us in the lavender fields, swirling viciously while separating into several smaller clouds. As the clouds separated apart, low moans and groans started to fill the air. I cuffed my hands to my mouth and whispered as quickly and quietly as I could.

"Elowyn, Kalani, we need your help! Josiah, where are you!?"

"That won't be necessary, fool." The brooding voice boomed, extending its hands from the shadows.

I grabbed at my neckline, gasping for air. The skeletal hands that broke from the blackened cloud clenched its fist at me in the distance, restricting my airways and silencing me with powers that I had never witnessed before. There was nothing I could do but watch as her tall, yet frail body came forth from the enshrouding cloud.

"The Necromancah!" Shajara shouted, juggling a decent size ball of fire in her hands.

"Put down your offense, Priestess of Astraga." the Necromancer ordered at once, "Lest you wish to make a . . . *grave* mistake?"

The Necromancer was not who I had figured to be. While the person towered in height and had a bone-stricken body much like Sagaru's in comparison, Kalani was right, this creature was even worse than Sagaru himself. The Necromancer was essentially female in appearance, and a mortifying female at that. It didn't make much sense to me, recalling that Kalani said his father Dante was the next Necromancer-to-be.

I listened to the bones in her hand crack as she let go of the vice onto my throat from such a distance away. I shivered and winced at such a sound and rubbed my throat while collecting my breath again. She approached Shajara and me gruesomely with her severely arched back. Everything that she touched in the lavender field instantly wilted away into coils of death beneath her pale bone-thin feet, leaving behind a dirty yellow ash that would take to the wind. A simple touch from the Necromancer would surely wither away anything within seconds. The flesh of the Necromancer festered and boiled with puss that lay sporadically stricken throughout her body. I watched her decrepit jaw hang half-hinged on one side of her face as low hisses of laughter escaped her wheezing lungs. My stomach had turned inside-out when she approached. The closer she managed to come, the stronger the stench of rotting flesh would flare into my nostrils.

I gagged several times as I heard her laughter become trapped in her throat, gargled and obstructed likely by a mass of clotted blood. A swamp-like colored puss boiled up from her jugular when she knelt down beside me and stroked my cheek with her emaciated hand. A singe of pain followed with her fingers and I held my breath, for the putrid odor was too much to handle.

"Now now, don't be shy." she spoke, her breath clumping out with profuse foulness. "We have something in common, dearie." She combed back what little mangled grey hairs she had from her appalling face.

"And what might dat be?" Shajara asked with her forearm covering her mouth.

In the distance, the several remaining dark clouds of smoke started to materialize into beings. One of those beings was Dante. I couldn't make the faces of the others. Their bodies were limp and drained of color. Their limbs moved sluggishly towards us like zombies that were reanimated from the dead. Dante still wore his military attire. It was torn, much like his flesh from the bomb that he died from.

"I'm so sorry ... Jackie." He vocalized deeply in paused groans. "I didn't mean to scare or hurt you."

I staggered backwards a little bit. "It—it is okay, Dante. Are you okay?"

The Necromancer let out a tiny giggle, "Of course he's okay. . . He's my puppet . . . For now. What we have in common, Priestess," the Necromancer croaked, shooting a glance at Shajara, "is that we both want that wretched Shaman gone."

"I thought you two were working togetha! What is dis?"

"Never!" she screeched. "He has gone completely mad. He is still starving for the souls of the living, stealing what he can from me! I will not tolerate this anymore!" she hissed, flapping her tongue like a snake. "His hunger is no longer satiated by what scraps I throw to him. Sagaru keeps on mentioning one soul, however." The Necromancer locked her beady crimson red eyes onto my face.

"No. Neva!" Shajara exclaimed, shoving her arm between the Necromancer and me.

A ghastly worm slid through the bare cartilage of the Necromancer's nose and looped into her mouth. She bit down, chewing on the crunchy worm as its pale pink guts seeped from her mouth. I watched, horrified, and whispered everyone's name again under my breath.

"Are you sure you don't want to take up the offer? I might just know how to rid Sagaru from the Plane for good," she said, resting her brittle bones onto her withering staff.

Her chipped claws entangled with Silver Threads that were draped over the top of her staff. These threads were not the sparkling bluish-tint that I remembered from Astraga. Instead, these strands were deep violet as if the blue was shining through a coating of blood. When placed together, they resonated a deep amethyst hue.

In the distance Dante groaned lightly, his eyes bearing a glimmer of hope to be freed of his torment. It broke my heart as I realized that Dante was simply a marionette to her, controlled relentlessly by the Necromancer. There was nothing he could do but obey her every command, much like the several others that lay spread out across the field, moaning in agony.

"I am positive! Da child stays with us in Astraga. You will never claim Jackie's thread, Sgrias." Shajara said strictly.

"Ah, I haven't heard someone speak that name in. . . eons." Her cracked lips smeared across her macabre face in a disgusting shape of unpleasant joy. "Very well then..." she spoke brokenly, tapping her thin fingers onto the staff in slight contemplation. "Perhaps you will change your mind later, Priestess."

In a wave of dismissal, The Necromancer's army of undead slithered back into the earth, rotting massive circles of lavender as they disappeared from view. I watched Dante retreat back into the earth. His face was somber, yet held an unbridled amount of forlorn hope. I could feel the pain in his eyes project into my mind as I watched. A man who served my country didn't deserve that kind of fate. I felt my resolve harden: I would free Dante of that foul, broken woman, no matter the cost.

The Necromancer gave one last piercing look at Shajara before a gust of lavender ash surrounded her rotting body, casting her into the sky and disappearing into the atmosphere. I felt the tainted Aether in the air from her presence, like a greasy, all-over itch.

Elowyn, Josiah, and Kalani had then appeared moments later with their guard up. I rose to my feet and wiped my cheek of the revolting ichor that the Necromancer left so generously behind.

"Ya too late," Shajara said.

"What's going on?!" Elowyn said with an impressive fireball burning in her hands.

"Yeah, we're here to help!" Josiah added.

"I said ya too late," Shajara repeated but louder.

"The Necromancer came," I said.

"What? How?!" Elowyn extinguished her flame.

"Just came forth outta nowhere. And Dante came as well."

I stared pointedly at Kalani for him to take over and answer all of our questions. "Explain." I spoke sternly.

Kalani at first looked shocked at my tone, but nevertheless carried onwards.

"Like I said, my father isn't The Necromancer, but one day he will be." Kalani murmured. His face grew blank and he kicked at some of the lavender ash, stirring it into the air with his foot.

"The Necromancer is Sgrias, who is now a woman that takes the threads of those who have fallen and uses it as a tool to manipulate the dead. When Sgrias takes the form of a man, she goes by the name of Sgrios. Souls that are often lost in the Astral Plane become tangled and misguided, especially when they are immediately pushed into the Fourth Circle so quickly. Sgrias exploits this and feeds off of their broken Silver Threads, practically injecting them with darkness. We don't know where she came from, but we assume that she has been around for as long as Sagaru, if not longer. It's a twisted ebb and flow to maintain the balance, some say."

"Why did you tell us that Dante was the Necromancer? You lied." I said.

"It wasn't a lie, so to speak, and I didn't say that entirely. I didn't get to finish the story in the pub. If my father is not freed of her binding, one day he will likely become the next Necromancer, the next 'Sgrios'. It's just a long story that I don't want to get into."

"Too late," Elowyn said, pinching Kalani lightly on the nose.

"Yeah, you have to tell us now. What if she gangs up with Sagaru?" Josiah spoke.

"I doubt that'll be the case. Apparently, she wants him gone," I said. "She seemed pretty pissed at him, to be honest."

Kalani rested against the willow tree. He tangled a branch around his rough, dry hand and let out a drawn sigh. He pulled the branch, snapping it apart and dangled it helplessly.

"There's a reason why we tie Silver Threads to the fountain statue in Astraga's square," he said. "It is to protect those who have passed. Theodore, the Heilige, has taught us that evil cannot touch the fountain, even if evil is able to break through the city's shield. The Heilige himself places the threads on the fountain to keep them from the Umbrage Walkers.

"Sgrias is a curse that has been laid upon the Plane, and we're not sure who cast it. Not even Theodore knows. He often preaches that our sins are the reason for the coming of the Necromancer, and that we should repent, but his words fall on deaf ears. Many people here act on young mindsets since our bodies are not restrained by mortal laws, inevitably causing us to become ignorant and selfish, giving into our wildest imaginations and using as much Aether as we possibly can. No matter how much fun it may seem to be in the plane, we should not extend our stay or abuse the power that is given to us. It's just wrong and is frowned upon. Sgrias collects the souls of the damned and she does for a good reason. If you've seen her visage, you'd know. Her body is not up to par, and is rather disgusting."

"Uh yeah, gross." I wrinkled my nose at the thought of her filthy stench filling the air again.

"Quite." Kalani said, "While she may remain immortal in the plane as most are, her body is flawed; her body often rots away at an alarming rate. With this happening, she is constantly forced to replace her body with another one. If she does not replace her body continually, we assume that she would disappear from the Astral Realm forever. Everyone who has tried to banish Sgrias has failed, succumbing to their own afflictions and, almost always, becoming simply another vessel."

"The vessels being her army of the dead, I take it. Like Dante," I pointed out after coming to the abrupt realization.

"Exactly," Kalani replied. "Sgrias twines her Thread with the fallen soul's Thread, merging them together. She'll simply pluck whichever strand she can find on her staff and incorporate it into her own, taking over that person's entire body and soul. My father will eventually become engulfed by Sgrias, and he will stand as her next vessel. "

"What happens to Dante's mind then?" Josiah asked.
"No Idea. Limbo maybe, we don't know. The Heilige teaches us that it's a different form of death, though if he takes that on faith or has some deeper knowledge, we don't know. Everyone takes the plunge eventually, some sooner than others."

"All we know is dat Sgrias prefers to play a passive card here in da plane. She isn't tha type of person to initiate an attack, unless given no choice. She'd rather stand aside and let da world turn in her favor. It's best not ta cross her howeva, she beholds immense powah and could take ya thread for her own in a split second. We tink she is stronga than Sagaru by multitudes."

"Why does she choose to be passive? And you said she has a thread of her own, how is that even possible?" I asked Shajara and Kalani.

I grew increasingly curious about this woman. Even if Sgrias was an abomination to us, something still gave me the inclination to know her story.

"Sgrias is the only known person to be able to reconstruct Silver Threads without the help of several people, which is why she is called Necromancer," Kalani said. "She has only returned a few souls to their bodies, but stopped however when she attempted to reconstruct her own Silver Thread and failed."

"Why would she return someone to their body?" I asked. "It makes no sense."

"You'd be surprised at how much a person yearns ta be brought back to da eart once dey've lost deir connection," Shajara said. "Confused souls will do anytin'. Da darkest deeds you could imagine, n' Sgrias is all about dark deeds, ya."

"But how did Sgrias fail at resurrecting herself?" Elowyn asked.

"We don't know if her power was too weak or if it was her flawed body that kept her from succeeding, but the attempt left the whole plane disturbed for months. We *do* know that beings were not meant to hold such power, and that's when she and Sagaru entered the Fifth Circle together. It's a circle that nobody dare treads, for fear of what may happen. It's what drives them increasingly mad. Sagaru failed at repairing his Silver Thread, just as Sgrias did, making him forever hunger for the souls of those who still live, while Sgrias now uses Silver Threads to obtain vessels so she continues to exist here in the plane."

"Howeva," Shajara said, "Sgrias' case was far worse. When dey returned from da Fifth Circle, her body started to rot instantly. Sagaru cackled at her, thinking that she'd deteriorate within a matter of minutes, but now Sgrias laughs at him in return, as he begs her for threads to feast on."

I waved my hand around quickly, exposing my very own Silver Thread that was tied to my knuckle. I bobbled it gently through the air as it wisped flowingly like the tentacle of a jellyfish in water.

"So there's more to these threads than we know?" I spoke.

The thread latched itself around my hand caressingly in warmth, gleaming brightly.

"Indeed," Kalani replied. "We assume that the threads are what give us power in the Astral Plane, that they allow us to manipulate the aetheric energy around us, aside from just keeping our souls attached to our bodies. Even if you happen to have your Silver Thread broken, your power can still exist to a degree, it's just that your soul is permanently severed from your body. As long as your thread is never manipulated or devoured, you'll still remain in the plane as a soul. If your thread is devoured or manipulated though..."

"Then chances are you'll become a spineless puppet like your father, or have your soul devoured whole, causing your mind to enter limbo. Maybe." I finished Kalani's sentence.

"Yes. Either Sagaru will devour you entirely and you'll disappear, or Sgrias will manipulate your thread and you'll become. . . Like my father a zombie of sorts. The only difference is that Sgrias does it to sustain her existence and Sagaru does it to keep his hunger at bay. It's pretty twisted, right?" Kalani kicked the ground after his voice cracked an octave higher.

I did it again. I crossed the line, oblivious to the fact that this was extremely personal to Kalani.

There is so much that I still do not understand about this

place. Even if I've resided in the plane for quite some time now, it's still very mind boggling. How is Kalani's father an Umbrage Walker? In order to become one, you must sever the thread of a Circle Walker. Did Dante attempt to make a dark bargain with Sgrias in order to get his soul back into his body, and in turn he was tricked? If so, she could turn every lost soul into an Umbrage Walker and wage impending doom on the plane.

All of these circumstances and scenarios in the plane were starting to take its toll on my sanity and it started to confuse the utter hell out of me. It's been hard to absorb all of this information in clusters at a time. They weren't kidding when they said that anything is possible in this place. I began to circle around in thoughts again until I came to the epiphany that I was almost recruited to Sgrias' army by Dante.

"Wait! When your father offered me his hand at the lighthouse..." I said, raising my finger in objection.

Kalani nodded and continued to answer my question before I had even asked. "It was likely he was being controlled by Sgrias, and she saw it as an opportune moment to collect another soul. You were lucky we came when we did, or else you would probably be standing aside my father at this very moment. He would've stolen your Silver Thread, had you taken his hand."

I didn't want to think of it anymore. The Astral Plane to me was supposed to be a realm where I could escape from reality, where people could gather together and enjoy their time away from the harsh realities of the world that burden them. The Plane was not supposed to be a place where evil attempted to consume all in its wake. It is wrong, and it was all thanks to people who overstepped their bounds by seeking to obtain a higher level of power. The Astral Plane was plagued from Elizabeth and her coven for what they had done, along with Sagaru and the Necromancer, too. They were a shining example of what greed will get you in return; never ending sorrow.

I did not know if I should have cast aside my anger towards them, but I chose not to. I could feel my blood move into my cheeks and forehead. Before I knew it I was fumigating in rage. Why do humans always find the need to exploit power to their own greedy demands?! I stomped off from the crowd and ignored them when they had called my name. Elowyn and Josiah ran to my side immediately but I had shoved them away, still pounding my feet into the ashy lavender field.

"Stay away from me," I said carelessly.
"Jackie? What's wrong? Come on, don't be like that."
Elowyn strapped her hands around my left arm.
"Back off!" I said, flinging my hand out of her grip.
"Hey! Don't treat her like that!" Josiah shouted.

"What're you gonna do, beat me up?" I mocked Josiah, laughing in defiance. I was still pissed.
Josiah pierced me by the torso, tackling me to the ground. We fumbled our limbs down the field, knocking each other occasionally in the face with an elbow or knee. Elowyn started to scream.
"Stop it, you two! Stop fighting!"

Her plea didn't matter in the slightest. By this time I was practically foaming at the mouth. Josiah had clenched his hands around my throat and started to bash my head up and down, smashing it onto the hard ground. A circle of fire set ablaze around the two of us, engulfing our bodies and nearly burning our flesh. My throat started to freeze by Josiah's hands and my breath became scarce as my lungs were pinched of oxygen. In the distance a small storm started to brew on the horizon.

"Oh no you don't!" I squeezed to speak through Josiah's strong grasp, nearly choking on my words. His green eyes fiercely flickered from the nearby flames. I grabbed his forearms and sent a blast of electricity throughout his body, flying him back several yards after he had lost his grip on my throat. I gasped for air when I gained my standing and started to charge. I nearly made it to Josiah's burnt body when Elowyn intercepted my attack. This in turn gave Josiah the time to gain his footing once more.

Tears began to fill in Elowyn's eyes. "Both of you stop it, right now!"

I raised my hand in unison to Josiah's, ready to deflect any of his oncoming attacks. With a ball of electricity charged in my hand, Josiah had sent several daggers of ice whizzing past Elowyn, who was standing between the both of us now. I returned the attack by exploding the shards of ice into pieces and tossed a sloppy fireball back at him as a counter attack. Josiah wound up a ball of fire himself and launched it at my own, colliding them together which had caused a small explosion to erupt. Elowyn was caught in the crossfire and struck down by the fire.

"Elowyn!" I screamed.

Her knees buckled as the smoke dissipated from her body. Right as her body hit the ground, she exploded into a million miniscule pieces of light. I watched as the tiny balls of light traveled vastly across the expanse of the plane. I ran passed where Elowyn had fallen and charged right into Josiah, pinning him to the ground this time as lightning streaked across the sky.

"LOOK WHAT YOU DID!" I screamed, "YOU NEARLY KILLED HER!" my voice roared.

I grew absolutely berserk and sweat started to roll off of me. I headbutted Josiah several times until the sound of his skull cracked. He did not fight back, his eyes trembling at what had happened. The tiny fireflies of light continued to encircle the two of us as I beat him with my bare hands. I continued to punch as hard as I could, cracking the bones in my hands. Josiah still did not react.

"Jackie! Enough!" Shajara exclaimed while flying me backwards with a gust of air.

Sharaja's magical strength was nearly impossible to surpass. It would take months, if not years, to attain her level of power.

I tossed and tumbled throughout the field and then watched Josiah rise soon after I was firmly planted in the ground. A stream of blood started to trickle down his forehead. I watched the red stream fill into the crease of his lips.

He mouthed the words "I'm sorry" before he finally exploded into a myriad of bright lights. I struggled to stand, as if I became Atlas himself, holding the entire weight of the world on my shoulders. The lights started to ferociously whip around the lavender field. I was too weak and the world started to flutter in my vision, causing me to collapse at the knees and send myself back into the waking world.

CHAPTER TWELVE

I instantly shot from my bed. Brutis stood his guard immediately, baffled at why I had leapt from my bed, but ready to bark at something. I clenched my head in excruciating pain. My skull felt like it had been smashed between two bricks and hot glued back together, and the knuckles of my hands were heavily bruised black and blue. I screamed out loud. It felt like my skin was on fire. I stumbled into the bathroom to scour the medicine cabinet. After I had knocked through a couple medications and creams, I slammed the metallic medicine cabinet shut and paused for a brief moment to look at myself in the mirror. What on earth had I done?

My skin was sunburnt, and I had a lump starting to gather on the top of my forehead. I winced as I poked the lump gingerly, throwing a few curse words to nobody in particular.

"Is everything alright up there, dear?" my mother called from downstairs.

"Yeah, ma!" I panicked. "Just woke up with a charley horse is all!"

"Okay sweetie! I'm off to work. Make sure you let Brutis out before you do anything today!"

"Okay, will do! Have a good day at wor–"

I heard the front door slam. Regardless of the door being gigantic and ridiculously heavy, my mother always found a way to weasel passed it quickly. I took a tube of aloe gel and slathered it across my arms when heading down the stairs and into the kitchen. I didn't realize how badly burned I was by Josiah. I was actually impressed at how quickly he could conjure a ball of fire. *Oh shit! Elowyn! Josiah!* I quickly reached for the cell phone that my mother had left on the kitchen island and dialed Josiah's number first.

After a few rings he had picked up. "Whuughtht–" he slushed out of his mouth with a guttural sound.

"Are you alright?! I'm—" I choked over the word.

"Uh, sort of, I have a splitting headache thanks to you. What's your deal, Jackie?"

"You're the one who tackled me!"

"Yeah, but you had no right to just get rude out of nowhere. What gives?"

I thought about hanging up. I didn't want to spill my guts to Josiah. I didn't want him to know about how upset I could get over such petty things. It just really drives me up a wall on how corrupt people are in this world, and they were apparently just as bad in the plane. What did it matter anyway? It's not like it'd solve world peace if I had confessed my reasoning for getting so upset at everything. The Astral Plane was growing onto me and quickly becoming my sanctuary to escape the world's shit.

"I'm sorry, really. I just lost it," I finally answered quietly.

"It's okay. You should check on El."

"I will."

Josiah hung up the phone without saying anything more. I took that as a sign that he was still upset. After I had dialed Elowyn's number, she immediately answered in a perky tone.

"HellooOoOo!"

I could practically feel her smiling.

"Uhm, is this...Elowyn?"

"Of course it is, silly. Whats up?"

"Are—you okay?" I asked perplexed.

"I am! You wouldn't believe what happened when I woke up. It's like I got sunburnt!"

"Me too!" I replied in excitement. "But you're not actually 'burnt burnt', are you?"

"Haha nope! This babe's gonna have a hot tan once this red goes down! Just in time for the ball, too!"

"The ball?" I scratched my head.

"Yeah, the masquerade, remember?!"

"Ohh yeah! Well I'm glad you are okay, and I wanted to apologize. I didn't mean to get you caught in the crossfire like that."

"It's okay, really! It was fun! I woke up and it was like a heat wave just flew off of me. My skin is already peeling. Amazing, huh?"

Something told me that Elowyn was really holding back on how she really felt, but I didn't bother to delve any further. I figured that if she wanted to express how she was feeling, she would. While she's the type of girl to say whatever she feels at any given moment, she can also be the type of girl to stretch the truth just to make sure that you're happy. It's admirable, really, but at times it's often bothersome.

"So I'll see you at the masquerade next, then?" I asked, feigning enthusiasm.

"Yes! Make sure to dress for the occasion, and don't forget to wear a mask, Jackie!"

"Roger that," I said and hung up the phone.

I scavenged through the refrigerator and eventually came to the conclusion that leftovers were going to be what I'd eat. By the time I had cooked the dry chicken and vegetables in the microwave and plopped the plate onto the table, I had completely lost my appetite. I didn't understand why, but I sat down and stared at the food mindlessly even though my stomach growled with hunger. I tossed the plate in the garbage and searched throughout the pantry to only realize nothing looked appealing at all, not in the slightest. A feeling of disgust washed over me. Imagining a morsel of food passing my lips churned my stomach.

It was so weird to feel this way. I didn't understand it as I tossed an unwrapped granola bar back and forth in my hands, trying to convince myself to eat it. A part of me wanted to just devour food but another part of me revolted at the thought. I threw the granola bar over my shoulder and turned on the television instead.

Well, what do you know—a hurricane. Here I figured that we'd be able to go an entire year without one, but it was silly of me to think that. After all, it's nearing the end of the hurricane season. One issue that my mother failed to realize when moving to Florida is that the house she decided to move into was right in the middle of a horrible flood zone. It explains why we got such a good deal.

A red banner rolled across the bottom screen of the weather channel while the prettied up, bodacious blonde female news reporter babbled onwards about the category. The amount of Botox and plastic surgery this woman underwent was shocking. I turned down the volume to avoid the loud screech that the Weather channel would soon make. It's probably one of the most annoying things in the world. Not the screech, but the fact that humans are so self-conscious about themselves that they feel the need to pump their faces full of plastic just to feel beautiful.

Is there something that I'm missing out on here? I honestly am at a loss for words as to why the world I live in is so damn skewed and jacked up. People like my mother, work themselves to ridiculous hours and go months without even having a day off, while girls succumb to the media and grow extremely debilitating mental defects about their body image, to where women feel the need to alter their face with a scalpel and buy the 'next best' cream that'll reverse the signs of aging, or vomit in a toilet after every meal they consume because they feel obese when in reality they're a toothpick in size. Even men fall victim to the media with all of these muscular, modelésque men parading around in television shows and magazines. I crunched my fist into a ball and started to tap my foot on the seat stool in hopes that it'd help me just forget about it all, but it was pointless. I took the creaky wooden chair and threw it across the room, smashing it into pieces against the fridge.

"AAAAAAAGH!" I screamed as strands of saliva flew out of my mouth and covered my chin. "WHAT THE HELL IS WRONG WITH EVERYBODY?!"

I thrashed back and forth, throwing various plates, glasses and utensils out of the cupboard, across the kitchen and into the living room. The louder the smash and the more glass that shattered across the walls, the more enraged and happier I grew. I had gone through half a dozen plates and several cups before I had released enough steam to finally calm down. My knees buckled and caused my body to hit the floor. I then let out several more murderous screams.

"I CAN'T TAKE THIS FUCKING WORLD ANYMORE!"
I had completely lost it. I darted my eyes back and forth across the glass littered floor, feeling the veins pop outrageously from my forehead. In the background I could hear the low humming of the television set as the plastic blonde newscaster announced the Hurricane's name - Lorne.

What a woeful name for a hurricane. It reminded me of lonesomeness, a name only given to those who are destined to live a nomadic lifestyle. Perhaps to be a one man army of sorts, needing no company other than themselves. In any event, I dazzled the idea in my head over and over while I could feel a string of drool escape my mouth and touch the floor. In the distance, a decent sized chunk of glass shined off of the television's light. I reached outwards to the glass piece and pulled it closer to me.

"Should I?" I whispered.
I held the glass piece to my forearm, slowly gliding it across my "sunburnt" skin. I did not break skin at first but instead played with the idea, leaving behind a tiny trail of dried skin flakes. I pressed harder the second time around, feeling the chemicals in my body course throughout my limbs, numbing the potential oncoming pain. I squeaked out a small laugh and bobbled my eyes back and forth. What if I was wrong? What if there wasn't anything wrong with the world, but instead something was wrong with me? I let out a ridiculously loud

scream and threw the piece of glass across the room. I'm stronger than this. The saliva broke from my face and slung onto the floor when I scooted my body upwards and leaned against the wooden cabinets.

"I am such a fucking idiot!" I shouted to myself.

An overbearing amount of indifference started to flood through me. The thought that I would self-harm put my mind into a state of unease. Never in my entire life had I dared think such a thing, even in my teenage years. What if my father really did commit suicide and made sure that his body wouldn't be found? What if the vision that Shajara showed me were true? In ways I felt refreshed, like I was able to "bleed out my demons" so to speak without actually shedding any real blood, but in other ways I felt grotesque, ugly, and tainted for thinking that I'd attempt such an odious act. Is this what actual people go through mentally when they're struggling to stay afloat? As I cleaned up the shattered glass across the entire floor, I kept thinking over and over if I had actually dug that shard of glass into my arm. Would it have made me become a better person or a lesser being? No. People who self-harm are not lesser, that's absurd. There could have been chance that I would've hit a tendon or worse.

After I collected all of the broken glass, I crouched down beside the pile and shook my head. What am I going to tell my mother? I didn't even think that far ahead. Now we have practically an entire cupboard that is empty and she's bound to notice eventually. It's not like we use more than two plates at a time anyhow. . . We're loners when it comes to family. I shifted throughout the broken glass and slowly started to piece together a ceramic plate that I had made for her when I was a youngster. I was not at all proud of the little creation, being that the paint markings on the plate were extremely novice. I was a young tot though and I had only just started to excel in art in school. A tear filled to the brim and I flicked it away when I completed the broken plate. On the plate, I stood with an obscenely large body and tiny head, while my mother stood taller than me with her natural blonde hair that I blotched on. I was only good at making stick figures at the time. A good laughter echoed out of me, a yearning laughter that spoke multitudes of how much I wanted to just go back in time again and have a regular family again. I even drew my father on the plate, with his darker skin and bulky arms.

It was almost like I was losing mortal possessions, one at a time. In fact, I actually was. First my mother's favorite vase, now a ceramic plate that she also cherished. To be honest, I didn't care as much as I should have. I already felt alarmingly detached from this world and the hole was only growing bigger and bigger by the day. Astraga is my new home. I swept the glass into a bin and tucked it away behind a few boxes in the garage. I prayed that she wouldn't notice anything in the cupboards went missing for at least a few days until I figured out how to compensate.

By the time night fell, Lorne had just begun to stir. Strings of lightning shot across the clouded black sky, and I was yet to feel tired. It was unusual for a hurricane to have lightning, but I still took all of the necessary precautions, especially locating the sandbags in case of flooding.

I raided the medicine cabinet once more and popped a few pills into my mouth to ensure a deep sleep. With a little elbow grease, I dug into the confines of my closet. After having to toss half of my clothes onto the floor, I found what I was looking for. A masquerade mask! It was a little damaged from the layer dust that had caked onto it, but with a bit of a wash it'd be good as new. Cid had given it to me, and the dirt on the mask was a perfect comment on our relationship. The mask's elastic band was a little crumpled and dried out, but I didn't mind. I used the mask as a part of a Halloween costume a few years back. I used to cherish it greatly but it lost its value once he stopped returning my calls and disappeared from the world on me. People tend to do that in my life and I've accepted it.

Cid chose it specifically for me since he knew that I liked royal purple at the time. The purple outlines meshed very well with the black frame, especially with the turquoise beads that were tied down by violet thread. My favorite part though was the black feathers that were spread across the top brim of the mask, giving the wearer quite the exotic and mysterious look. I placed the mask carefully on my face and fluffed around my hair. I really had gone off the deep end when it came to maintaining my image. I like to think that my thick hair looks good on me when tangled in weak waves. For some reason the dye that my mother and I fiddled around with really didn't stick all too well. If anything it had faded into a barely noticeable dirty blonde. Along with a little bit of hair growth, I had the perfect ombre look. I nuzzled Brutis deep into my arm and slowly drifted off into a deep slumber to the distant sound of rain.

"I told you to dress for the occasion, Jackie!" scolded Elowyn. I opened my eyes in Astraga to see her standing before me, a hand on her hips.

"But I did!" I argued back, clicking my fingernail onto the masquerade mask. We stood in a small gap between shops, just off the main street, keeping clear of the press of people starting to assemble.

Elowyn rolled her eyes and spun herself around, dazzling her beautiful emerald dress before me. I heard footsteps behind me, and when I had turned, Shajara was standing there in a sapphire dress that sparkled like a thousand shooting stars. No longer did she sport her war-torn rags that tugged at her breast and hipline. Instead, she stood as she always had, a combined posture of fierceness and elegance. The warhawk hairdo that I was used to seeing was gone. Instead, her hair was respectfully placed down in braids, tied together by one giant band which flowed over her shoulder.

"Shajara, I..." I trailed off.

I had lost the ability to compliment.

"Quiet, child," she quickly cut me off. "Dis be da only time you see me in a dress. My respects are due to da Heilige, and tonight we honor da dead, ya?"

"That's right," Kalani added. He stood next to Josiah a few steps away, affixing Josiah's wardrobe at the neckline.

By the time I had seen everyone dressed up in their proper attire, I started to feel slightly underdressed. I adored Josiah's appearance. He wore a silk-white button up with a black tie and black suspenders strapped over his shoulders. Josiah had even placed a flat top hat onto his head which held his dark hair properly in place. Everyone had even gone the extra mile and put on fancy dress shoes for the occasion to match their outfit. I shuffled my bare feet in embarrassment at noticing this.

"Dun worry," Shajara whispered into my ear, sensing my discomfort. "Dere is a seamstress in town dat can sew ya up no problem."

"We'll all meet together in the Cathedral courtyard, okay?" Kalani spoke.

Everybody nodded, splitting into their own direction. I followed behind Shajara, weaving in and out of the mass of people and tried my utmost best not to step on the skirts of her sapphire dress. We came to a halt in front of another small shop with a carved image of a needle and thread hanging above the door. Shajara knocked smartly on the wooden door and walked inside without waiting for a response.

"Shajara, my dear." An elderly woman's voice echoed through the cobwebby shop. She waved her hands in the air to greet Shajara. They both embraced in each other's arms as the various lanterns throughout the room glowed at different levels of light.

"Who might this be, darling?" the elderly woman peered

over Shajara's shoulder with her beaming brown eyes and bent nose.

She took on the perfect stereotype of what a storybook witch would look like: ragged white hairs sticking out wildly all over her head, a bent back, and a voice that could put knots into wooden planks. I felt her bony fingers press against my skin as she quickly measured my body in every angle possible.

"Gertrude, dis is Jackie. A Circle Walkah." Shajara's voice took on a lilting tone and she spoke as if reciting something from memory. "Today we be attendin' da masquerade, and we need joo to work ya magic!" She spoke while encouraging me to raise my arms up for measurement.

"Well, Jackie," Gertrude said, "I think we have just what you're looking for." she said in a high-pitched squeak. Gertrude looked down at my feet and a moment of disgust unfurled on her face, making her nose appear even longer. "And we'll cover up those feet as well."

Gertrude herself wore tiny grey slippers on her feet. I guessed that she wasn't what was considered an active Circle Walker, being that she was rather on the elderly side. Maybe she was dead. Or maybe she just slept with slippers on.

"Isn't it a taboo here in Astraga if you're not dead? Wearing shoes and all?" I asked.

"Oh no my dear, not at all, especially for occasions like tonight!" the old witch lady replied with a wrinkled smile, sticking a pin into my loose shirt and tugging it backwards. She carried on her business, drifting in and out of the backroom while humming my measurements over and over. The flames within the lanterns grew brighter as Gertrude walked closer to them and then dulled as the distance between her and the lanterns became greater. I peered over at Shajara, who was tinkering with her lavender colored masquerade mask, struggling, I think, to make it less feminine-looking.

"Shajara?" I asked, staying carefully still with all the pins in my clothes.
"What'chu want, mon?"
"Are you and Kalani. . . you know. . . an item?"
Shajara quickly looked up from the mask and planted her eyes on me. "What'cha say now?" she tilted her head and approached me.

"Well, it's just that you two seem pretty close. Is he a Priest of Astraga himself, like how you're a Priestess?"

Shajara looked back down at the mask in her hands. I watched as she continued to fiddle with it. Eventually she spoke.

"He was once a pupil of da Heilige, but dat ended quickly afta he tried to free his fatha from the Necromancah. Kalani was nearly banished from da Plane for goin' against da Heilige an' his teachins. It's forbidden ta resurrect someone form da plane without da consent of da Heilige first."

"Why wasn't he banished, and why haven't I seen any other Priests or Priestesses?" I asked.
As Shajara and I chattered, Gertrude quietly went to work and slipped a pair of fancy dress shoes in my direction on the floor.

"I intervened. At da time, I had just earned my Priesthood. I defended Kalani to da Heilige and now he owes me. And what, am I not good enough for yah as your guide?"
"No! It's not that. I'm just curious."
"You will meet a few of dem at da ball, I'm sure. Some of da Heilige's council walks among da dead, so ya best be

respectful, ya?"

"Roger that. And you still haven't answered my question about . . . I mean, if you and Kalani are together."

"Dat's because it's none yah business, child." She looked up at me from under her eyebrows.

"Hey!" I said, pulling over the loose white cotton shirt that Gertrude handed me. It looked like a pilgrim's shirt, especially with the cowhide string that laced back and forth up the middle of the chest.

"You know you can tell me. I can keep a secret."

"Love is forbidden in da Plane."

"Why?" I asked.

Shajara whapped me on the forehead with her masquerade mask and looked at me jokingly. "Because, we dun need any spirit babies floatin' around in Astraga! Now stop askin' all dese silly questions, ya?"

Gertrude let out a raspy giggle. I thought about what Shajara had said as I watched frost begin to collect in the window sill of Gertrude's lantern-lit shop, etching the corners in blue veins of ice. Weather in Astraga was sporadic and spontaneous. It all depended on how much Aether was drawn from the atmosphere at the given time. I imagined that if all of the Circle Walkers in Astraga had used magic at the same time, an entire storm would erupt and send the Plane into a frenzy.

By the time that Gertrude had draped a dirty quartz necklace over my collarbone, the nearby window had completely glazed over in frost, eventually exploding the window panes.

Shards of glass flew throughout the room. All at once the lanterns exploded too, burning brightly and then extinguishing into a withdrawal of smoke. Sharjara had grabbed my arm and started dragging me into the street. Snow befell lightly onto the City of Astraga and I could see my breath in the cold. Pieces of gargoyles from above lay in the snow like black words on a page—

the cold had come so quickly that they had burst from the pressure of the water.

"Dun't come out!" Shajara yelled at Gertrude before slamming the door shut.

Shajara sprinted down the brick roadway of Astraga, and I followed as quickly as I could. For her being in a dress, she sure knew how to maneuver without any complications. She was more than capable of keeping ahead of me. Shajara gently pressed against the people of the crowd to slip by and eventually we made it to the central Square of Astraga only to find that we were too late.

"Where is it?!" I shouted, panicking, looking at the space where the statue of the lovers had been. The statue was gone.
"It be alright," Shajara panted. "Da statue has been moved for da ceremony, dat's all. Must've cost quite a bit of Aether ta move such a sacred ting, no wonda the windows had shattered earlier." she confided.
Shajara then approached a person I had never seen before who was standing not too far from us.
"Jackie, meet Jonathan, a Priest of Astraga." Shajara spoke.

The absurdly tall man turned his attention when Shajara draped her arm across his shoulders with some effort. You could tell she struggled to match his seven feet in height, but she managed to do it gracefully. Jonathan extended his incredibly long arm with a welcoming smile.

"Greetings," he spoke in a soft, humble tone.
His eyes had never met with mine. I shook his large hand and nodded courteously.
"Hello." I replied back, observing a set of strange scars around his neck.

"Shajara has told me quite a bit about you. Shall we?" He gestured toward the Cathedral.

Shajara walked ahead of us, giving me the chance to speak with Jonathan.

"What's it like being a Priest for the Heilige?" I asked.

"Well," he inhaled deeply. "I could say many things about what it is like. But I could only give you a small piece of it. We are ultimately here to serve Astraga and minster to the new Circle Walkers that discover the Astral Plane. It's a blessing, really."

I had trouble keeping up with him, being that his legs were much longer than my own. His black dress shoes clicked loudly on the brick road. They were penny loafers.

"You were ordained by the Heilige himself?" I asked.

"Indeed. In 86' I was appointed Priest after half a decade under Theodore's tutorship. It was a joyous year, if I say so myself."

"You seem really young. You're practically my age." I said, growing increasingly curious.

Jonathan gave a surprised laugh, attempting to dismiss my curiosity by shaking his head. I did not falter and continued to send a barrage of questions his way.

"How old are you?"

"In Astraga? Old," he smiled innocently.

I peered down at his shoes.

"Those shoes seem to be pretty old, too. They look like they're from the eighties." I commented. Jonathan did not respond.

"Ah!" He exclaimed cheerfully. "A beautiful piece of architecture, wouldn't you agree?" Jonathan breathed quietly, leaning back his head to take in the entire Cathedral.

"Shajara and I helped rebuild this Cathedral and added our own little twist," he looked down upon me. "It stormed for a solid three weeks afterward from all of the Aether that the Council absorbed to manifest such an amazing structure. It's a wonder that people managed to craft such a breathtaking piece of architecture back hundreds of years ago in the waking world."

I brushed the light snow off my shoulder and smiled. "I agree. It's astonishing. Did you use Aether to move the statue inside of the Cathedral, also?"

"Yes." Jonathan replied back. "Sorry if it may have caused any disruptions."
"You did startle us, but it's reassuring to know that the statue is still in good hands." I spoke back, heading into the Cathedral with him.

CHAPTER THIRTEEN

Dozens, if not hundreds of people had gathered into giant groups within the courtyard of the Cathedral, each person dressed in exquisite attire. Court jesters spread sporadically throughout the crowd in their exaggerated harlequin costumes to entertain the guests, jingling the bells affixed to their curved shoes, dancing with baubles in hand. In the far corner of the courtyard, a minstrel was accompanied by several musicians who were playing various instruments —I saw a harp and several lutes—while the minstrel himself recited a soft ballad to the onlookers who gathered around him. A little girl who couldn't have been much taller than my waistline brushed passed my leg, gaining my attention. I was able to see a small glimpse of her face before her velvet blue gown had disappeared into the crowded area. I followed her as best I could.

I shifted among the elaborate crowd while masks of all shapes and sizes, colors and trinkets were worn by the partygoers. Cracked porcelain masks with sullen shadows for eyeholes, some masks suspended on sturdy rods with massive multicolored feathers that leapt from the top. No matter how politely I tried to maneuver around people, I would end up brushing against their gorgeously frilled and embroidered dresses. The clanking of jewelry mixed with music and high-pitched laughter, and, before I could retrace my steps, I became lost within the crowd. I spun around the crowds of people as best I could before my hand was taken by a stranger. I was whirled around several times in dance. To and fro I went, with a woman whose face was only covered by a half mask. I eventually broke apart from the crowd, leaving the stranger to trail off elsewhere, likely to her friends.

A giant maple tree lay planted in the courtyard's ground where the little girl remained seated under, picking the crimson colored leaves off of the ground. It was Ariella, and she was not alone. Deborah was accompanied by her side, laughing with joy as one of the court Jesters amused them with silly gestures and mime-like movements. My heart swelled at this, realizing that Ariella wasn't trapped alone in the plane upon her gruesome death at the concentration camp. Who knows how long Deborah had been visiting her. Be it years or not, it soothed my mind knowing that Astraga had the ability to still unite family and surpass the rules of mortality that we humans are restricted to. I looked upwards into the snowing midnight sky and grinned. The translucent shield of Astraga that was hanging overhead in the atmosphere glimmered a bit.

"It's a pleasure to see both of you together," I said to the twins, tipping my masquerade mask.

Deborah was surprised to see me on the plane rather than at a bingo table. I myself wasn't used to the sight of twins having a massive age gap. Ariella gave an innocent smile to me and continued to play with the jester. Deborah turned her attention toward me.

"How are you here?" Deborah asked.

"I've been visiting for quite some time now," I responded with a mysterious smile. "And I've been fortunate enough to have met your sister," I added, nodding my head towards Ariella.

Deborah at first seemed concerned, almost wary of me. Her narrow eyebrows eased up after a few seconds of staring me down and soon enough she bared a courteous smile instead.

"Well it's good to know that I have a dancing partner with Ariella." Deborah said cheerily.

I chuckled and quickly nodded before a familiar voice had called my name in the distance.

"Jackie!" Elowyn shouted excitedly.

Elowyn was hanging off of one of the many vine-wrapped pillars that dotted the courtyard. She waved her hand to beckon me over and I followed. Josiah was speaking with Kalani under the Cathedral's colonnade, not too far off, but Shajara was still out of sight.

"Tonight is going to be a blast!" Elowyn exclaimed, beaming down at me.

The court jesters, minstrels, and the other performers scurried out of the crowd and lined themselves in rows before everyone. A chipper-looking woman in the line cleared her throat and quieted the noise.

"Hello everyone and welcome to the Astragian Masquerade!" she boomed to the crowd.

A heavy applause and a few cheers let out.

"Tonight we are fortunate enough to be in the presence of quite a few great figures that shaped Astraga into what it is today. We are pleased to announce that Heilige Theodore himself will be amongst our revelry, along with his council, so with all due respect, please be on your best behavior! There will be *no* use of Aetheric magic within the courtyard!" she said, peering at everyone in a serious manner.

"Now if everyone would please follow me into the nave, we will let the *real* festivities begin!"

The people roared in glee and flooded the inside of the Cathedral; I felt myself swept along with Elowyn by my side. A dazzling spectacle was laid out before us. Enormous stained-glass windows depicting ancient beings and complex scenarios climbed the walls throughout the upper part of the nave; nearly all of the images I was unfamiliar to. The central window captured the battle that had happened between Heilige Theodore and Elizabeth when she and the coven had defied Astraga.

"Isn't it just beautiful, Jackie?" said Elowyn, staring up at the windows.

A few jesters had promptly gathered together and started to perform tricks for the crowd using magic, clumsily juggling balls of fire and tossing them through one another as a means of entertainment.

"Yeah El, it sure is. Everything here is magnificent."
"Look! There's a window with Shajara painted on it, and those must be the other Priests and Priestesses beside her. Wow!" Elowyn awed, fascinated.

Sure enough, there was Shajara's image on in the window. The only other person that I could identify out of the other eleven people was Jonathan, who was the tallest of everyone shown.

The statue of the star crossed lovers stood firmly in the center of the room, glittering brightly from all of the Silver Threads that draped it. Elowyn and Josiah took off into the crowd to dance, while Kalani stood off to the side, carefully watching the partygoers. It was one of the most festive and beautiful events that I had ever attended. People of all ages were welcome to attend and enjoy. Ballroom dresses and shawls gracefully traveled through the room as the sound of expensive shoes tapped on the glossy marble floor.

"He's coming!" a young man in the crowd yelled, pointing to the front of the nave.

"The Heilige!" another shouted joyously.

Jonathan and Shajara were standing beside each other in one row and were accompanied by two more couples at their side, while the other row on the opposite side had three couples as well. All twelve Priests and Priestesses of Astraga stood, waiting patiently for the Heilige to approach. The walkers of Astraga had stopped their dance and turned their attention onwards when the music slowly faded away. In the distance he stood between the two rows of his council, clutching onto a rather large staff which held a generous-sized crystal affixed on the very top. A jubilant cheer rumbled in the crowd but was soon deafened by his gesture.

"Greetings, Walkers of Astraga! It brings us great happiness to see so many of you here tonight. We have many thanks due to the council of Astraga for constructing such a wondrous event. Please, if you would put your hands together for the hardship that these men and women undergo to assure your safety while walking the plane!"

The entire room burst into applause, led by Heilige Theodore. He lifted his crystal staff for silence and continued his speech.

"For every year that Astraga remains afloat in the plane, we are fortunate to see our numbers rise. Some who stand with you in this room have walked the Astral Plane for decades— if not centuries—while others have just begun their journey. We undoubtedly welcome you all with open arms and hearts, be you a newcomer or an ancient walker of this otherworldly haven. We only wish that you treat the plane with care, and that you do no harm to your comrades."

A streak of lightning lit up the surrounding stained glass windows of the Cathedral, momentarily bringing life to the elaborately painted scenarios.

"Tonight we must celebrate and rejoice, for we are the people who have shaped this realm! Without further ado," Heilige Theodore spoke, motioning his hand towards the court musicians to resume their instruments.

The nave filled once more with heavy laughter as the people began to dance. I slid up to Kalani, who was standing apart from the crowd.

"What's up?" he asked, still carefully watching the dancers.

"I was wondering if you knew anything about Jonathan."

"Who?"

"Jonathan, you know, the Priest?" I pointed into the distance where Jonathan was taking Shajara's hand in dance.

"Oh, Jonathan, right. He's a very respectable fella. He's been around for a decade or two, and he's never misguided any of his walkers. If he keeps it up for another century, he might be looking at replacing the Heilige. If Theodore ever steps down, that is."

"No, no. I mean, what do you know about his past? There are scars on his neck, where did he get those?"

Kalani paused and gave me a quick glance in the eyes. The look of indifference on his face said it all. He looked back at Jonathan and Shajara dancing and then momentarily back at me, never fully responding but instead giving a slight shrug of his shoulders before heading off.

"If you must know," said a voice unbeknownst to me, "He hanged himself."

I turned around quickly. A man who was about my age was looking at me. He approached and nodded, a sly smile growing on his skinny face. The pale color of his skin was frightening, but not as frightening as the cold of his hand.

"Donovan," he spoke in a thick British accent when I shook his hand.

"Jackie," I said. "You were one of the Priests standing next to the Heilige."

"That I was, yes," Donovan replied. "Jonathan had a troubled life in the waking world. You wouldn't have guessed it by how generous he is now, but he was heavily bullied throughout his years. Children and even some adults had pestered and picked on him, tossing him around like a rag doll."

"He should have swung back if people were throwing him around! He's a giant." I insisted on saying.

"Oh he did, but it was pointless."
"Defending yourself is never pointless!" I quickly stated.
"Physically it is, when you are born blind at birth."

Boy, did I feel like an absolute idiot. I choked back on my words and really didn't know what to say anymore. Quite embarrassed, I could feel the blood collect in my cheeks.

"When he came to us in the plane, we were lucky enough to find his Silver Thread. It was nearly torn to pieces when he took his own life. A Silver Thread is very sturdy indeed, but also quite frail. Everything that you do, both in the plane and even in the waking world will have an effect on your thread. We may be able to repair and mend threads, but you should know by now that only a select few can fully reconstruct them if they're completely torn apart. Jonathan is happy here though, especially since he was given the gift of sight upon his passing. Now his thread rests peacefully on the statue of the lovers, right next to my own."

Donovan kept a sly smile on his face as he excused himself from the conversation. The vibe he gave off when speaking was almost phantom-like. The lightning outside continued to bolt through the atmosphere, and rain started to pelt away at the Cathedral walls and windows. I assumed that the use of Aetheric magic during the masquerade was to blame. Every so often in the massive crowd, a person would burst into thousands of tiny lights and be sent flying through the Cathedral, reminding me that nearly everyone here would eventually wake. The near-inaudible buzzing that filled my ears as the warm balls of light whizzed past would hum into my eardrums and send a sensation of tingles throughout my body.

I was taken in hand by a stranger and pulled into the crowd, but this time the stranger was male. This scent of this strange man's cologne reminded me strongly of back home in the

Midwest. You know how a friend's house can have a very particular smell, or how even a certain region or place may have a lingering scent, be it good or bad? This was one of those moments, and the smell was eerily familiar.

I didn't question his bold move, but followed him as we paraded around the people. Despite his brown eyes being shadowed by his detailed Venetian mask, they chimed inside of my head like an urgent warning; a sharp reminder that I knew this man but I couldn't place my finger on it.

"People sure are friendly here," I said, spinning round.
"Of course. We're all a family of sorts," he replied.
My heart let out a large thump. His voice, I remembered his voice from somewhere!
"I know you, don't I?"
He looked directly at me with a smile curling onto his face.
"Do you know me?"
"Don't play games with me!" I let out a coy laugh, "I remember you from somewhere. What's your name?"

The charming man opened his mouth to speak, but my entire perception of sound had ceased to work. All I could see were his lips moving and his head shaking in approval. I nervously laughed and shook my head from side to side and he ended up frowning in return. A loud ringing screeched in my ears, followed by the ground shaking at a tremendous rate. Was I waking up? No! I was far from ready to wake up just yet!

I wasn't. In fact, none of us were waking up.

I was trampled by the crowd, people scurrying quickly to get out of harm's way. After the ringing had dulled, loud screams darted from every direction at once. The windows shattered into a hailstorm of glass. Shadows emerged from the floor and took flight into the air, shaping into the form of dark figures while heavily robed people flew into the Cathedral and seized the ground.

"THE STATUE!" cried a hoarse voice, "GO AFTER THE STATUE!"

A flock of dark shadows crept across the floor toward the statute, but they were soon confronted by a few of the council members. While everyone was in a state of panic, I sprinted through the crowd to the back of the nave to be with Shajara, but she had other plans in mind. She lunged over a few fleeing Circle Walkers and, in an instant, took the form of an enormous white tiger in midair. She looked back into my direction and motioned for me to join in. And that is exactly what I did.

With a fireball wound up in my hands, I charged headfirst into the chaos. My fist lodged deep into one of the nearby Umbrage Walkers, making them eat the blistering fire that crackled in my grasp. Kalani, Elowyn, and Josiah had also called themselves into the action, fighting valiantly across the Cathedral.

"Protect the statue at all costs!" Jonathan shouted after smashing an Umbrage Walker's skull into the ground. A burst of dark energy exploded on impact, sending the tainted walker back to the waking world.

"We must not let them take the Silver Threads! Band together!" yelled Kalani.

Shajara let out a bellowing roar after tearing apart her enemy and swiftly swooped across the floor to finish another. The Heilige himself stood to the occasion by planting his crystal staff deep into the marbled floor to defend the city of Astraga. The sound of discarded plastic and porcelain masks crunched on the floor continuously as the fighting prolonged.

"This is an outrage!" Theodore boomed, sending a tremendous amount of electricity in several directions. "The shield of Astraga has broken! To arms!"

Through the utter devastation and ongoing antics of war, Sagaru eventually appeared to join the combat. Silver Threads ended up flying throughout the air, some completely severed and others still practically intact. With each thread that Sagaru was able to obtain, the stronger he grew in power. He devoured the threads while plowing his way through the people, carelessly indulging his insatiable hunger for power.

"ENOUGH!" roared the Heilige as he sent a calamitous amount of energy throughout the entire Cathedral. I felt the entirety of Astraga shake as it tossed everyone to the ground. The weather raged on while various streams of light and dark balls of energy smeared the rooms from the waking people.

"I WILL NOT TOLERATE THIS IN MY CITY! BEGONE!" Theodore ordered.

Enormous pillars of bright, white light had spontaneously struck down throughout the Cathedral, vanquishing any evil that may be in the vicinity of it. The light was so strong that it would cause an entire whiteout of your vision. The heat that these pillars gave off was astounding to say the least. Any closer and I could have been instantly incinerated. Once the monstrous beams of light dissipated, Sagaru's echo cackled throughout the halls.

"Run you coward!" I screamed, "You'll never amount to anything!!"

I kicked a nearby slab of crumbled limestone and hurried over to a severely injured Umbrage Walker. I took his collar into my hands and shook him violently.
"WHY WOULD YOU DO SUCH A THING?!"

"WHY!" I screamed. A few strings of my saliva flew out and landed on his bloodied face.

It was the first time I had ever really encountered an Umbrage Walker—other than Sagaru, Dante, or the Necromancer—up close. The veins in his neck pulsed outwards and were as dark as coal. Unintentionally, cold gusts of icy wind started to trickle outwards from my hands, creeping onwards and eventually taking hold of the Umbrage Walker's body. Within a matter of seconds, the Umbrage Walker had frozen solid.

"ANSWER ME!" I shook his frozen body forcefully.
"Jackie!" Donovan shouted from across the room. "We have more pressing matters."

I turned to him; he was standing over Elowyn, who lay in a heap of emerald fabric. Donovan calmly fought a pair of Umbrage Walkers, keeping his body between them and her. I dashed over to her side.
Her lips trembled and the color started to rapidly flush from her face. I cradled her shaking hands in my own and dusted off the debris that had collected on her emerald gown.

"It's going to be okay. It's not that bad." I assured her.
"Jackie. . . I'm c—cold. I—"
"Just hold on, we're going to get you help. I promise."
A small puddle of blood had started to surround her body. No matter how much I pressed onto her stomach, the wound wouldn't stop bleeding.
"Wh- why am I not waking up?" Elowyn stammered.
Shajara lowered her head and remained silent. Nobody would make eye contact with me or Elowyn. She repeated her question but everyone still opted to remain quiet.
"ANSWER HER, DAMNIT!" I cried out.
"She's bleeding out." Jonathan spurted out quickly.

"CLEARLY," I said in a panic. "Thank you for the fucking observation, genius!"

"No, she's bleeding out in the waking world. Her actual body is bleeding."

"How is that even possible?" I screamed.

"She has sustained too much damage, Jackie." Shajara said, her head still lowered, "Her thread is gone."

I shook Elowyn's hand violently. No thread appeared on her trembling hands.

"It be only a matta of time before she foreva remains in da plane."

"I want to g-go h-home," Elowyn whimpered fearfully.

I hushed Elowyn softly and combed back the golden strands of hair from her face. She let out a few involuntary tremors.

"We have to do something!" I demanded. "Don't just stand there, Josiah! DO SOMETHING!"

"What can I do?!" Josiah choked back.

"SOMETHING – ANYTHING!"

"That's it." Kalani interrupted.

"SGRIAS!" Kalani howled throughout the Cathedral. "I know you're out there!"

A sweeping wind of ash and debris collected on the ground before us, forming several pools of dark matter. From the ashes once again crept Sgrias, even more hideous in appearance than before. Her body seemed to be entirely made of crawling insects. Her dark army of mindless beings stood in the distance. With her twisted dark staff, she squirmed closer and relinquished a stench so foul that the hairs in my nostrils singed.

"You called?" she spoke in slow, wheezing breaths.

By the looks of things, Sgrias didn't have much time left before she'd have to find a new vessel to leech off of.

"I'm ready to offer up my thread," Kalani said.

"Dis be madness!" Shajara exclaimed, placing herself in front of Kalani. "You can't do dis!"

"You heard . . . the Priestess. You can't do thissss...." she cackled, coughing up a massive glob of discolored mucus.

"I can and I will," Kalani answered. He wiggled his hand, revealing his Silver Thread and untied it very carefully from his finger.

The crimson pits in Sgrias' eye sockets emitted a sharp spark of greed. Shajara moved out of the way when Sgrias reached for the thread, but Kalani took a few steps back.

"On one condition," he said.

"And . . . what might that condition be?" Sgrias licked her cracked lips. Her white, rotten tongue made my stomach roil.

"See that girl over there?" Kalani pointed over to Elowyn. The state that Elowyn was in was grim. She seemed as though she could barely comprehend what was going on.

"You reconstruct that girl's thread from scratch."

Sgrias tapped her fingers onto her staff momentarily, seeming to think deeply about the proposition.

"Doing so will . . . cost me greatly . . . but I accept," Sgrias answered.

"And you free my father from your reign," Kalani added.

The room went silent; the suspense of Sgrias' decision was starting to grow unbearable.

"An eye for two eyes? I think not." Sgrias hoarsely laughed and turned. She snapped her bone fingers for her minions to follow.

"Wait!" said Kalani quickly. "All right, just help us return the girl's thread."

Sgrias toyed with her staff momentarily, her dead, unmoving eyes staring deeply onto Kalani.

"Done."

A civil argument broke out between the Council of Astraga whether Kalani was permitted to do such a thing.

"Under no circumstance will you do this, Kalani," Donovan said sharply.

"Can't the Heilige help mend her thread instead?!" Josiah asked.
With his staff in hand, the Heilige wobbled his way towards the crowd.

"After the battle that just took place, we are far too weak." Theodore mentioned, itching at his beard. "Even if we had our full strength, we wouldn't be able to reconstruct this poor girl's thread, for it has been swallowed whole by evil. Without any actual thread, it can only be reanimated from nothingness. Something only this wicked creature likely possesses the ability to do— a most detestable creature in our view."

"Saint Theodore, your words warm my already rotting heart." Sgrias replied.

The Heilige ignored her and turned to Kalani. "While we do not condone your method, Kalani, we will allow this. But by doing so, you give up your rights to step foot in Astraga again so long as you are ruled by this—this thing that stands before us."

"You cannot allow dis to go on!" Shajara cried.
The Heilige waved his hand to dismiss Shajara's outcry.
"I accept this consequence," Kalani said formally.
"Understand that you place your mortal body in jeopardy, young one," Saint Theodore added. "It is likely that you will no longer be able to rise in the waking world, so long as Sgrias holds your thread."

"I understand," Kalani bravely replied.

"It is a brave and foolish thing. This poor girl has family and people who love her in the waking world?"

"Yes, Heilige," Kalani answered.

The Heilige nodded. "Then so be it," he said, and finally faced The Necromancer one last time. "Continue on with this foul sorcery. Once the girl's thread has been restored, you shall be gone from Astraga, and you shall never return. Your foulness offends the very air. Do I make myself clear?"

"Crystal," she coughed and smirked.

"You've gone mad!" Shajara shrieked at the Heilige. "How could you do dis?!"

"Hush now, Priestess," he nodded with a genuine smile. A small wink also came from him and was directed specifically at her. "We must not impede any further before it is too late."

Without wasting a second more of time, Sgrias ordered her minions to scatter around in a large circle. She spoke in the broken rhythms of a foreign, blackened tongue. As she spoke, she walked slowly around the interior of the circle. After every menacing click of her decaying mouth, she spat acid at her minion's contorted bodies, causing them to combust into a multicolor of changing gaseous essences. By every minion that had combusted, a thread on her twisted staff would singe off. Eventually her minions dwindled from a dozen, to half that, then down to four. Kalani's father, Dante, still remained.

The Necromancer at first struggled to coerce the vaporized minions into a whirling tornado of massive energy. The ground of Astraga started to tremble from the weather that continued to grow. Further and further the vapor compacted together in an immense display with her wicked guidance. Horrific screams echoed out from the faces of the minions as they stretched and twisted in attempt to escape the black magic.

In the battle to control the demented spirits, Sgrias' brittle body buckled slightly at the knees. A thread started to take form in the center of the vapors, sacrificing the souls to create such a sacred object. One by one the colors of the gaseous cloud would disappear, the moans and teeth-cringing screams following thereafter. It was done. A Silver Thread had been created.

Sgrias fell to the floor, her body depleted to nearly nothing. She lifted her frail limb and extended the Silver Thread out to Kalani. He had honored his end of the bargain and motioned for Josiah to follow. With the Silver Thread retrieved by Josiah, Kalani took his own and handed it over to her. Sgrias barely was able to withstand another motion of her arm when putting Kalani's thread onto her staff before her body turned into a pile of ash, leaving her staff to drop and make a loud thud on the debris-littered floor.

Confused faces plastered the group of surrounding people. I was confused too—did Sgrias accidentally push herself too far? Had she overexerted her black magic to the point where it consumed her whole? A sharp gale howled through the broken windows of the Cathedral and swept away the remains of the Necromancer.

Josiah ran over to Elowyn and desperately tied the newly formed Silver Thread onto her finger. Elowyn had already gone cold. I shook her in my blood-drenched arms a few times. Elowyn stared off into the distance without blinking. She remained still as ever. Her vision was still transfixed onto nothingness, an abyss that only the dead could possibly comprehend.

"Elowyn!" Josiah shouted. "Come back to us!"
Nothing had happened.

I carefully placed Elowyn's body into Josiah's arms. Kalani

himself started to sway back and forth. He held his hands to his head and dropped to his knees, screaming like a maniac.

"MAKE THEM STOP!" pleaded Kalani. "MAKE THEM STOP!" Kalani's skin flushed immediately. It was apparent that his mind had started to dissolve into madness. Cracks and blisters started to form on his arms and legs. Donovan, Shajara, and a few other Council members hurried over to Kalani to help him in any way possible.

"Get away from me!" Kalani screamed, swinging violently. His voice cracked as his mind broke.

The staff of Sgrias rattled ominously on the floor. Shajara leaped for the staff, ready to destroy it. The way she darted after the staff spoke of an entirely new depth of anger that humans rarely reached. Her attempt to claim the staff in her possession had failed. Instead, Shajara was sent flying backwards by an unknown force when she came near it.

A loud gasp of air filled Elowyn's airway. She jerked upward and clutched at her heart. Josiah gave a short scream and latched harder onto Elowyn.

"Get back!" shouted Donovan.

The staff of Sgrias sprung into the air before us all, spinning madly in circles. Out of nowhere, Dante's controlled body had seized up, locking stiff at the joints. Faster and faster the staff spun around, rapidly collecting particles of Aetheric energy from the air. Dante's bones cracked several times. An explosion of shadows and smoke engulfed both Dante and the staff.

A sinister laugh shrieked from the shadowy mass of smoke, and Sgrias was no more, for Sgrios had been reborn.

CHAPTER FOURTEEN

The harsh lights of Sgrios' wicked eyes had gleamed through Dante's own skull.

"Ah," he sighed nostalgically. "It has been too long since I've had the opportunity to vessel such a lovely creature."

Sgrios twisted his neck jerkily to the side with a slight twitch of his head. The more we watched him struggle to maintain his posture, the more it became apparent that he was not used to having a new body. For a split second, I was tempted to go after Sgrios in his feeble state, but I couldn't muster the courage. Hadn't Dante suffered enough in his lifetime and his afterlife? The entire world had turned its back on him when he perished at war, and now even his body wasn't his own anymore. Sgrios leaned heavily onto his staff and quietly approached Kalani, who was wailing in agony.

"Shh, my child, come with me. We have much to do together, you and I." Sgrios said and wrapped his shaking arm around Kalani's broad shoulders.

Kalani did not fight against the Necromancer, and when he had looked back up, I could see the veins had darkened in his face. Kalani's eyes had quietly filmed over into blackness.

Shajara reached out her hand towards Kalani, but she knew that he was no longer the human he used to be. He was now a slave to the Necromancer, bound completely, and his father had officially lost his soul to the Necromancer too.

"Leave." The Heilige demanded.

A stiff grin twisted itself onto Sgrios's pale face. The Necromancer retreated into the shadows with Kalani under his arm.

"It's okay, Sha." Donovan moved closer to Shajara, ready to comfort her. She slapped away his hand and refused to look any of us in the face.

"Don't touch me." she said and started to march off.

"That is no way to treat a fellow Priest." The Heilige said.

Shajara turned a glare onto her leader. "DON'T. CHU. DARE." The inflection in her voice cracked when she pointed sternly at the Heilige. "We lost him because of YOU! You of all people should not have agreed to allow dis!"

Shajara's accent thickened in her rage to the point where I could barely understand her.

"We did it in order to save a young girl's life." The Heilige responded in a humbled tone.

"WHAT LIFE?!" Shajara bellowed. "LOOK AT HER! SHE IS STILL LIFELESS AND YOU KNEW DIS WOULD HAPPEN!"
Shajara had made a valid point. Elowyn hadn't spoken a word since she was revived and her eyes never blinked, still staring off into whatever – or wherever it might be.
The Heilige bowed his head and resumed his silence.
"What?! You have nutin' to say for yaself?! YOU ARE DA HEILIGE! WE ARE SUPPOSED TA LOOK UP TO YOU!" Shajara

grabbed him by the collar of his robe.

"Enough!" Jonathan ordered and separated the two by intervening. Shajara flung Jonathan's arms off of her and stomped out of room.

"What did she mean by 'you knew this would happen'?" asked Josiah.

I looked up at the Heilige but he still chose to remain silent and he too soon walked off into a different direction.

Elowyn's body had exploded into a myriad of lights, stretching their distance across the entire Cathedral and eventually fading. Soon Josiah had followed in the same way, but a tiny ball of light still resided for the time being. I played with the warm ball of fuzzy light with my hands, captivated by the thought that this could possibly be Josiah's pinky toe, or maybe even a finger.

"You'll tell me what Shajara meant, right, Jonathan?" I asked.

Jonathan scraped off a bit of dried blood from my check and nodded. "Come with me."

We had strategically stepped throughout the crumbled Cathedral and made our way down to the pub. The place seemed to be vacant; in fact all of Astraga seemed to be vacant now. Crissy the bar maid approached us with two full steins of brew and set them quietly on the table. Jonathan sat quietly for a brief period of time with a look of pensiveness on his face. Several times he opened his mouth to speak, but refrained and bobbled his eyes off into a different direction to likely think further.

"Approximately fifteen years ago, the Heilige conjured an emergency meeting between the council. A fellow Priestess had broken her Silver Thread by accident when dealing with a band of Umbrage Walkers in the plane, exceeding her power and ultimately falling to them. Luckily enough the Umbrage Walkers weren't all too smart and didn't retrieve her thread. The Heilige sensed this and recovered the Priestess's body immediately, along with her thread and called for a resurrection."

"Why should the Umbrage Walker have taken her thread?" I asked curiously.

"These threads also behold a profound amount of power to them and allow us to use Aether in the plane more effectively. Without them we can still cultivate magic and the use of Aether of course, but with them we are stronger, much stronger in fact."

"So that is the reason why Sgrios and Sagaru also collect them, to gain power." I said.

"Exactly, now this Priestess also had a physical body in the waking world. She had an actual life. A husband, children, and an entire career laid out for the remainder of her life. The Heilige was deeply saddened by this and as aforementioned, collected his council together and preformed the ceremony. Despite being one council member short since the Priestess was the victim, the ceremony was still successful. Something had changed however. When the Priestess was reunited with her body once more, she had forgotten years of her life in the waking world and also forgot much of what the Astral Plane was. Her mind had basically reset itself and the council did not know what to do."

"Well what did you guys decide to do?" I leaned inwards.

"We did the best we could and dismissed her from her duty as a Priestess of Astraga. With that we assigned a fellow Priest to watch over her in the waking world and also in the Astral Plane to make sure she'd be all right. The Heilige covered it up as best he could but slowly over time the Priestess started to regain her memories back. She was given a rare case of amnesia and the doctors assumed that she must've hit her head pretty hard when she was sleeping."

"That's it? You guys didn't tell her what happened?"

"We didn't have to. She eventually remembered and she was fortunate enough to still have an actual life outside of the plane. She went along with the doctor's diagnosis and played coy to prevent the Astral Plane from being revealed. Not that it'd matter, since everyone around her would think that she was insane if she did say such things."

"That or she REALLY did hit her head a little too hard." I

laughed despite the unfortunate circumstance.

"Exactly," Jonathan replied and guzzled a good amount of the bubbling brew within his stein.

"So what is going to happen to Kalani? I mean, his thread was sacrificed and as far as I know, he's from Hawaii."

"Hard to say what is to happen to him in the plane, but as far as the waking world goes, he'll probably be placed in a coma so long as he cannot return back to his body."

A feeling of uncertainty had washed over me. Now I know why Shajara had taken such a bold stance on the entire situation. Kalani knew what he was doing and Shajara also knew that his body would become forfeit so long as he offered up his thread. Not only that, but it was starting to become more apparent that they were very close to one another.

"You're not kidding, are you?" I asked with a glimmer of hope that Jonathan was pulling my leg.

"I wish I were, my friend. Entering a coma is the best option we have, and we can only hope that he doesn't stop breathing."

I sighed, pulling in the stein closer to me. "And the reason why Kalani started to go insane was because his thread was detached from his body?"

"Yes. This is a first as far as I know, but those who have lost their thread seem to fare just fine without it after some time. It's likely that darkness has started to corrupt him. Never had the Heilige honored such deeds either, I was surprised myself."

"I still don't understand." I replied.

"Our bodies and minds are connected in some strange, cosmic way, Jackie. I can't fully describe it, but when your soul detaches from your body, you're susceptible to anything."

Jonathan continued to directly speak to me. "You are never more alive than you are right now at this very moment and if baffles me why people such as yourself seek out the Astral Plane so much. Sure, it's a realm where you can have an untold amount of fun and exploration, but by the passing of every day your body withers to a small degree once you surpass the apex of adulthood.

This is common knowledge and you know this of course, but once your soul is torn from your physical body —" Jonathan paused for a moment and looked off into a different direction. "It's like you lose a piece of yourself that you can never regain."

"Is that how it felt when you stepped off the stool?" I asked carelessly.

Jonathan glared at me, his eyes filling with what looked to be discern.

"I don't know who told you or what you intend to get out of me from that brassy statement – or maybe you could have guessed from the markings around my neck, but I still valued my life in the waking world even after my death. Yeah, fortunately I have gained the ability to actually see things in the plane when I arrived, but I would sacrifice a thousand years in darkness just to know what it felt like to live one year back in my body. I knew no better back then when I was just a youth. When you're born without something that you're supposed to innately inherit, you don't exactly find out what you may be missing out on until later in life, or in death for that matter."

"Like when people tease you and start to bully you?"

"Sure, you could put it that way." Jonathan muttered. "What has gotten into you, Circle Walker? Your instigation is becoming offsetting." he said.

"I'm sorry," I quickly said, "it's just that . . .You know, you're not the only one in the plane who has suffered in the waking world, Jonathan. Everyone suffers to some extent. We all have our hardships," I spoke in attempt to lessen the severity of my crude behavior. "there are many other people; like Ariella."

"Isn't she just a peach?" Jonathan wrinkled his face in a cheeky smile.

"She is." I replied.

"It breaks my heart to see that she had left the waking world at such a young age. So many years she could've lived. She hadn't even the chance to fall in love, or the chance to share her first kiss with a boy; an entire lifetime just taken out from beneath her feet at the hands of a grown adult who should've known

Cody Hathaway

better."

I was in hopes that Jonathan would be able to understand why I exactly tread into the Astral Plane time and time again. It was a bittersweet release from the actual world, a place where I didn't have to think of the need to constantly get up and take care of myself. It was a place where I wasn't judged for not having a job or a place where I wasn't scrutinized by my peers or society as a whole for being the person that I am. The Astral Plane didn't have a media or a mecca of social networks that people were subjected to. To be honest, I was starting to think that I didn't fit in at all back in that world.

Jonathan and I continued to speak to one another while drinking and every once in a while Crissy would come by and add two cents into the conversation at hand. Rays of sunlight started to peek through the dirtied windows of the tavern and I watched as particles of dust occasionally stirred up from the floor.

"Do you think that we'll be able to save Kalani?" I asked Jonathan.

"As a Priest of Astraga, I don't know the answer to your question. We can only hope so, should we ever get back Kalani's thread, that is."

"And in time before he rots away," I added.

"Indeed. Do not fret though. I'm sure you've heard this plenty of times but, anything is possible in the plane."

I let out a bummed laughter. "Yeah, Kalani used to say that."

"He's a wise man. Shajara and Kalani go back for quite some time now."

"You're right." I drifted off and started to pay attention back onto the shifting particles of dust in the sunlit tavern.

"This'll be my first sunrise in the plane." I mentioned.

"Well, it is good that you acquire a full night's rest." Jonathan prompted.

"I was supposed to share my first sunrise with Kalani and Shajara though." I said with the feeling of a frown starting to surface.

"Then I suppose we'll just have to make sure that happens!" Jonathan spoke and tossed his stein of beer onto my face.

When the ice-cold liquid hit my face, the floor beneath my feet grew heavily unstable and before I could chew Jonathan out for his jerk move, I was waking up to the sound of Brutis yelping in his sleep from a doggy nightmare.

Hurricane Lorne didn't have as much force as I anticipated it would. Water hadn't even breached the sandbags I placed down but I suppose it was better to be safe than sorry. The weather was still quite nasty however and the wind gusts were pretty stellar from time to time. I really hadn't collected myself entirely upon waking up and Brutis himself seemed to be quite out of it. I tore off the Masquerade mask from my face and tossed it onto the nearby couch, recollecting the thoughts of the entire night. It was truly a blessing to partake in such a beautiful event that night, regardless of how it ended. I could still vividly remember the flowing gowns and the Venetian masks swirling around the ballroom, or how the elaborated etched fabrics of beautifully colored costumes sent soft gusts of air across my skin. It was like I was placed in the smack dab middle of a Venice carnival. Who was that Brown-eyed man that I stumbled across before the Cathedral was invaded, and why did it feel like my heart was missing something?

I shook out my daydream when Brutis started to scratch at his collar with his back paw. A substitute news anchor on the Television baffled onwards about the Hurricane conditions and what precautions should be taken throughout the week while I still somewhat pondered to myself about Astraga and what exactly might soon unfold for me in the Astral Plane, let alone those who I tread with.

Oh shit! Elowyn! I quickly dashed for the cell phone and auto-dialed her number through the contacts list. Not even two rings into the call she had picked up. Shockingly to my surprise, Elowyn was still as cheerful as ever.

"Herro?" Elowyn answered the phone.

"Elowyn!? Are you alright?!"

"Uh yeah, why wouldn't I be, silly?"

"Oh, I don't know, maybe because you were PROFUSELY BLEEDING in my arms last night in Astraga." I noted sternly.

"Oh right, that, hehe. Nope! Still healthy as a clam on my end! I woke up with some a sore tummy, but that's all!"

"Phew, I was really worried. You know you could have lost your memory or even worse, right?!"

"HI JACKIE!" A familiar voice echoed through the phone on Elowyn's end.

"Is that Alexandria?!"

"Why yes, that is Alexandria, Jackie!" Elowyn coughed. "I was just about to tell her about the killer workout we did last night!"

I panicked. To our knowledge, Alexandria was completely clueless to the Astral Plane. It never dawned on me that we kept it secret from her for so long.

"What's an Astraga?" I heard Alexandria ask curiously.

"Oh nothing!" Elowyn giggled in reply. "Just a –really– intense workout that Jackie and I made up to give us killer abs. I mean –really– intense."

"Gee El, put any more emphasis on the world 'really' and she might believe you." I snorted.

"*Shut up, Jackie.*" Elowyn whispered through the phone.

"Well it's good to see you're not dead! I have a few more phone calls to make. Have you checked up with Josiah?"

"Yeah, he's good. He can't get ahold of Kalani though." Elowyn responded.

"I don't think we will be able to for some time. We can talk about that later. We don't need Alexandria snooping around right now."

"Agreed, Jackie! See you around."

"See ya."

"There you are, dear." my mother spoke when circling the kitchen island to visit the refrigerator.

I was startled to see her at this time of day. Usually in the morning she's already all dolled up and ready to leave for work. Today wasn't the case however, as she already had her hair dangling off the right side of her shoulder and was dressed in full pajamas.

"Uhm, don't you have to go to work or attend an interview?" I asked, confused by the given scenario.

"Nope, I actually just got home."

Figures.

"What's that for?" my mother pointed at the Masquerade mask with her head tilted slightly.

"Oh, that's uh, a masquerade mask."

"Didn't you get that some time ago?"

"Uh, yeah, I was actually just looking back through some old stuff and I thought it would be neat to maybe pull a Halloween costume together soon."

You know, I'm just going to go on a whim here and assume that I obtained the uncanny ability to think on my toes from my father's side of the family. I really cannot even count the amount of times that I've saved my own ass from getting in trouble due to this, and I'm starting to think that taking improv classes one day might be a good thing for me to excel at.

"That means your birthday is also coming up, sweetie, is there anything in particular that you wanted?"

"Yeah, my own family back." I thought to myself.

"Can we move out of this forsaken state? This bipolar weather is driving me insane." I asked, tossing the TV remote near the Masquerade mask.

"Honey, we just moved! It was no better in Illinois than it is here."

"I guess you're right, but back there I had a life, mom."

"And down here I have a very busy life!"

I started to get mildly agitated. As much as I wanted to enjoy a day with my mother, it never really worked out because our personalities often clashed. No matter what I said, she'd have the perfect answer to counterattack my plea. I reached for the

Masquerade mask in hopes to steer my attention elsewhere, twirling the silk string bands through my fingers.

"How about you take off for work on my birthday and we can do something fun, like head over to Key West, or maybe visit the coast?" I asked.

"You know I can't do that, Jackie."

I sighed and dropped the masquerade mask onto my face, still twirling the bands between my fingers. "At least father did things with me on my birthday."

"Excuse me?"

"You heard me." I whipped back. There was no holding back any longer.

"You're always too fucking busy for an actual real life outside of your work life! You guzzle down an entire pot of coffee like its water!"

"Well to be fair, it really is made with water." My mother replied, choosing to not make eye contact.

"STOP! Don't give me that sarcastic ass remark! You haven't taken out your earrings in god only knows how long. This is the first time I've actually seen your hair down in months! By the time I open my mouth to say good morning, you already have one foot out of the door. When I go to tell you goodnight, you're calling me with an excuse as to why you're not going to come home that night."

I yanked the masquerade mask from my face with the strings still looped throughout my fingers and continued to berate her after I stood from my seat.

"I've had take-out and frozen pizza for dinner more times than I would like to count, mother!" I shouted.

"Well then cook for your damn self!" she snarled, slamming the refrigerator door shut. "You're a grown human being, learn how to act like one." she added.

"You're missing the goddamn point, mother! There are times where it feels like you don't even exist! I shouldn't wake up to be surprised by your presence still in the house, let alone I shouldn't feel like I'm the only one in this entire house. This place is huge and there is so much wasted space, even Brutis gets lonely when you're not home! Why did we even move to Florida?! To run away from your depression involving Dad's disappearance?! Guess what?! It's not your damn fault!"

I smashed the masquerade mask onto the kitchen island with my fist, shattering it into several pieces. It felt as though steam started to excrete from my ears, especially at the fact that my mother didn't bother to even reply. Instead she made a signature move of hers and took her leave without saying another word. It isn't often that my mother buckles out of an argument, but when she does decide to take her leave abruptly, she knows that she is in the wrong.

"Just going to walk away like you did for father?!" I screamed down the hallway.

I got nothing. No response, not even a whimper. The only thing I heard was the sound of her bedroom door slamming shut. A few droplets of blood dribbled out from my palm where a piece of the mask decided to embed itself in. I raised my hand while swearing at nobody in particular and a tiny stream of warmth stated to trickle down my forearm, and that is when it dawned on me.

I may just know how to kill Sagaru and get him out of the Astral Plane once and for all.

CHAPTER FIFTEEN

"You're absolutely insane and I will not be a part of this."
Josiah spoke, completely dismissing the brilliant idea I had
pitched.

"Come on, Jo! It's going to work, I know it."

I tried my best to coax Josiah into the plan. No matter how
many times I pitched the idea, he just wasn't having it. He
continued to reject the offer and ended up storming out of the
room.

"Just hear me out!" I pleaded, chasing after him.

"No! There is no way that I'm going to potentially murder
you in order to get rid of Sagaru. It's completely out of the
question and you are one crazy person for thinking I would even
partake in this."

"It's not that bad, man! All we need to do is wrap my Silver
Thread around his finger and then somehow get my body to wake
up. Once we do that, just place the pillow over my head until I
stop fighting back."

Josiah's face went into absolute disbelief to where he even
threw up his hands in the air. "And what if your plan doesn't
work? What if Sagaru doesn't wake up in your body once you tie
your thread around his finger?"

"It's *bound* to work, Josiah. Trust me! Remember when
Kalani told us about how Elizabeth's coven started to swap bodies
through the Astral Plane? That has got to be how her coven did it
— by exchanging Silver Threads."

"Do you not remember that we literally almost lost
Elowyn? Hell, we just lost Kalani. What makes you think I'm going
to allow you to do such a foolish thing?" Josiah said, sternly
pointing his finger in my direction.

"How else are we going to get rid of Sagaru, huh? I'm open to suggestions."

Josiah had trouble forming an articulate sentence to combat the conversation at hand. He made a very good point. There may be a chance that the plan doesn't work. The plan could even backfire on us. I hadn't sifted through all of the potential flaws, but it was the best sounding idea that came to mind when I saw my masquerade mask strings wrapped around my finger. Josiah let out a troubled sigh and drew closer towards me. He placed his hands on both sides of my head and pressed his forehead against mine.

"Listen. I care about you and so many other people also care, Jackie. If you do this, you are potentially putting your life on the line. You're only twenty one years old. Don't be a fool and martyr yourself for something you believe may be right. We can find a different way. Sagaru hasn't even haunted us in our dreams lately."

I took Josiah's firmly planted hands and cuffed his them into my own, dropping them to waist height.

"I understand that, Josiah, and I care about you too, but we literally, like you said, almost lost Elowyn, and to who? To Sagaru. If we let him continue to terrorize Circle Walkers such as ourselves, he may end up taking our lives for good. Should he gain possession of our Silver Thread, he will devour it whole or offer it to the Necromancer in some twisted, dark exchange. Do you understand?"

Josiah nodded firmly. "Yes, I understand that but what if it doesn't—"

"It'll work Jo, trust me. " I spoke in a reaffirming tone.

"But Shajara will not allow you to do it."

"She doesn't have to know, nor will she."

Josiah disbanded from my grasp and carried his mind elsewhere for a brief moment to collect his thoughts.

"Elowyn will be our wake up call, literally." I said, "She will be able to wake us both up at a certain time, and once that happens you will take the pillow and suffocate me before he's allowed to react in my body. After I stop breathing, resuscitate me immediately. If you need me to teach you CPR, I can do so."

"No, that won't be necessary. I'm well aware of how to give someone CPR." Josiah mentioned.

"Good because I actually failed it in Med. term class." I spoke, letting out a small chuckle.

I reached into my waistband and pulled out my father's old Desert Eagle. The magazine was nearly full since my father touched it last except for one missing bullet, and I've always wondered what that one bullet was used for.

"If push comes to shove, I want you to use this. We cannot let it get out of hand." I placed the gun into Josiah's hands.

With Josiah's mouth at first agape, he managed to pick his jaw back up and speak.

"You're absolutely bat shit insane!" he said, shoving the weapon immediately back into my hands. "One bullet will take your head clean off of your shoulders, you idiot! My entire apartment complex would call the cops, let alone there'd be a giant hole in my wall!"

I really didn't know much about weapons, but I believe it, especially with the astonished look that remained plastered on Jo's face. I never really gave it much thought but to be taken out by my old man's own gun would be pretty insane indeed.

"Put that thing away. If push does come to shove, Jackie, I'd rather incapacitate you than DECAPITATE you, geez."

"Well I'm still open to suggestions!" I added, tucking the gun away after checking the safety lock.

"Don't worry; these guns will subdue you instead!" Josiah said bravely, flexing what arm muscle he head.

"Yeah, okay." I snickered.

It was really awesome of Josiah to turn a serious situation into a laughing matter. I really needed it. I am honestly terrified of the thoughts that have been circling my head, should I lose my life in the situation, but after what happened to Elowyn, I'm willing to take the risk to ensure of Sagaru's demise. With Sagaru gone from the Astral Plane, Astraga will be a much safer place. Not only that, but the Necromancer Sgrios will no longer have a potential partner to collaborate with if they ever chose to form an alliance. Having those two working as a team could cause alarming risk in the plane, especially with Sgrios' army of undead and Sagaru's gathering of Umbrage Walkers put together.

Over the next few days I had dabbled in the Astral Plane and continued to practice the use of Aetheric magic. Both Josiah and Elowyn accompanied me, but we chose to keep our appearances low on the radar in hopes that Sagaru or any unwelcomed visitors wouldn't show up. We figured hiding out in the Lavender fields would be our best option.

Shajara had taught us a technique known as "Phasing" some time ago when Kalani was still around. The technique allows us to phase between the Astral Plane and the waking world, while still remaining out of our bodies. It's a general Taboo to do once you leave your body and enter the Astral Plane, as the Heilige frowns upon this practice. Lucky for us Walkers, humans who are still alive think that it's the actual dead they may be communing with when we actually do successfully visit the waking world as a spirit. I suppose you could say that they are half right being that the actual soul itself does leave the body when you project into the plane, but there is still a chance that when they do have a supernatural encounter, that it actually is someone who has passed on.

Unfortunately for us not much action went on for us in the Lavender fields at night, so we took our ambitions to the cities and hit the populated streets. Have you ever felt lIke a fly on the wall, or a shadow on the pavement? This is what phasing often felt like because no matter how much the three of us tried to stand out from the crowd, humans would simply walk by without hearing the faintest sound. We'd scream at the top of our lungs and would even charge our bodies into the middle of the streets to have cars and even humans walk right through us as if we didn't exist. It was somewhat terrifying to think that this might be what it feels like to be dead.

To be forgotten, alone, but still be able to see everything prosper around you. To watch people move around you without ever being able to interact with them. Imagine spending decades, or centuries perhaps, watching entire civilizations of mankind rise and fall, watching inventions become the apex of our culture, just to watch them rust and become outdated within time. Eternity never seemed so frightening before until now, especially without a voice to be heard.

Weather varied between the plane and the waking world. Often times the plane would just have cloudy nights or a few dry lightning spells, whereas the cities of Florida was still feeling the after effects of Hurricane Lorne. Josiah would dare us to picture what foreign countries would look like, in hopes that we'd be able to actually travel the world in the matter of seconds but Elowyn was too afraid to tap into that kind of magic. I agreed with her and we promised that it's better to leave that kind of magic alone for now. Even though we were going against the Heilige himself by practicing Phasing, we still tried our best to abide by the laws of the plane. It's not that Phasing itself was outlawed by authority; it was just considered a practice of magic that should NOT be exploited. Before Kalani lost his soul to the Necromancer, he'd often tell us tales of his comrades who went mad from doing it too much.

The actual dead who didn't have a Silver Thread anymore were especially vulnerable to this, feeling the need to phase back into the actual world because they were still attached to a mortal feature, such as an object or even their loved ones. I still felt that regardless of all of the dark events that have taken place – from Jonathan's suicide, Ariella's unfortunate murder, and even the witnessing of Kalani sacrificing himself in order to save Elowyn – I've been able to grasp a stronger hold on how much I should value my life. Sure, I may not always show it, especially when I'm having a mental battle with myself, but I've started to understand how much humans take their lives for granted. I think that we humans in today's society forget that we're not immortal, especially at a young age.

"What is going on here?" an unknown voice called out to the three of us.

At the time, we were tinkering around with an older group of people who stumbled haphazardly out of a local bar in the city. We didn't even at first pay attention to the voice that called out to us because we figured that it was just another human in the waking world on the streets.

"What are you three doing?" The voice sternly called out as she sent a small gust of wind towards our feet, causing us to tumble through the inebriated group of people and onto the ground.

The woman stood tall, taller than me actually. With her stern posture, she placed her hands firmly on her hips and cocked her head upwards to gain a good glimpse of us through her spectacles.

"Who the hell is this broad?" Josiah muttered as we all quickly scrambled to our feet.

"Josiah!" Elowyn snapped back, tugging on his arm.

It was a priestess of Astraga, but we weren't exactly sure who it may be. I remembered her face and that same exact pose sticking out in my mind when I recalled the stained glass windows in the Cathedral, before they were shattered during the Masquerade. A long, dark brown braid draped down one side of her shoulders and met near the bottom of her rib cage. Her lips were plump and eyes sharper than ever, although the tint of her eyes were warmer in comparison to her hair. She, like Shajara, wore very unique clothing. They weren't war-torn rags or fur, but instead she dressed in strange skin-tight leathers and even sported really interesting combat boots. If you were to ask me, this woman has likely seen her fair share of battles as well. Most Priests and Priestesses of Astraga seemed to dress differently from what I've noticed.

"Cora is the name if you must know," she retorted to Josiah specifically. "And I do believe that you all are taunting these poor, innocent humans by phasing out of the plane, am I correct?"

Elowyn and I let out a loud gulping noise while Josiah chose to remain bold. I don't know what had gotten into him lately.

"It's not like they can hear or see us, lady." Josiah called out.

Cora took a few steps closer to the three of us and the sound of her dirty boots clonked on the pavement. "No, you are lucky they did not hear or see you. If you practice it enough, they will."

Josiah whirled his finger around to signify that he didn't even give a rat's ass and whistled to add onto his abrasive standpoint. That is however the last time we'd ever see Josiah act so rebelliously against a figure in the Astral Plane, as Cora took the opportunity to grab his whirling finger in her hand. She bent it so far backwards that you'd assume she was trying to expose his bone.

"OW OW OW, OKAY!" Josiah screeched, twisting his arm to go with the direction of the bent finger.

"You will not disrespect me and you will not Phase again, so long as I am not nearby to keep an eye on you petulant children. Understood?"

We all nodded in unison while Josiah put more much more emphasis into the head nodding.

"Good!" Cora nodded with a sarcastic smile, letting go of Jo's finger. "It's unfortunate that we've met under such circumstances, but I'll have you hooligans know that I'm assigned to watching over the plane and those who phase out of it. I'm accompanied by another Priest who goes by the name of Samuel, and trust me – you do not want to get on his bad side."

"I am quite curious though," Cora added to her speech when walking a few paces away and turning back to face us. "What are three Circle Walkers doing — who are still very alive in in the waking world might I add — dabbling in the practice of Phasing behind their Tutor's back, hmm?"

We all exchanged varied looks of concern at one another before I mustered the courage to speak on our behalf.

"You see, one of our "tutors" so to speak, befell to Sgrios, ma'am." I said.

"Ah, Kalani." Cora replied, nodding her head while seeming to recall the events that unfolded during the Masquerade.

"Shajara has not been seen since the event occurred." Elowyn added.

"This is true. She did storm off, and I don't blame her in all honesty." Cora spoke.

"Why do you say that?" I asked.

"Well it's no secret that they are lovers, or were at least." Cora snorted loudly, "You could barely breathe with all of the stagnant sexual tension in the air."

"Hey, have some respect!" Josiah demanded, still trying to crack his finger into the right position again.

"You are right, my apologies, but you still have yet to answer my question. What exactly are you all doing exactly, phasing about without any guidance?"

"Just seeing the broad spectrum of our capabilities is all." I replied quickly in a sly manner.

"I assure you," Cora spoke, inching in closer with a wicked eyebrow raised, "You're capabilities are endless. Do not lose yourselves in this twisted place that we inhabit, we wouldn't want your story to be told among the other dozens of tragedies we all have heard about."

I didn't know whether to be intimidated by Cora's statement or to take more caution from here on out. Regardless, Cora went on her way and dismissed the three of us without any further questioning.

"Guys, I don't know if we should do this anymore." Elowyn spoke in broken pauses.

"We're not giving in. There is literally no other way that we can get ahold of each other once we are able to place the Silver Thread on Sagaru's finger. Phasing is the only option we have to contact you, El. We just have to practice more." I said assertively.

And that is exactly what we did. We practiced for hours

upon hours and days upon days, this time trying to hide even lower on the Radar than before by phasing in our own homes. We didn't need Cora or even Samuel gaining any insight into our intentions, let alone Heilige Theodore himself. We strictly forbid ourselves from stepping foot near Astraga in the meantime, and luckily enough for us, Shajara had not appeared in the plane since the Masquerade incident involving Kalani happened. As much as I felt sorry for what happened that night, I'm sure Elowyn carried most of the guilt on her shoulders even though she couldn't control what had happened.

The three of us made a solemn oath to keep our devised plan a secret, no matter the circumstances. After nearly a week's worth of trial and error, we made breakthrough progress by being able to interact with an object within the waking world; a lighter that was placed on a nearby table. It wasn't much, but it was just enough to signal to Elowyn when we needed her to wake us up at the right time.

"The plan is settled. Elowyn will stand guard and keep an eye on the lighter while Josiah and I venture into the plane to find Sagaru." I stated.

"But how are we going to find him? He kind of appears when we're in turmoil." Josiah noted.

"That is exactly how we are going to summon him; when he thinks our defenses are down." I said. "All we need to do is create a spectacle, and preferably outside of Astraga so nobody is harmed."

I'll admit that I was quite nervous. I didn't even know if this plan was going to entirely work, but it was the only thing we had going for us. As dusk started to approach, I contemplated on the idea of calling my mother in hopes to make amends for the recent argument that we had before I went through with this insane plan. I tapped the white lighter anxiously on the table before my train of thought was broken by Elowyn snatching it from my possession.

"It's alright, Jackie. Everything is going to work out. We have the upper hand." Elowyn tried to speak convincingly. Her attempt to eliminate the discouraging and tainted thoughts in my head was very admiring.

"Thanks, El. I don't even know if I'll be able to get to sleep tonight."

"Don't worry about that." Josiah said, pointing to his apartment medicine cabinet. "I have a few sleeping pills just in case."

"We're not supposed to abuse substances to gain access into the plane." I replied in a discomforted tone.

"I know. It's just in case. Live a little. Relax."

I wish I really could, and I really wish I could play it off like how well Josiah was doing, but I could feel a piece of his mind drifting off when his eyes would shakily dart across the room. Josiah by no means has been a timid guy since I met him, but tonight could be an exception. Nevertheless, we all gave one giant group hug together before Josiah and I popped an Ambien.

"I'll be here when you rise." Elowyn confirmed, setting the white lighter on the correct marker. "I promise."

"Thanks, sweet cheeks." I winked.

Elowyn resumed her spot in the corner of the room while Josiah and I waited patiently for the sleep aids to kick in. It wasn't exactly easy to slip into the Astral Plane via astral projection when you have a pill that is attempting to dictate your brain chemistry, but nevertheless we accomplished it after some time.

Immediately upon arrival into the plane, Shajara had already been waiting for us. The heels of her bare feet rhythmically tapped onto the dresser and the gleam in her heterochromatic eyes said it all; she knew. An awkward silence filled the room while Shajara's body language spoke plenty to both Josiah and I. She abruptly folded her arms, still kicking her crossed legs onto the dresser and even then flared and eyebrow, making her demeanor even more intimidating.

"Well?" Shajara scolded. "Someting dat you wish to tell me?"

"Uhm, not really," Josiah said shamefully, never making eye contact with Shajara.

"We're in the dog house, aren't we?" I asked.

"Did joo really tink dat I wouldn't find out?" she asked and leapt from the dresser to approach us.

"It's not that we –wanted– to hide it from you, Sha." I replied softly.

Shajara raised her hand to me and pressed her thin fingers tightly together. At first I thought she was really going to go in for the backhand, but she restrained.

"I should slap da stoopid right out of yoo both! Tinkin' dat you could both get away with phasin' without my permission! I told jah! Da Heilige does not support phasin' one bit, ya?! I have eyes n' ears all over da plane, inside n' outside of Astraga! Saint Theodore would revoke ya right den and dere, and I have half a mind to report'cha to em'!"

Wait. Shajara knew that we were practicing phasing likely because of Cora informing her. . . But what Cora doesn't know is the reason *why* we were phasing, therefore Shajara doesn't either. I quickly glanced over towards Josiah right as he was opening his mouth to speak.

"We just wanted to stop Sa–"

I quickly knocked into Josiah's side to make it look like an accident, purposefully knocking him to the ground. When Josiah's confused stare locked onto my own, I shook my head as nonchalantly as possible and muttered to him: *"she doesn't know"* with utmost silence.

Shajara took it upon herself to yank my body into her grasp and clutched her cold hands around my neck and chin at the same time, cocking my head forcefully to face her.

"She doesn't know –WHAT–?!" Shajara growled, her facial expressions roaring in rage.

You know, I never realized how demoralizing the color blue and green could possibly yield until they're in the form of eyes that are practically burning into your skull by every passing second. I knew that if I didn't act soon, all would be for naught and the plan I ever so disastrously devised on sheer whim would foil. I clenched onto the hand that Shajara had me suspended by and let out a strong pulse of energy from the tips of my fingers to send her flying backwards. She broke right through the bedroom wall. Josiah scrambled onto his feet in absolute shock and started to shake his hand at the hole that Shajara's body had left.

"Wh– What the hell?! What're you thinking!?" Josiah stammered. "Have you gone mad?!"

"Sure, why not." I snapped back. "We need to create some tension in the plane and what better way to do that than to piss off a hotheaded Jamaican?! We need more people, we need to relocate, and we need to use more Aetheric magic, immediately. Understand?!"

Josiah nodded without thinking twice. "What do you want me to do?"

"I want you to head to Astraga as quickly as you can and cause a scene. There should be plenty of people hanging around the city square. Rally anyone and everyone, the more the better. If you can gain the attention of some of the Priests and Priestesses, by all means – do it. Just make sure you don't hurt anybody in the process unless you have to defend yourself."

With that being said, Josiah sped off without a second more to waste. I felt like a hypocrite but it was foolish of me to think that I could tiptoe around the plane and get rid of one of the most notoriously known figures without getting caught. It was now or never and I didn't even know if the urgent decisions I just made were going to work at all. A terrifying feeling started to bubble within my gut at the thought of failure. That dreadful feeling intensified inside of me when I saw Shajara starting to crawl out from the wall that I just put her through.

"Da nerve you have..." Shajara snarled.

She whipped back her warhawk hairstyle into place with a violent neck crack and mocked my bold move with a taunting chuckle. With the snap of her fingers she casted out an array of spears in the form of ice and bolted them swiftly into my direction. All but one I was able to successfully evade before a burst of pain shot through the ankle region of my right foot. The battled ranged onwards between the two of us, destroying

Josiah's entire apartment complex in the process. Lucky for us, none of the real damage would ever show in the waking world. It was likely that Elowyn was probably filing her nails in the middle of all the commotion. Gah, I could have really used her help at this point.

"I dun know what has gotten into ya, Jackie," Shajara yelled when taking cover behind a burning piece of furniture, "but once da council comes to my aid and we're able to subdue ya, you will be banished from da plane. Mark my words, Jackie!"

"I'm so sorry, Shajara! Really, you don't understand!" I cried out. "Just know that it's for a good reason!"

"Sending a Priestess of Astraga through a wall for a good reason?! Explain yaself!" Shajara screamed and tossed a few bolts of electricity blindly from her cover.

"I can't! Just trust me!"

I wound up a hefty fireball in my hands but I had to unwillingly extinguish it soon thereafter. I was ambushed by both Jonathan and Donovan when they appeared from each side of the crumbling apartment walls. I hadn't realize how strong Donovan was himself when he released powerful multi-elemental attacks that I hadn't seen before. After being scalded by fire and nearly put out of my misery by a strong current of electricity, I knew that it was time to flee. Being outnumbered by three veterans of the Astral Plane was asking for immediate failure, even taking on one alone was risky business.

"Catch me if you can." I said, winking at them. I bolted through a dilapidated piece of wall and into the night sky. I couldn't even look back at this point for fear that one of them would grab ahold of me before I could reach Astraga. The faster I sped throughout the atmosphere, the more I counted my blessings and hoped that Josiah was able to successfully go through with our plan. Right as I breached through the Stratosphere, I was flanked by an immense amount of energy that sent me tumbling away from my path to Astraga. Donovan had caught up with me.

CHAPTER SIXTEEN

I spiraled downwards, helplessly out of control like a pigeon whose wings were clipped in midair by a rifle. The wind whistled into my ears and the further I plummeted back to the Earth, the further the feeling of hope had separated itself from me. With every ounce of willpower and strength I gathered, I tried to move my body but it was useless, as the lethal blast of lightning that Donovan shot from his hands had paralyzed me from the neck down. All I could do was watch as the ground below started to grow in detail and size, forming fields, streets and the like. *"So damn close"* I thought to myself.

My vision never ceased as I thought it would, because at this time I should have departed from the Astral Plane and back into the waking world by now. The closer I came to impact, the more I realized that I would have to take the brunt of the force head on and I realized that this wasn't going to end pretty after freefalling for a dozen or so miles. I closed my eyes tightly and remembered all of the good times I had shared with everyone in the plane. I knew I was going to survive the fall, but I also knew that I'd never be welcomed back after what idiot moves I executed. Hopefully they could forgive me someday.

During those fleeting moments I recalled it all. The petty fight that Josiah and I had fallen into that nearly burned Elowyn to a crisp, the time I first laid eyes on Shajara and Kalani, or the time where I talked to Kalani's father, Dante, at the lighthouse because I accidentally projected myself there when I was first getting used teleporting places in the plane. That is when I realized that I was an absolute idiot and started to concentrate heavily on the foundation of Astraga in hopes that I could make it there before it was too late. I pictured the Cathedral, the Pub, and the square bustling with hundreds of people from all across the world. I remembered the brick pavement streets that wound throughout the city and the beautiful marbled statue which draped thousands of Silver Threads. I could hear Gertrude's witch-like laughter fill the room as she played seamstress to people in her shop, and I watched as Ariella darted throughout the tight-knit crowd, chasing after a child who couldn't have been much older than her. The harder I imagined the floating city, the louder the useless banter of the people started to fill my ears and soon enough I could feel the soggy brick street beneath my feet.

You'd think that it'd be a million to one chance of working, but nonetheless it did. When I had opened my eyes after strongly envisioning what I yearned desperately for, it materialized before me and I was actually standing at the edge of Astraga. My body was still a bit thrown off at the drastic change of environment and I ended up collapsing to the ground shortly after with a slight tinge of vertigo, still feeling the effects of Donovan's incredulous lightning attack. I let out a long, grievous sigh followed by a strong amount of maniacal laughter that I had outsmarted him without a second to spare. In the distance, the sound of a small explosion went off and I knew exactly why. Josiah had been keeping up with his end of the deal.

I made myself throughout the winding city streets until I heard a second set of feet starting to scurry close by, but the distinct sound alerted me that these particular feet had shoes on them. After I darted my vision in several different directions, Ariella appeared and pointed towards the Astragian square in fear. I took that as incentive enough to where I needed to head. I thanked Ariella quickly and proceeded to give a small nudge to head her in the opposite direction of the action. A few more explosions shot into the starry sky and smoked started to choke the nearby air.

Nothing prepared me for this moment, and I mean nothing. After being trampled on by dozens of Circle Walkers, a small army of Umbrage Walkers infiltrated the city of Astraga and brought with them creatures that I had never seen before. I couldn't even conceive on how they existed. Dark tendrils shot forth from the ground, breaking through the city pavement and constricting whatever they could in reach while other darkly animated creatures that resembled deformed bat-like leeches took flight and preyed on those who fell short of escaping. I watched as the newly deceased animals and walkers amalgamated together to form monstrous and bizarre Chimeras, carrying tremendous power in their wake, controlled unwillingly by the Umbrage Walkers. A familiar hand swooped out from the horrified crowd and snatched me back to my feet in one strong haul.

"Good to see you again!" Josiah spat out as we inevitably ran into a thick cloud of smoke and stagnating debris. I held onto Josiah's grasp until we broke out of the cloud and towards the outer city. We looked back at the ongoing destruction that was taking place while the people of Astraga still evacuated as quickly as possible, passing us by like a blur of speeding cars down a congested highway.

"What the hell are those things?! I told you to cause a ruckus, not summon creatures of hell upon people!"

"Trust me, I didn't summon those hideous creatures!" he said between breaths. "Sgrios appeared right as I reached Astraga and he decided to bring an army with him."

"Well, yeah, I can see that!" I shot back at Josiah sarcastically while patting away the ash that accumulated on my pants.

"Jackie, now is not the time to be a—"

Before Josiah could finish his scolding, a hail of fire bombarded the immediate vicinity and sent us both directly apart from one another. An all-out war broke out between the conflicting forces and we were caught in the middle of it. Kalani could be seen at the forefront of the battle, stripping Circle Walkers of their threads by tearing their bodies apart with bestial vigor. The disgruntled look on his pale face flared brightly from the fires that surrounded him as thick, black blood pulsed through his throbbing veins. It was there in that moment when he caught a glimpse of me in the distance that I knew we had officially lost Kalani for good. There was no going back for him, or his troubled father.

If I had known of Sgrios' intentions to attack Astraga beforehand, I would have never launched Shajara through a wall or caused a scene earlier with the other council members, as this war was a disturbance enough to hopefully get Sagaru out from hiding. A loud crash of thunder and lightning split apart a good chunk of the land nearby, causing the ground to tremble in aftershock. The plane grew heavily unstable as the use of Aether continued throughout the battle. I engaged into combat with an Umbrage Walker that stood not too far away and held my ground as best I could before being knocked back by an unrelenting force. With my sight still dazed, a familiar war cry soon bellowed from behind me and when I cocked my head backwards, a monstrous white tiger with those unforgettable eyes leapt unforgivingly onto the Umbrage Walker and tore them to pieces in a matter of seconds.

Even though I shouldn't have been as ecstatic to see her, I couldn't help but rejoice when Shajara sank her teeth viciously into that Umbrage Walker. Joanthan, Donovan, and even Cora appeared on the battlefield to fight against the pestilence of dark forces that were controlled by Sgrios and I assumed that Samuel was the beast of a man who stuck closed to Cora's side and watched her back. Amid the chaos that continued to reign throughout Astraga, I was able to get some words in edgewise to defend myself for why I had chosen to blatantly lash out on Shajara.

"Very smooth, Jackie," Shajara snarled after she had transformed back into her original body and tossed the head of an Umbrage Walker out of her grasp.

"Er, at least I'm apologizing now!" I said.

Not even ten seconds of our conversation had played out before we found ourselves fighting off those horrifying bat-like leeches back to back.

"Listen, Jackie! We need to find and protect da Heilige! Can I trust you to find him?!"

"I don't think disbanding right now is in our favor, Shajara!" I shouted across the field, swooping to the ground to evade an oncoming predator.

Venomous ichor projected out from a nearby leech and eroded an entire slab of earth that acted as a barrier between the two of us. After winding up a steady amount of energy, I blew away the Leech with a molten blast of fire.

"Even though we are outnumbered, without da Heilige we are hopeless! You must find him, now!" Shajara cried.

"Do you know how dangerous that sounds?! We can't risk it! I'd rather di—"

"GO, NOW!" Shajara screamed, elbowing me in the back of the head.

"Ow! Okay, okay!" I stuttered and disappeared into the crowd.

After traversing a good distance into the onslaught, I dove headfirst to tackle down an Umbrage Walker who at the time had Josiah pinned to the ground. With monstrous pressure I crushed the Umbrage Walker's skull into the earth with my hands and left their twitching body to fend for its self until it dispersed into a thousand remnants of dark energy. I secretly wished to myself that they'd have a migraine that'd last for a week in the waking world.

"There's no time!" I shouted, "We need to head into the City. Come on!"

Josiah unwillingly nodded and gathered himself back to his feet and carried onwards. The entire city of Astraga had been cast into flame and smoke and there was no sign of it letting up anytime soon. Once Josiah and I had reached the Cathedral steps, a massive explosion within the nave of the cathedral went off and the sound of broken stone and rubble started to litter the city streets around us.

"BEGONE!" Saint Theodore roared, scattering a team of

Umbrage Walkers and hideous beasts apart when he pierced his staff into the floor. The Heilige refused to move from his rightful spot, protecting the statue of the star-crossed lovers with all of his strength. If the statue is to fall into the hands of evil, they would gain an untold amount of power through the Silver Threads that lay strewn across it.

For every Umbrage Walker or hideous amalgamation that fell, two more rose in their place and soon enough a hefty crowd of two dozen twisted creations and tormented walkers alike opposed the three of us.

"Stand together!" Josiah cried out.

"Let none pass!" Saint Theodore ordered, wiping the sweat and collection of dirt from his dark skin.

A wicked crackle of lightning snapped through a gaping hole in the Cathedral and circulated across the ceiling momentarily, followed by an intimidating rumble that shook Astraga to it's core. A standstill was met between the opposing forces until a foolish Umbrage Walker took it upon himself to initiate the first attack. The Heilige raised his hand in defense to the whip of energy that the Umbrage Walker sent out, reflecting it back and slicing him clean in half with barely any effort. I shot a quick glance at the Heilige in astonishment and he reciprocated a response by jerking his eyebrow askew and cocking a half-assed smile in triumph.

"Anyone else care to dance?" Saint Theodore chuckled, his serious demeanor now lightened by his cocky jest.

A distinct and familiar bout of laughter echoed once again throughout the halls, filling every inch of the room with corruption. It was the one I was waiting for: Sagaru. A collection of pitch black smoke encircled all of our enemies, hiding them into the shadows and eventually revealing the demented Shaman once more after the smoke had subsided. The colored feathers still remained tied to the horns of the animalistic skull that rested on his head. He tilted his head upwards just enough to reveal those bright golden pupils that danced hungrily inside of his beady onyx eyes, unforgiving to the world around him. Despite the wicked smile that stretched across his horrific face, it bore determination to get what he came after: the statue.

I locked eyes with Josiah and we both nodded our head ever so slightly in agreement.

"Prepare yourselves, Walkers." The Heilige spoke, pointing his staff directly at Sagaru. Sagaru snarled at Saint Theodore's action and shrugged his arms.

"Now, now, that is not how you treat a guest, is it?" Sagaru slithered back, his foul breath protruding from his mouth in clouds of visible vapor. The temperature in the plane had suddenly dropped a significant amount. The walls themselves started to lightly coat with sparkling sheets of ice and crept all the way to the ceiling, forming decent sized icicles along the way.

"You are no guest here, vermin." Saint Theodore retorted back.

Sagaru pressed his jagged fingernails against his cheeks, drawing in a sarcastic gasp as if he were offended. "How could you say such a thing?!" he spoke, taking a slight step forward in hopes that it'd go unnoticed.

The Heilige sent a generous bolt of electricity to the foot that Sagaru extended, causing him to hop backwards in shock.

"You encroach on territory that you are most unwelcomed upon, Sagaru." The Heilige stated.

"And you dare attack your own brother, Theodore!" Sagaru exclaimed.

An immediate silence ensued after, dampened by the thought that the Heilige himself had a secret or two of his own. Josiah turned his attention towards the Heilige in confusion and I continued to keep my eyes affixed onto Sagaru, never deterring interest. I swatted my hand from left to right quickly, trying to expose my Silver Thread without being noticed.

"Pay no mind to this buffoon who spews inconsiderate statements and utter falsehood!" Theodore spoke, taking a prompt stance to approach Sagaru closer in anger.

"Oh, but it is true." Sagaru winked, tapping his sickly finger behind Saint Theodore and towards the statue.

"Enough!" Saint Theodore belted out and extended his staff. He expelled a devastating amount of energy towards Sagaru, causing his body to be sent flying backwards a great distance. A band of Umbrage Walkers reappeared from the ground in clusters of ash and smoke to aid Sagaru. With the witnessing of this, the Heilige clamped his hands tightly together and started to whisper under his breath, speaking the names of his trusted council and one by one they appeared to match Sagaru's small army.

"Why must it come to this?" Sagaru said. He shook his head once he emerged from beneath the rubble that toppled over him.

"Now!" Shajara yelled, leaping forth into the crowd with both hands aglow from the molten fire she conjured up.

A mild fight broke between the two opposing groups and the sound of breaking bones and blood spatter muffled the raging storm outside of the Cathedral. Jonathan and Donovan had locked into battle with several Umbrage Walkers while Cora and her comrade Samuel fought valiantly to subdue the hideous creations that continued to form from the remnants of discarded bodies. I shoved myself quickly throughout the crowd, often having to dodge any unwarranted attacks that ricocheted from nearby fights until I was able to reach Sagaru.

With Josiah in my sight, I waved my hand quickly again to expose my Silver Thread again and tugged it carefully off of the knuckle of my finger and charged forwards, latching my grip onto Sagaru's body as best I could.

A sliver of a moment befell me where I lost all coherence when I slipped off my thread. I lost the ability to breathe, the ability to feel and understand how to function. Any form of cognition had come to an immediate halt, my body and mind ceasing to move forwards naturally. The tips of my fingers no longer carried the ability to register the feeling of what it was like to touch someone or something, much like how my very own nose was incapable of picking up the scent of debris or the amount of iron that choked the air from all of the blood that plastered the Cathedral walls. Soon enough the hearing in my ears flushed to absolute silence and thereafter my vision itself started to darken. I essentially became brain dead, albeit briefly.

I lost my connection to the Earth, to the waking world, but more so to my very own body. I became absolutely detached and separated both mentally and physically. I was isolated, and never had I felt the feeling of absolute aloneness like until now. If nothingness had a feeling, this would be it.

CHAPTER SEVENTEEN

The sound of a thousand missiles streamed throughout my eardrums. Back and forth my body sway, my arms still numb from removing my Silver Thread. Sagaru relentlessly tossed around to break me of my hold and even sank his vicious fangs into my skin at some point. I saw Josiah dive forwards through the crowd to aid me, but it was too late. I had lost all muscle function and flew some yards away. My Silver Thread drifted carefully to the ground beside me, glistening like a sweet blue Hyacinth that had just been freshly picked from a garden.

Ongoing battles continued to proceed around me. Shajara single-handedly catered to the Heilige's side through every second of it, capable of taking down the entire room should she have to. I kept my last glances focused strictly onto her and watched as her warhawk of beautiful hair whipped sharply in rhythm with her body. Even with those gorgeous locks doused in blood, she remained the strongest and most outstanding woman that I have ever met. I reached my hand out towards Shajara, but it was then crushed beneath an Umbrage Walker's heavy boot. It didn't matter, as I couldn't feel the pain anyways.

Tiny moments of vertigo started to swirl through my head and I knew that I was close to losing it all. The Umbrage Walker knelt beside me and dangled my own thread over my lifeless face, mocking my horrid defeat. She wiggled the tip of her tongue on my thread to taunt me further until a massive fist swooped in from the side and cleared her head clean off of her shoulders in one amazing strike. The ringing ceased and soon enough audible sounds started to rush into my ears. Josiah grabbed ahold of my thread and cuffed my underarm over his shoulder to lift me up as best he could.

"Hold on, Jackie!" Josiah exclaimed, staggering away from the Cathedral.

"Only you would save me from the brink of death, Jo." I said in attempt to muster up the last bit of my strength.

"Shut up, you've saved my life before and you know it. We're getting you out of here."

"Egh – We can't do that yet. Not without the Silver Thread on Sagaru." I replied.

"That can wait." Josiah said firmly.

"Hell no it can't! I didn't come this far for nothing."

About three steps later I had disbanded from Josiah's grasp and turned around, more determined than ever, even with a weakened soul. I shook my head of any remaining vertigo, straightened my backbone and charged onwards. Sagaru was enjoying the victory of capturing another Silver Thread by the time I had made it back to the nave, guiding it down his throat with his sickly fingers.

"There's nothing more relishing than watching a human lose their life." Sagaru hissed outwards, licking his fingers one by one.

"Have you no sanity?" I asked, clutching my own thread tightly behind my back.

"An immortal?" He squawked back at me, "You're asking an immortal if he's sane?!"

"Very much so," I replied carelessly.

Every second that ticked away started to prolong into agonizing hours of what to do next. As Sagaru carefully approached, I quivered in fright, thinking that I could fail once more in this pressing moment, something of which I could not afford.

"Perhaps you need a reminder, arrogant child," Sagaru said while inching close to me as possible. "To be an immortal means you are undying. Undefeatable by any and all who should stand against me!"

"Are you sure about that?" I asked, grabbing ahold of Sagaru's arm and quickly fastening my Silver Thread around his skinny wrist.

Sagaru looked down for a brief moment before he decided to gleam his onyx eyes back onto me. The Silver Thread quickly converted from its original faint blue hue to a twisted, deep royal purple.

"Silly child, what is this? You offer me your thread?" Sagaru questioned, mused by my strange act.

"Even gods at some point must perish, Sagaru." I stated. Sagaru tilted his head sideways in confusion at my statement before his eyes widened with the realization that I was up to something.

"Do it now, Josiah!" I screamed.

I clamped my grip on to Sagaru as tightly as I could and Josiah phased immediately out of the plane. Sagaru writhed back and forth with his body, but I was unrelenting and refused to let go, even if the plan had failed.

"What are you doing!?" He screeched, finally breaking free after separating the two of us with a blast of dark energy.

"I'm sending you away, and for good." I replied with a wicked smile identical to his.

Sagaru momentarily charged towards me, practically seething from his ears. He was caught off guard by a sudden moment of dizziness, causing him to lose balance and trip over one of his deceased Umbrage Walkers who lay lifeless on the floor. His words started to collide together and worsen by every moment before he tore the animal skull crown from his head, likely hoping that it'd help alleviate his dizzy spell.

"Holy crap, it's working!" I shouted and pointed my quivering hand at Sagaru.

"YOU WILL PAY FOR THIS, YOU ARROGANT CHILD!" Sagaru boomed, clutching his head with his hands.

Outcries from Sagaru wailed onwards as he once more felt the weight of the world start to press down on his shoulders. It is a feeling we humans were all too aware of — a feeling that he hadn't felt in centuries. His body started to uncontrollably shake until he ultimately burst into an impressive array of dark, energetic balls of matter which took flight immediately out of the Cathedral. The impression on Shajara's face was priceless when she watched Sagaru deplete into thin air, but this was only half the battle.

"Um. . . Did I just see what I tink I just saw?" Shajara asked, absolutely floored by the impressive feat.

"And. . . Was that Sagaru who just left the Astral plane?" Jonathan questioned, confused by what he just witnessed.

"Shajara, Jonathan." I spoke when peering at both with great concern. "I need to go. I need to go, now."

And that is exactly what I did. I left the entire battle behind and everyone involved. Granted Sagaru's army of Umbrage Walkers had also retreated once they witnessed Sagaru's disappearance, there wasn't a second to spare. Over and over I pictured Josiah's apartment, down to every detail that I could possibly remember. From the aged tiles on his laminate kitchen floor, to the gross shag carpet he inherited from his mother as a moving out gift, even down to the doilies that his mother insisted he take to decorate his furniture. Josiah also started to fancy lavender candles ever since the day he had a seizure, just to make him feel comfortable from that day forth.

Feeling the ground shift beneath your feet when traveling in the blink of an eye has always caught me off guard. I wound up off balance, diving face-first into Josiah's apartment living room wall. I phased out and into the waking world and gathered myself back together, heading immediately to where I could see both Elowyn and Josiah shaking my body with extreme force.

Elowyn pounced on top of my body and wound up her hand, slapping me upside the head in hopes that it'd wake me from my deranged stupor. My jaw slightly unhinged and my eyes barely opened in reaction. Even though I had been visiting the plane for months, I still hadn't gotten use to the sight of seeing myself out of my body. I crouched at the bedside and continued to encourage both Josiah and Elowyn to continue.

"Just keep trying!" I shouted. Neither of them could hear my voice.

"Oh for Christ's sake!" Elowyn cried out, grabbing me by the shoulders and shaking profusely.

"Un gri' Kro'stelvian! Melhaleim ishmaji un demis!" my lifeless body choked out in broken gasps of air, rising from the bed and knocking Elowyn to the ground.

Right when Josiah approached to detain my body, he was sent flying back from my own possessed hand and destroyed the nearby countertop in the process, littering shards of glass across the bedroom floor. I watched helplessly as the color in my once innocent eyes transitioned from a tranquil blue to a torturous black, like droplets of dye rushing through a bottle of water. I was no longer in control, for Sagaru's soul had once again entered the waking world through my body.

"Never in the six hundred years that I've walked the plane, have I witnessed such magic before." Sagaru breathed out, twisting my vocal chords to fit his own demonic tone. He flexed my fingertips outwards with his control and retracted them back into a clenched fist with delight, fascinated by what it felt like to be in a physical body once more.

Elowyn grasped ahold of a nearby pillow with a covert hand, inching her way towards my possessed body while Sagaru remain momentarily perplexed. Beads of sweat started to form on her upper brow before she swatted them away nervously. Her eyesight quickly took notice of Josiah writhing in pain on the ground. A glass shard had impaled his lower right abdomen during the fall and there was no telling the severity of his injury from just a sudden glance. Regardless of the situation at hand, Elowyn pressed on.

"You know, pesky girl," Sagaru spoke scornfully with his

back still turned to Elowyn, "A friend of yours is bleeding to death on the floor while your other friend remains trapped in the Astral Plane, yet you believe that you can suffocate me with a measly piece of cloth all by yourself?"

"How pathetic," Sagaru whispered under his breath, shaking his head.

"Obviously you underestimate me!" Elowyn exclaimed. She dove after my controlled body and tightly wrapped the pillow around Sagaru's airways, clinging on with all of her strength. Sagaru thrashed about to break free of her hold, smashing her body against the wall several times. Mortifying screeches muffled through the dense pillow and Sagaru started clawing at Elowyn's arms in desperation.

"May you suffer a most unpleasant death, Sagaru!" she screamed, tightening her grip.

"Elowyn, you can do it!" I cheered, anxious to see Sagaru fall.

In one last great effort, Sagaru charged backwards into the wall with incredible speed and all went still at the sound of a horrendous CRACK that followed thereafter. Elowyn's grip on the pillow immediately went limp, her hands dropping to her side before she slowly started to slide down the now-indented wall. Sagaru gulped for air in broken bouts of relief, the muscles in my throat convulsing at the sudden demand for oxygen. With his breath caught once more, he focused back onto her and clenched her throat with savage hold. A stream of blood started to trickle from Elowyn's forehead, flowing downwards passed her eyebrow to wrap around the edge of her Jaw.

"Have you any last words before I pulverize your skull into the ground, you bitch?!" Sagaru exclaimed, shaking his head and spitting on the floor to mock her last moments alive.

"Y- Yeah." Elowyn squeezed out of her throat, "Enjoy hell."

The sound of a gunshot fired off inside the apartment bedroom. I watched Sagaru lose all control of my body and topple to the ground, the darkness then retreating from my eyes and reverting back to the innocent, soothing blue they used to be. A fresh stream of gun smoke slowly escaped from the bullet hole that now lay permanently ingrained on the side of my head, just above my left temple. Josiah's hands shook uncontrollably with his finger still on the trigger, tears flowing down his cheeks.

"I had to do it." He muttered three times over.

"If not, he would have killed you, Elowyn." Josiah said, his voice trembling just as much as his hands.

Elowyn wiped the minor amount of blood spatter off of her face with her eyes still bulging out of their sockets in immense disbelief. She crawled forward shakily and cradled my lifeless head within her lap. With her bloodied fingers, she closed my eyes shut from their deceased stare and sobbed uncontrollably, rocking back and forth. Hundreds of tiny, shadow-like streams of smoke started to seep from my body, ejecting outwards and dissipating into the air. My Silver Thread followed by appearing not too far away, drifting softly down to the floor like a strand of hair, split in two.

I collected the broken thread in my hands and examined it for a few moments before Cora appeared and knelt beside me. I hadn't any words, really. I was dumbfounded to say the least.

"Are you alright?" she asked, gently closing my hands together and bringing them to my chest.

"You know, Cora, I'm not sure." I replied and looked at her directly. "Aside from being murdered, I believe that Sagaru is now officially gone for good from the Astral Plane. I'm glad that my friends are okay though."

"Come on," she said, lifting me up. "Let's take care of that thread."

"Josiah!" Elowyn screamed, flailing her hands for him to come near. "Jackie's still breathing! Listen!"

Josiah scrambled to his feet, ignoring the shard of glass that was embedded in his abdominal wound and rushed over to listen carefully. Surely enough it was true, my lungs continued to draw in air even despite the gunshot. The two panicked together back and forth, unaware of what exactly to do next until their brainstorming came to an end. Josiah and Elowyn ultimately decided that it was best to bring my body to the hospital immediately. For hours they remained in the emergency room, bombarded by a staff of medical professionals and few policemen who were asking a bountiful amount of questions left and right.

On the trip to the emergency room, Josiah and Elowyn devised an elaborate scenario that would serve as the foundation for a lie that would hold the record after all that we've already lied through thus far in this hellish journey. The story stands that three of us had decided to have a night out on the town in Tampa, where I served as the designated driver while Elowyn and Josiah were allowed to get roaring drunk. During our eventful night, the three of us ran into some bad company down the road, leading to Josiah getting stabbed, myself shot with a .22 caliber pistol, and Elowyn developing a severe concussion from someone beating her senseless.

Yes, the Police tested both of their alcohol levels via Breathalyzer, and even drew blood from my own body to confirm the story. Yes, the story fit perfectly because Josiah tossed an aged bottle of Crown Royal in the back seat before driving to the Emergency room, chugging it along the way and even forcing Elowyn to do the same. And yes, my friends are the best kind of shit heads a person could ever ask for.

"Officer, I've already described this person to you four times now, what more do you want from me?" Josiah asked, including a hiccup at the end.

The heavy set, bearded officer gave him a stern glance and closed his miniature notebook. He then tucked away his pen into the pocket that was next to his badge and walked off without any further questions.

"Really, Jo?" Elowyn punched Josiah's kneecap. "You just described Kalani, the Heilige, and your second cousin from Alabama as our attackers."

"And?" He shrugged, "Would you rather I described what Sagaru and Sgrios look like? Besides, I hate my second cousin from Alabama."

The nearby nurse who was cleaning up the mess of medical equipment stopped what he was doing for a brief moment and gave the two a bewildered look. Elowyn tilt her head out from the side of the hospital bed that Josiah was resting comfortably on and gave the nurse an innocent smile. Moments later a doctor whipped around the corner of the Emergency room, nearly snagging the end her overly bleached doctor's coat on a nearby counter's edge.

"Jackie is in stable condition." the doctor affirmed. "There was a significant loss of blood, however we cannot rule out just yet if your friend is going to suffer any mild or permanent brain damage. While the bullet only grazed the temporal bone of the skull, some of the brain was also impacted by bone fragments that we had to remove. Whoever shot at your friend doesn't have very precise aim, thankfully."

Josiah's face turned red as a cherry.

After a drawn out sigh, the doctor continued to speak. "It would seem as though no serious damage has taken place other than that, but there is no telling when your friend will wake up, or if your friend will wake up at all. We're afraid that Jackie has slipped into a coma."

In a nearby room I sat aside my deathbed, firmly holding onto my broken Silver Thread. I detested the way I looked with a heaving mass of gauze bandages wrapped tightly around my head. A giant tube was shoved down my throat along with several strange wires weaving around my body that hooked up to various machines. They also stuck an IV in my inner elbow but the most dreadful part was the disgusting hospital gown the hospital staff dressed me in.

Shajara poked her head out from behind the hospital curtain, keeping her respectful distance.

"May I come in?" she quietly asked.

I nodded.

After taking her seat, Shajara planted her arm across my shoulders to console myself, occasionally rubbing and picking away at the crusted blood and debris that caked onto my face.

This was the first time that Shajara had really shown me any type of deep affection, and while I used to have a maddening crush for such a gorgeous woman, I couldn't help but now idolize her as an astounding human being who I looked up to.

"You know, Jackie, you'za brave soul." she spoke. "A little stupid, ya, but definitely brave."

I cracked a good laugh and leaned into Shajara's embrace. "Thanks, Sha. You're quite the firecracker yourself."

I continued onwards with my true thoughts, clearing my throat and speaking as clearly as one could.

"You have been a wonderful teacher to me here in the plane. You've taught me many tricks of the trade and kept watch over my friends and I while we embarked on our own journey in this insane place. At times you can be a hotheaded, unpredictable ball of fire, but I like it that way. I'm sure it's no easy task trying to watch over us, and please do not feel like you've failed at protecting me. It was my own stupidity that wound me up here. I'm sorry for attacking you earlier, and I'm very sorry for any taboos that I may have committed. Saint Theodore is going to tear me a new one."

"You be quiet now, ya." Shajara insisted. "I'm proud of ya, takin' out one of da most notorious people that this place has had to dealt wit' for such a long time. Pretty crafty one, you are." She admitted. "N' don'cha worry about da Heilige, I am sure you be in his favor now."

"Even after this?" I placed my broken thread into Shajara's hand.

Shajara withheld deep breath, attempting to remain calm as possible. A glimmer of concern sparked through her mesmerizing eyes and a few jumbled words left her mouth at most. Unfortunately she couldn't form an articulate sentence and to my surprise, not too far off in the distance I could hear a familiar voice wailing to see her child.

Shajara took this as cue for her to quietly leave. "Come visit me in Astraga once you've made peace, Jackie." She spoke softly before melding into thin air.

"My baby!" my mother cried out before collapsing to the floor. "My beautiful baby!"

A few medical staff entered into the room to comfort my mother, but she refused all hands that dare went near her.

"GET AWAY FROM ME!" she sobbed, flailing her arms in all directions when standing again. "Keep your damn hands off of me! Leave me to my child!"

The few nurses rushed out of the room hastily, drawing the hospital curtain behind them. My mother tossed her purse carelessly on the ground and braced her frail hands tightly around my own, weeping uncontrollably.

"I am so sorry!" she choked out in whimpers. "I should have been there for you!"

"No!" I cried out, "Please mom, don't do this."

I knelt beside her and tried to brush the tears that streamed down her cheeks. It was of no use.

"First I lost your father, and now I've nearly lost you!"

She continued to weep at my bedside and all I could do was watch painfully and think of how miserable the situation was at hand. She made a good point. First she lost the love of her life and now she lost the only child that she ever had. As much as I wanted to say "I told you so!" I simply couldn't muster the words because I had inadvertently abandoned her, especially after treating her like absolute garbage the night prior when we got into a petty argument.

Heavy bags started to welt under her eyes that bore a most unforgiving shade of red and blue. She dabbed away at the tears while still caressing my hand. Three drenched tissues and several apologies later, I couldn't take it anymore and bowed out. I leaned in to give her one last kiss on her forehead and said my goodbyes.

"I love you. Be strong without me."

I traveled to the only place I felt at peace. I wasn't yet in the mood to surround myself with people, and I knew that the lavender fields were the one place that I could rightfully go to and collect my thoughts. Once I propped myself up against the weeping willow tree, I tried to tickle my hands by brushing them against the blades of grass but my sense to touch was still very weak. I could barely even smell the lavender anymore. The aroma that once intoxicated me now was meager in comparison; lackluster at best. Jonathan was right. After separating your soul from your body, your senses seem to weaken quite drastically.

"Don't worry." She spoke and took a seat beside me. "Ya senses will get betta in time, ya."

I nearly jumped in surprise at Shajara's sudden appearance. She plucked a nearby blade of grass and placed it between the palms of her hands and up to the knuckles of her thumbs. After wiggling her eyebrow and licking her lips, she blew onto the piece of grass in order to generate a whistle but failed in doing so.

"Bah!" she grumbled and tossed the grass into the warm breeze. "I was neva good at dat anyways. Kalani tried teachin' me plenty a' times, but I just couldn't pick it up."

"Shajara, a practical legend, if not a queen of the Astral Plane, who could single-handedly take down an entire army of Umbrage Walkers is defeated by a piece of grass? No way." I chuckled.

Shajara bonked me on the head and narrowed her eyes. "Don't test me, Circle Walkah."

"How did you know that I was here, by the way?" I asked curiously.

"I'm assigned to watch ova you, Jackie. It's my duty." she winked.

I plucked myself a piece of grass that outstood from the rest and preformed the whistle correctly. Shajara nodded with a warm smile on her face.

"Dat be it!" she stated.

"In all honesty, I was never really fond of the way it sounded."

An absence of conversation fell onto the two of us thereafter. In the time that we didn't exchange any words, we peered off into the vast distance of the lush, royal purple fields and watched the gusts of warm wind swoop through the beds of flowers like giant waves toppling over one another in the oceans. An overwhelming sense of calmness came over me. Knowing that we'd never have to deal with Sagaru again was a feeling I wouldn't trade for many years to come. If you ask me, it was worth it. Sure, Sgrios still exists and could at any moment raze Astraga should he choose to, but he was a problem in itself that I worried far less about. The sun started to barely peak over the horizon's edge, giving life to the lining of where the sky met the earth and filled the clouds with an exuberant amount of light.

"Things are pretty fucked up, Sha." I mentioned.

"Why do you say dat?" she replied after glancing over at me.

"We were supposed to share the first sunrise with Kalani and the others. Now he's a mindless zombie, his father is Sgrios incarnate, I lost my connection to the waking world, and the only thing we have to show for it is that we defeated Sagaru."

Shajara played with her warhawk a little bit, itching at the scalp while being fully aware of what I was speaking about. She chose to resume her silence for the time being instead and carried her eyesight elsewhere.

"We'll save him before he loses his soul to Sgrios, right?" I asked.

"If its da last ting I do." She stated. "And we'll get chu back in ya body in no time."

"Promise?" I smiled and looked at her.

"Promise."

I was always worried that when my life was to end, there was going to be an infinite amount of nothingness waiting for me on the other side; an entire region of pure darkness that I'd never be able to escape from, no matter how much I ran. I worried that the realists would be correct: once you die, you simply just rot in the ground as a corpse and your body becomes nutrients for critters and maggots alike, your mind ceasing to soar onwards. I've had such absurd fears encumber, cripple, and restrict me throughout my entire lifetime that I became completely oblivious to the beauty of the world around me, and never for a second did I stop to think that I'd find my own heavenly abode at some point.

And yeah, I still do choose to believe in many other things that humans generally don't pay much mind to. I believe in Karma, and I believe that there are incomprehensible, supernatural powers at play that we would never be able to fathom ourselves, let alone control. So in retrospect to the journey that I've endure thus far in my hectic lifetime, I've come to but one conclusion: we're all just chasing after our own little paradise in this strange universe. I just happened to stumble across mine a little bit sooner than expected.

Made in the USA
Monee, IL
18 September 2022